Easton

in the VALLEY

A Novel

People Are Talking About Easton ...

Rebecca Price Janney's *Easton in the Valley* is a balm to the soul! History lovers and patriots will especially delight in this gentle read that brings both modern day and historical Easton to life, giving readers a glimpse into colonial history both then and now. Through warm characters and settings filled with detail, Janney weaves the stories of historical characters entering the struggle for a nation with the story of a woman whose parents are facing the struggles of their later years. *Easton in the Valley* invites readers to honor and embrace the whole of their heritage in both its difficulties and its triumphs.

—**Marlo Schalesky**, multi-published, award-winning author of *Waiting for Wonder* and *Wrestling with Wonder*

You will love the characters and brilliant weavings of the present and the past in Easton in the Valley—two stories for the price of one as the stories speak of independence then and now.

—**Janet Holm McHenry**, author of the Best-selling *Prayer Walk*

The dual story line of a present-day researcher and an eighteenth-century colonial sheriff is almost like reading two novels at once—and it's hard to decide which is more engrossing! Janney's training as a historian, as well as her skill as a storyteller, give her a unique ability to make this juggling act work. I hope she gives us more adventures of Erin and her ancestor, Peter Kichline.

—**David E. Fessenden**, author of *The Exploding Speakeasy*

Easton in the Valley immediately drew me in. The characters were so engaging, I wanted to keep turning pages to find out what happens to them.

—**Valerie N. Moran**, genealogist

When I sink my teeth into a good book, I can read for hours and hours. What a joy it has been reading Rebecca Price Janney's "Easton Series". Any lover of historical fiction will find these books to be a true blessing!

—**Scott Shultz**, Junior Past National President—Patriotic Order Sons of America

Thank you for this great story, which centers so much about ancestry and home … I thank you for a wonderful book.

—**Missy D.**

The story speaks to me on so many levels … Rebecca's writing style is wonderful. It is so readable. She's a great storyteller.

—Carolyn B.

The characters are so real. Their struggles are so real. I care about them deeply.

—Dan R.

No matter where you grew up, thinking about "what it was like" so many years ago is beautifully portrayed through this book and relatable to all. I love a book that makes me eager for the next in the series!

—Debra G.

It is amazing how many things in the books I can identify with.

—Cheryl Q.

Rebecca Price Janney

Easton

in the VALLEY

A Novel

Elk Lake
PUBLISHING™

Cover Design: Jeff Gifford
Interior Design: Anna O'Brien
Editor: Deb Haggerty
Published in Association with WordWise Media

PUBLISHED BY: Elk Lake Publishing, Inc., 35 Dogwood Dr., Plymouth, MA 02360
Library Cataloging Data
Names: Janney, Rebecca Price (Rebecca Price Janney)
Easton in the Valley, Rebecca Price Janney
[#pages] p. 23cm × 15cm (9in × 6 in.)

Description: Elk Lake Publishing, Inc. POD paperback edition | Elk Lake Publishing, Inc. digital eBook edition | Elk Lake Publishing, Inc. Trade paperback edition | Elk Lake Publishing, Inc. 2017.
Identifiers: ISBN-13: 978-1-946638-18-2(POD) | 978-1-946638-19-9 (ebk.) | 978-1-946638-20-5 Trade

Key Words: Genealogy, American Revolution, Pennsylvania History, Revolutionary War, Romance, Family

Dedication

For my mother, Helen Price Perio, 1925-2016
and my mother-in-law, Ann Kurtz Janney, 1934-2016

Acknowledgments

Each time I've sat down to write this second book in the *Easton Series*, I've had the pleasure of this wonderful place's company, along with the characters I've grown to love. I'm grateful for the assistance of many people who've shared their insights and knowledge about Easton and its history so I could create a more accurate picture of times long ago, including Renee Drago, Northampton County Pennsylvania's Archives Officer, who never seems to tire of my inquiries, and Richard Hope, who's written several books about Easton history, including one about mills. He's also pondered along with me where Peter Kichline and his family actually lived on Northampton Street. There's also Christopher Black of the Bachmann Players, who skillfully portrays Robert Levers during Easton's Heritage Day celebration, and who has recently created a group of reenactors known as Kichline's Flying Camp. I'm grateful for his enthusiasm for Peter Kichline and for all the Camp's members, including Patricia Burton and Donald Rinker, who are so supportive of my writing efforts. Then there's Tom Verenna, Nancy O'Hanlon, and the late Jane Moyer, librarian of the Northampton County Historical and Genealogical Society/Sigal Museum. Thanks also to Sharon Gotthard of the Easton Area Public Library's Marx Room, and the Reverend Michael Dowd of First United Church of Christ for his encouragement and for sharing his deep knowledge of the church's history. I'm also grateful to Heidi Fisher Patrick for helping me with my German!

I also want to thank my agent and friend, Dave Fessenden, and Deb Haggerty at Elk Lake Publishing for their support. Thanks, too, for the love and encouragement of my best friend and the love of my life, Scott Janney, and our beloved son, David. Finally, I'd like to thank my father, Joseph Perio, for the way he loves my writing, but especially me.

"Multitudes, multitudes
in the valley of decision!
For the day of the LORD is near
in the valley of decision."
Joel 3:14 (NIV)

CHAPTER ONE

Erin's graduation day was perfect—almost. Most of her family and friends mingled in the backyard, punctuating their conversations with sporadic bursts of laughter. In the kitchen, steam ascended from trays of chicken marsala, mixed vegetables, baked ziti, and mashed potatoes, but the beef lay puddled in congealing gravy, as if begging to be left alone.

"I can't figure it out." Pat Miles glanced over her daughter-in-law's shoulder at the sorry mess.

"What's wrong?" Wearing her signature worried expression, Erin's mother looked up from putting Kaiser rolls into a Longaberger basket.

The beef was drawing a small crowd, which included Erin's son.

"I don't think even Toby would eat that." Ethan wrinkled his nose and pulled away, although his dog sniffed around the table as if he thought nine-year-old boys should have better judgment.

Erin bent over to examine the aluminum chafing dishes. "I think I found the problem."

"What is it?" Pat also crouched down for a better look.

"The fuel canister isn't burning."

Al Miles wandered over. "Is there some problem, ladies?"

"The fuel isn't lit under the roast beef," his wife said.

"This is just awful!" Audrey wrung her hands.

Erin put a hand on her mother's shoulder. "It'll be okay, Mom. Don't worry."

Her father-in-law came to the rescue. "Let me have a look."

Al examined the canister and concluded. "It's empty, a dud."

Erin thought fast. "I could just put the beef on the stove over low heat." She pressed her fingers around the top and bottom of the aluminum pan to see if it was sturdy enough.

"Don't we have extra canisters in the house, Al? You know, the ones we take camping?" Pat asked.

His face brightened. "That we do! I'll just run back home and look for one." Then his perpetually smiling face took on a sheepish look. "Uh, where do you think they are?"

Pat gave a laugh as light and thin as herself while looking first at Erin, then Audrey. "If I fail to put the ketchup anywhere other than the right-hand door of the refrigerator, precisely between the Welch's Grape Jam and the A-1, my husband won't find it."

Instead of getting defensive, Al broke into a smile. "Yes, but I have other talents."

"That you do," said his wife of nearly fifty years. "The Sterno's in the basement, on the left-hand side, in the back near the Coleman stove, in a small box."

Al pressed his lips together and squinted. "I think I know where you mean. Okay, I'll be right back." He turned to his only grandson. "Ethan, would you like to go with me? If your grandmother's instructions are accurate, and they usually are, I shouldn't be more than a few minutes." His eager expression made his ruddy complexion appear rosier still.

"I don't know, Grandpa. I really want to play outside with my cousins. And Mom, shouldn't Jake be here by now? I don't know why he's not here yet." Ethan seemed torn, a kid who'd always struggled with decisions both large and small. He'd once told his mom, "I just don't want to miss out on anything." She felt the same way about life.

"There's still a half hour before the party starts, and his parents usually run late," Erin said. She hadn't known her son's best friend ever to be on time, and they had been right behind her minivan in the Villanova parking lot. To be fair, the place had been jammed with graduation traffic.

"Okay, Grandpa, I'll go. Can Toby come?"

"Sure!" Al reached into a pocket and produced a Milk-Bone™, which he held out to the dog. "Here you go, Toby."

Erin laughed. "You carry dog biscuits in your pocket, Dad?"

"Doesn't everyone?"

Toby, however, seemed to know better things when he smelled them, in the form of a medley of enticing aromas filling the kitchen and his senses. He refused to budge.

"I know when I've been rejected," Al said with a mock pout. "Let's go, Ethan."

After they left, Erin pulled a list out of her pocket to see if she'd forgotten to put out anything. "Olives!" She went to the refrigerator for the container she'd purchased the day before at the local deli and put it on the island next to the pickles.

Audrey frowned at them. "I've never seen olives like that before. They aren't green."

Erin smiled. "No, they're not, Mom. I thought I'd get something more special for the party."

"You should use Grammy's cut glass dish for olives that fancy." Audrey pointed to them as if they were the crown jewels.

"Great idea! I'll be right back." Erin walked into the dining room for the dish she kept in the china cabinet only to find her best friend Melissa standing over the cake, her blonde brow puckered. "Is something wrong?"

She cocked her head and pointed. "Take a look."

Erin drew closer. "What in the world!"

A large purse sat on top of the cake looking like a float from a fringe festival. She recognized the object at once—her mother's enormous east-west hand bag, the one Ethan had given her last Christmas. Audrey's signature wad of facial tissues poked out of the top as if this were a gift bag.

"Why is my mother's purse in the middle of my graduation cake?"

"That's your mother's?"

Erin nodded. She'd never seen a purse on a cake before.

"I guess we should remove it," she said, her thoughts heading into a spin cycle. Why had her mother done this? Could she have been distressed about something? She didn't seem upset—a little anxious maybe about the graduation party going well, which was typical of her, but not upset. Even so, what would have possessed her to slam her purse onto Erin's graduation cake? *Is Mom being absentminded?* She decided against that notion. *Absentmindedness is my department. The absentminded used-to-be professor who wants to be a professor again.*

"How long do you think her purse has been sitting there?" Melissa stood staring at the object.

"My brother brought her just as we arrived and the caterer showed up—about a half hour ago. I didn't have time to talk to her or show her where to put her things." She said this as if the purse-cake situation might not have happened if she'd taken more time to be with her mother. Not so deep-down, Erin felt embarrassed, like a little girl whose mother had never quite been in step with the other moms in the neighborhood. "Ethan grabbed Allen and Tanya right away and took them to the family room to show them his Lego tower. I kind of lost track of my mother."

Melissa leaned closer, and Erin smelled her signature gardenia scent. "I hesitate to say this, but do you think something might be wrong with her?"

Erin felt a chill run up the side of her right calf. "Her eyesight hasn't been good for a while."

"I had a great-uncle, Neil, who went really deaf. My great-aunt, Tina, told him to put the cat out back, and hours later, she couldn't find Snowball—or was the cat's name Rocky? I forget. Anyway, hours later, the cat had wandered back into the kitchen—they had one of those doors so the cat could go in and out—but something wasn't right. My great-aunt said, 'Why is our cat black?' Neil replied, 'Didn't you tell me to paint the cat black?'"

Erin couldn't help but laugh, although her rather serious problem remained. "Maybe we should take Mom's purse off the cake. Hopefully, there isn't too much damage underneath."

"Yes, let's. I'll help."

Erin lifted the heavy bag and found white icing mixed with black and blue smears from the lettering. As Melissa grabbed a Villanova University napkin and started rubbing off the icing, Erin swallowed hard.

"The cake is ruined," she said, noting the smeared diploma and black cap, then reading aloud the disfigured message—"Congatlon Dr. rin les." She suddenly thought of her grandmother. "This falls under the category of what my Grammy Ott would've called 'The Wreck of the Hesperus.'" She looked from the confectionary disaster to Melissa, who had started to snigger. Then they burst out laughing.

"What happened here?" Robin, Erin's neighbor, stared down at the cake she'd obviously taken hours to create.

"It had a close encounter with someone's purse." Erin didn't want to go into the whole story, just to salvage the situation if at all possible. She still rued the day the fashionable Robin had seen her at the bus stop wearing aqua slippers with a blow dryer motif, a Flyers hoodie, and pink maternity pajama bottoms. Erin disliked looking foolish, and this situation seemed somehow worse than even that earlier one.

Robin's eyes were the size of dinner plates. "O—kay," she said slowly.

"Can you fix it?" Melissa asked.

The diminutive woman tilted her head first this way, then the next. "I think so. I'll just run over to my house and get the leftover icing. It's a good thing I didn't toss it. I must have had a premonition or something." She rushed from the dining room.

"Are you going to say anything to your mom?"

"I don't know, Melissa." Erin pursed her lips and looked out the window where her nieces and nephews crowded around the next-door neighbors' colossal mastiff.

Melissa followed her friend's gaze. "That is one seriously huge dog."

Erin chuckled. "One day the UPS man came just as Steffy, that's the dog, came lumbering over to Ethan. As the driver handed me a package, he said, 'I see you got your son a pony.'"

Melissa laughed. "She seems gentle, though."

"Yep, she's the proverbial gentle giant."

A voice interrupted them from the doorway. "I didn't see the cake yet. You know how I love a good one. Pat told me it was in here."

Mom! What am I going to do now?

Melissa cast a wary glance in Erin's direction.

"Uh, yes, Mom, the cake is here, but there's, uh, a slight problem, and Robin, my neighbor who baked it, is going to fix it."

Audrey walked over to the long box and looked inside with her fading hazel eyes, the ones similar to Erin's color. "Somehow—that—doesn't— look, well, right. I can't quite make out what it says." Audrey looked at Melissa. "It's my eyes. I'm getting the macula."

Melissa frowned at first, then brightened. "Oh, you mean macular degeneration."

"Uh-huh." She turned to her daughter. "What happened? The cake looks all smooshy."

"Yes, well, uh, Mom, you see we, um, we found your purse sitting on top of it." Erin felt like she was five years old and frightened of being scolded for saying the four-letter word she'd seen graffitied on the side of a print shop on her way to school.

"My what?" Audrey spoke as if Erin had, indeed, cussed right out loud. Scowling fiercely, she demanded, "What do you mean you found my pockabook on the cake? Why would I put my pockabook on your cake?"

To Erin's vast relief, Melissa discreetly slipped out of the dining room. "Well, Mom, I don't know. I was wondering that myself." She ventured into the wilderness of their relationship, wondering what she'd find among the trees. "Do you think you didn't see the cake when you put your purse down?"

"Why would I do that?" Then, just a moment later, she broke into a storm of tears. "I'm telling you, Erin, my eyes are getting worse. If I did that"—she pointed to the cake—"what else am I going to do?" She started wringing her hands again.

Audrey's negativity and messy boundaries were among the reasons Erin had kept her emotional distance until last year. "I don't know, Mom," she said, feeling helpless.

Robin came whirling into the room with an armful of baker's gadgets and tubs of icing. Erin felt it only right to introduce her to her mom, even though she wished Audrey were in a different room just now. "Robin, this is my mother, Audrey Pelleriti."

"Well, hello. It's very nice to meet you." Robin put her things down and shook Audrey's small hand. "You look a lot like your mom, Erin. Is your dad here, too?"

"Uh, no." *Why is everyone suddenly poking every one of my sore spots today? This is supposed to be a happy day.* She struggled against a sinking feeling, willing herself into cheerfulness. "It looks like you came armed for battle, Robin."

"Yes, and I aim to beat this mess."

Erin balanced a plate of food on her lap while she talked to her brother and his wife. Everyone else was either in the kitchen, sun room or outside where the sound of children at play wafted through the open dining room window.

"That's quite a combination." Tanya smiled as she nodded toward Erin's plate containing a piece of the cake she'd just helped cut and over which she'd sprinkled a half dozen olives and a handful of raw, red onions. Robin had managed to deftly recreate the confection from its collision with Audrey's handbag.

Erin blushed, well aware of how other people tended to regard her culinary quirkiness. "I know, I know."

"We have a little something for you." Tanya produced a small, rectangular package she'd wrapped with silver paper and topped with a tiny blue and white ribbon.

"Oh, how nice!" Erin put her plate on the coffee table and accepted the gift, finding a silver necklace inside bearing a sparkling sapphire. "It's gorgeous! Thank you so much." She hugged Tanya, then Allen, who gave a shy smile.

"We wanted to give you something with Villanova's colors," her brother said.

Erin fastened the slender chain around her neck. She hadn't worn much jewelry today except for diamond studs in her ears, her usual three rings, and the Pandora bracelet Jim had given her, posthumously, for their anniversary the previous year.

"It looks beautiful," Tanya said.

"Speaking of beautiful, I really like your hair." Erin had always admired her sister-in-law's dark, silky tresses. "I think the longer length looks nice."

Tanya smiled. "Allen does, too. But yours is really pretty, and I think it's longer too. I just love your blonde highlights against the brunette. Your hair is just that way naturally, isn't it?"

Erin nodded. "As for the length …" She leaned closer and whispered, "Mom doesn't approve. She thinks women over twenty-five should keep their hair short."

"I think that's how she was raised—how women did things back in the late fifties and early sixties," Tanya said.

Erin picked up her plate and took a big bite of cake with its mishmash of flavors. Then she said, "Thanks again for bringing Mom today. It would've been hard for me to pick her up when I had so much to do here for graduation and the party." Although her mother was still driving, Audrey would've never ventured as far as Lansdale on her own, not even in her younger days. Anything past Bethlehem seemed like the ends of the earth to her.

"No problem," Allen said.

"I wish Dad could've been here, too," she said, then added, "and Bridget. I didn't say anything to them about the party because I didn't want to hurt their feelings."

Allen pressed his lips together and nodded. "We didn't either when I saw him a few days ago. I figured you didn't invite them."

"I wish things were different between him and Mom."

"Me too."

"How is he?"

"Doing well," Allen said. "He's still out riding a bike and going fishing every morning."

"Isn't that amazing?" Tanya asked. "How old is he now?"

"Eighty-one," Erin and Allen said at the same time.

"I hope I'm like that when I'm eighty-one," Tanya said.

They were quiet for a few moments while Erin finished her cake, washing it down with a cup of lukewarm coffee.

"So, what's next?" Allen leaned forward as a ray of sunlight bounced off his thinning brown hair, then into his matching eyes. He sat back again, avoiding the glare.

Erin was being asked this a lot lately, understandably so. In the year since Jim's death, she'd thrown herself first into tracing her family tree and joining the Daughters of the American Revolution, Valley Forge Chapter. Then when Ethan started fourth grade, she'd hammered down on finishing the doctoral dissertation she'd been working on for three years. Now, less than a month after the first anniversary of Jim's death, she was officially Dr. Erin Miles. It only stood to reason she'd start looking for a teaching position, and she truly did want to be back in the classroom. But she also wanted to continue researching her family history and maybe become a volunteer genealogist at the historical society or with the DAR. She hadn't admitted this to anyone yet, however, not even to Melissa. Wouldn't those activities seem like underachieving after her ambitious dissertation about the career of Samuel Miles, her husband's ancestor, Revolutionary War hero, and 18th-century mayor of Philadelphia? Yet, she wanted so much to know more about any connection he might have had to her six-times great-grandfather, Colonel Peter Kichline of Easton, who'd served in the same battle as then-Colonel Miles. Because she'd focused her study of Miles on his political career and had a tight dissertation deadline, Erin hadn't had time to consider any link. Now she wanted to, but how could she if she jumped right into a teaching position?

She told her brother and his wife, "I haven't quite decided yet."

"Where would you like to teach?" Tanya asked.

"Probably one of the colleges or universities around here."

"There are plenty of those," Allen said.

Yes, there were. Erin imagined herself going online to find out which ones were looking for a full-time professor of American history, but somehow ruing the process. The bold truth was she wanted a job to come to her. She didn't have a lot of psychic energy after the grueling dissertation defense, plus she was still grieving, though not as intensely as the first year. She hadn't returned to Hatfield College after they denied her the full-time history position she treasured, and she knew teaching jobs in general were extremely hard to find. She was enjoying involvement in the DAR and looking forward to her first State Conference. What she really wanted, in addition to a job appearing magically, was to research Peter Kichline and her other ancestors with a vengeance.

CHAPTER TWO
Saturday, February 5, 1774

The Rev. William Hanlon quoted from the book of Ecclesiastes. "'To everything there is a season, and a time to every purpose under the heaven.' This, Peter and Sarah, is your season for marriage, to begin a family of your own, to take your place in the life of the community that has nurtured you since infancy."

Sheriff Peter Kichline smiled at his oldest son and namesake, liking the sound of seasons of happiness and fresh beginnings, especially for Peter Jr. and his beloved bride. In fact, Peter Sr. was embarking on a new season in his own life, one he fervently hoped would be as low in drama as the last one had been characterized by it.

"We look forward to a long period of marital felicity as you learn to live together as husband and wife," Hanlon said, "but God's ways are often not our own. We must take each day as a gift."

Easton's former school teacher, now a Presbyterian minister serving congregations on both sides of the Delaware River, knew the Kichline family well. When he'd first arrived in the nascent village eight years earlier, he was teaching his way north to Yale College and a pastoral career. He'd also become good friends with the sheriff, who'd just lost his wife of sixteen years. Not only did Hanlon often visit the Kichline home to use the library, he'd also wooed and won the sheriff's housekeeper and niece, Phoebe Benner. At that same time, Peter was emerging from his own mourning to marry Anna, the daughter of his dear friends, Caspar and Margaretha Doll. Now, in the absence of a regular pastor at the German Reformed Church, Hanlon had come to perform the ceremony at the log schoolhouse where the congregation worshiped.

"I promise to love and cherish you always, until death do us part." Peter Jr.'s brown eyes gazed steadily into his bride's.

His father just hoped death wouldn't disrupt this union the way it had his own—twice. When he'd married Sarah Doll's sister a year after his first wife's death in 1766, he'd hoped to have Anna even longer than the fulfilling years he and Margaretta had known. Unfortunately, just six years later, three miscarriages had taken their toll on his youthful bride—her last pregnancy ending in her death, as well as the baby's.

Peter Sr. glanced at the former Catherine Gwinner and smiled, touching her lightly on the right forearm. When his wife of three months beamed back, he prayed silently, *May she outlive me, Almighty God. May I never again experience the heartache of losing a wife.*

The Caspar Dolls had moved from Easton to a Plainfield farm a few years earlier, but they'd kept their town house, which Peter Jr. and Sarah were going to inhabit. Sheriff Peter and Catherine greeted the bride and groom in the dining room—filled with enough food and drink for the entire village, most of which had managed to squeeze into the house like so much sausage.

"God's blessings." Peter shook his tall son's hand.

"Thank you, sir."

He leaned forward and kissed Sarah's soft cheek. "May you have a long and fruitful life together, my dear."

"Thank you, Father Peter." Her face shone like lamplight.

Peter noticed his closest friend, Robert Traill, standing by the table holding a plate while examining the multitude of dishes with a grin as broad as his midsection. The sheriff walked over to Traill, Catherine on his arm.

"Well, hello, my friend." Traill shook Peter's hand. Then he bowed toward Catherine. "Hello, my dear."

"Hello, Mr. Traill. The food looks delightful, doesn't it?"

"Indeed. What did you make?"

"As a matter of fact, I baked the apple and shoofly pies." She nodded toward them. "Susannah baked most of the bread."

"Ah, she's becoming quite the young lady, as well as a good cook." Traill elbowed Peter. "Before you know it, she'll be taking a husband."

Peter felt a lump form in his throat but managed to make light of the comment. "Hopefully, not for a while yet, good sir. After all, she's not even fourteen." He managed to change the subject. "Robert, I'd like you to meet some of my family who came from Bedminster for the wedding."

Traill cast a longing look at the food he'd have to leave behind for the time being, then put down his plate and followed Peter into the living room. The sheriff stood aside to allow Catherine to step through the doorway first, watching her limp as she made her way to the window and a row of chairs. Peter followed, careful to bend under the lintel so he didn't leave part of his forehead on the wood as he went through. Easton's low doorways seemed to lay in wait for his six-foot-two-inch frame. He walked over to his mother, warmed by the smile she cast in his direction— her firstborn, the baby of her German youth in the days when her own marriage had been young and full of promise.

"Peter!" She held out her arms to him, and he went to her, kissing her wrinkled cheek, remembering when the skin had been firm and rosy.

"I'm so glad you're here, Mother. I wasn't sure you'd be able to make the trip in the cold."

"I don't go long distances very often these days, but I so wanted to meet your new wife, and to be here for Peter Jr.'s wedding. I'm just sorry we didn't make it in time for the ceremony."

He noted the way her seventy-plus years had not only carved deeper lines into her face, but also intensified her character. Long ago in the dark days after his father's death, with a new baby and two lively boys in tow, she had soldiered on in the power of the Almighty to whom she prayed constantly—as if he were right there with them. And so he had been.

"She insisted she come along." Andrew, Peter's younger brother, could've passed for his twin except for slightly more delicate features, a nod to their mother's side of the family.

"I tried to talk her out of it, but she insisted if our wives were going to make the trip, she would, too." Charles Kichline, the youngest of the three brothers, spoke up.

"I see Father Koppelger wasn't able to come," Peter said of his stepfather's absence.

"I'm afraid not, my son. He is plagued by rheumatism."

"You must send him my best regards. I'll plan to visit you this spring." Then he added with a smile, "When at last I have more time."

His mother reached for Catherine's hand. "Aren't you lovely, my dear. I wish you and my son a long life together."

"Thank you, Mother Kichline."

Peter began making introductions to his wife. "I'd like you to meet my sisters-in-law. This is also Catherine, Andrew's wife, and Susannah, whom my brother Charles was fortunate enough to wed at his advanced age." He winked at his younger sibling, whose jaw had just dropped. Peter watched as Charles caught on, and they shared a laugh.

After greetings and embraces, Peter presented Robert Traill to his extended family, then he offered to get a plate of food for his mother. She wouldn't have to brave the hungry horde surrounding the table.

Her gray-blue eyes flashed. "First, I'd like to see my grandchildren—well, at least Jacob and Andrew. Susannah was here just a few minutes ago. My, how that child has grown!"

Robert Traill bowed. "I'll be glad to get your food, madam."

Peter gave his portly friend a once-over. "I wouldn't trust him, Mother."

Traill laughed, slapping the sheriff's back. "In your case 'no.' In your dear mother's case, she can trust me as far as the day is long."

"I'll be happy to get her meal," Catherine said. "Perhaps my new sisters-in-law will join me so I can learn all I need to know about managing a Kichline husband."

Peter laughed as he entreated the ladies, "Do be kind."

His sisters-in-law Susannah and Catherine laughed too as they linked arms with his wife and walked toward the dining room.

"I'll get the boys, Mother." Peter turned to leave.

"Son." Her voice stopped him. "May I have a word?"

He turned back, guessing what might be on her mind. "Yes, of course."

"If you will excuse me," Traill said. "It was a pleasure to meet you, madam."

"I assure you, the pleasure was mine." As he walked away, she motioned Peter to sit next to her. "Your wife is lovely—and so young."

"Thank you, Mother. I'm hoping she'll outlive me." He said this with a mixture of humor and sadness.

She nodded. "I'll pray for a long life together." After pausing for a moment, she said in a soft voice, "I couldn't help but notice how she limps.

Did she hurt herself recently?"

Catherine's hobble had caused most of Easton's single and widowed men to pass by one of the town's most intriguing females—witty, kind, intelligent, and strong. He could just hear the likes of Richard Bell discussing her as if she were a sheep or a cow: "That one won't be good on a farm—too frail, and she might not be able to bear healthy children, if any at all." If Peter were completely honest with himself, though, her infirmity had given him pause as well. He was a stalwart man, but he didn't think he could stand losing yet another wife. He gathered his thoughts and shared his new wife's story.

"Catherine was born in Connecticut. When she was very young, there was a carriage accident in which her mother and father died. The horse came down hard on her leg, and while the break did mend, she was left with a minor limp."

His mother knit her brows, nodding. "How unfortunate to have lost her parents so young and in such a way. Who raised her?"

"She had four older brothers, who brought her with them to Pennsylvania where they lived for many years."

"Yankees?" One eyebrow shot up.

He nodded his head. Yankees had been a continual thorn in his side as Sheriff of Northampton County, a group insisting the northern hinterlands of Pennsylvania belonged to Connecticut because King Charles II had granted the land to them. The problem was, he'd also deeded the same vast tract to Pennsylvania, which had already begun settling the land when the Yankees arrived.

"Three of her brothers ended up returning to Connecticut," Peter said. "The other one, who was very fond of Catherine, moved down here and married an Easton woman two years ago." His eyes searched the room to see if he could locate Frederick Gwinner and his wife, Maria, but without success. He continued, "Catherine lived with them until our marriage."

His mother remained silent as she placed her blue-veined hand on his arm. Peter sensed an approving spirit from her—a spirit of understanding, and his heart was gladdened.

A fire crackled while the wind danced around the windows as if looking for a way to penetrate the stone house on Northampton Street and entertain its occupants. In the candlelit parlor, Peter and his two brothers were the only family members still awake following the day-long festivities. His younger sons, Jacob and Andrew, along with their sister, grandmother, stepmother, and two aunts filled the chambers on the second and third floors. The sound of someone snoring slid downstairs and the men grinned at each other when they heard it. Peter and his namesake were both night owls, but tonight his eldest son was down the street beginning a new life with Sarah Doll. He missed the young man already.

An elderly woman poked her head in the doorway, wearing a fierce expression. "*Gibt es noch etwas, Herr?*"

"*Nichts danke, Frau Hamster.*" Peter assured her they didn't need anything just then.

She bowed as if he were King George III himself and walked toward her quarters behind the kitchen.

"Who, or what, was that?" Andrew asked, his sides beginning to shake with barely contained mirth.

Peter managed to keep a straight face. "That, my dear brother, is Frau Hamster, our venerable housekeeper."

"Wherever did you find the likes of her?"

"She came with Catherine; she's a devoted family servant who once vowed undying loyalty to her ladyship." He took a sip of ale, trying unsuccessfully to conceal his own amusement.

Charles shared the conclusion he'd reached. "I certainly wouldn't want to be at cross purposes with her."

"I assure you, her bark is worse than her bite, as they say."

"Then she likes you?" Charles asked.

"I'm happy to say she does."

"Speaking of cross purposes …" Andrew placed his pipe on a table. "What do you make of the hubbub in Boston?"

"What specifically are you referring to? The so-called Tea Party or the Crown's response?" Peter thought he knew which way his brother's sympathies lay.

Charles grimaced. "A most unfortunate series of events."

"I wouldn't call them unfortunate," Andrew said. "The authorities have been leaning hard on the people up there for eight years, ever since the Townsend Acts, and they aren't the type to go down without a fight. If I were there, I would've been dressed like an Indian myself, flinging the blasted tea into the harbor!"

"Indeed, you would." Charles's eyes twinkled. In appearance, he was stouter than his brothers, built more like the father whose death had occurred when he and Peter were very young and Andrew still in the womb. Charles was known as the quiet brother, a man every bit as strong-minded as Andrew, but in a different way. Charles took his time weighing points and counterpoints before acting, a process sometimes lasting years. After all, he hadn't taken a wife or started having children until the age of thirty-nine; he and his Susannah were currently up to four. Peter, on the other hand, approached decisions in a way reflecting aspects of both brothers— combining Charles's more careful deliberation with Andrew's vigor.

"We will see what interesting events unfold in the coming days," Peter said. "On the one hand, the colonies have enjoyed relative peace under the Crown for over a hundred years. On the other, Britain's repressive policies since the French and Indian War have reflected their treatment of us as unruly children, unable to care for ourselves."

Andrew slapped a hand against his right thigh. "What parent has his hand in his own children's pockets, I ask you?"

A log on the fire slipped from the grate, and Peter rose to push the glowing wood back with a cast-iron poker. He kicked at the sparks with his boot.

"Speaking of coming days," said Charles, seeming eager to end any conflicts between his siblings, "what will you do when your term as sheriff is up? What great public service is next on the horizon?"

Peter leaned against the fireplace, feeling the warmth at his back. "I'm happy to say after serving two terms, I'm looking forward to retirement in a few weeks—to running my mills alongside Andrew and Jacob, now that Peter has taken up fulling." He grinned, his face flushing, as he pictured himself sitting before this very hearth with Catherine on such a blustery night. They'd be reading Milton together while someone else minded Northampton County. "I'd like to spend some time getting to know my new wife better, maybe have more children."

Andrew pursed his lips. "What about the new church building I heard everyone talking about at the reception? No doubt you'll get involved."

"I am already." Hadn't he put sweat equity as well as funds into the first school in 1755 and been a champion of the courthouse construction a decade later? Of course he'd be helping build the church. "Community involvement will always be important to me. I just would like to keep my activities closer to my own fireside in the coming season."

"To whom much is given ..." Both Charles and Andrew echoed the words they'd heard repeatedly as boys and young men.

Peter smiled. "Indeed, but I won't be sitting above pounding hooves riding all over this vast county chasing down outlaws. I am fifty-one after all." Why were his brothers sniggering anyway?

CHAPTER THREE

She jumped from her desk chair when the phone rang, feeling very much like her boss had caught her writing a personal email at work, except she had no boss because she had no job. Toby, rudely awakened from a nap in the middle of a sun spot on the floor, started barking in his throatiest bassett hound manner. Guilty as charged. She knew she shouldn't have been on Ancestry.com when she was supposed to be looking for a teaching position.

"Hush, Toby. Shhh." Three rings later, he stopped howling and leaned against her left leg as she took the call. "Hello."

"Hey, Erin, it's Allen. How are you?"

Her brother rarely called on a weekday. In fact, he rarely called. She sat down again, waiting for whatever news he had to deliver. "I'm doing well, and you?"

"I'm fine. That was a nice party. Tanya and I enjoyed ourselves a lot."

"I'm so glad you were able to make it."

"How's Ethan?"

"Doing well, looking forward to summer vacation."

"When does that start?"

Erin glanced at the DAR calendar with a portrait of American First Ladies who'd been members. There were stark contrasts between the more contemporary figures of Laura Bush and Nancy Reagan and their nineteenth-century counterpart Caroline Harrison. "June 17 is his last day, so about five more weeks."

"I think the kids get out earlier up here." He was momentarily silent. "The reason I'm calling is Mom had a little accident yesterday. She's alright, but she was shaken up."

Her pulse quickened. "What happened?"

"She was going to work, and when she turned into the parking lot from South Main Street, she misjudged the entrance. She jumped the curb and hit a big planter on the sidewalk."

"Oh, wow! Thank God, she wasn't hurt. What about the car?"

"She took it to Shades Auto, and they said the cost would be around $600 to repair the damage to the front end."

"Yikes! The old car might not even be worth $600," she said.

"That's what Matt Shade told her."

"Is the car drivable?"

"He says so, but apparently, it doesn't look so good."

"What do you think she'll do?"

Erin had feared something like this might happen—had tried not to think too much about the possibility. Her energetic mother was barely acquainted with the concept of retirement, which was a major reason she was still on the job at the age of seventy-eight. What would Audrey do if she were no longer able to work, do her own shopping, or banking or … Erin stopped the flow of thoughts to focus on what Allen was saying.

"I advised her not to have the car fixed. Erin, I don't know how much longer she can drive." He corrected himself. "Honestly, I don't think she should be driving at all anymore. She could've hit someone on the sidewalk or slammed into a telephone pole and been seriously injured or worse."

This seemed like a good time to tell him about the cake. "I totally agree. Actually, something happened at my party, and I wasn't able to tell you with her there." She described the surprise she felt when she saw their mom's Dooney and Bourke decorating the top of her cake.

"She what?" Allen's exclamation ended in a low whistle. "I can't believe she put her purse on your cake!" Erin pictured her brother shaking his head in disbelief. "She couldn't even tell the difference between a table top and a cake? She really needs to give up driving, Erin."

"I'm with you all the way, but I have to be honest—I sure don't want to be the one to tell her." She quickly added, "And I'm certain you don't relish the thought either."

After a pause, he said, "She asked me not to mention her accident to you. I think she's afraid we'll both gang up on her about driving, and she's trying to downplay what happened."

This didn't set well in her spirit because pretending not to know something put her in an awkward position. She stepped lightly. Things had been good between her and her brother this past year. She was getting to know him, as well as the rest of her family, better, and she didn't want to upset the delicate balance. "I'll bet she's scared. I know I would be. Allen, I just don't know how to act as if I don't know about the accident when I do. I don't want to lie."

"I understand, but please don't tell her I told you. I said I wouldn't."

She was between a rock and a hard place.

Small talk filled the initial part of her conversation with her mother the next day, then Erin waded a little deeper. "So, Mom, what have you been up to?" Maybe Audrey would volunteer information about her mishap.

Dead air. Then, "Have you talked to Allen lately?"

Here we go. Erin was ready for her dodge, having rehearsed what she would say before making the call. "I had a nice long talk with him and Tanya at the party."

"I'm glad they could come and that they brought me. You know I don't like to drive all the way down to your place." Silence. "So, he didn't tell you what happened to me?"

More dodging, like she was in a bumper car at Easton's old Bushkill Park. "Did something happen to you, Mom?"

"Yes, something happened to me."

Erin chafed at her mother's habit of turning a question into an answer using the same words. "So, what was it?"

"What it was is I had a little accident." Her voice took on a defiant tone.

"Oh, that's too bad. Are you alright?"

"I'm fine. My car isn't, though."

"Tell me what happened." Erin felt like she was finally off the hook.

"Well, I was going to work, and when I pulled into the parking lot the sun was right in my eyes, you know how it does that. I ran over the curve and hit a planter. Now, who in heck puts a planter on a sidewalk?"

Erin wasn't about to go there. "I'm so glad you weren't hurt, Mom. What about your car?"

"The front end's all smashed up. I took it over to Shades', and they said it would cost $650 to fix it."

"That's a lot of money."

"I know, but I can't afford a new car, and I have to get to work."

Now she was in the deep end, and Erin had never been an especially good swimmer. "Uh, Mom, I hate to say this, but your car was built during the Reagan Administration. I don't think you could even get that much for it."

Audrey's voice went up an octave. "I know, but what else am I going to do?"

She hadn't spoken to her daughter like this since Jim's death, and her tone felt like a turning point for Erin, a moving forward. She wasn't exactly at peace about the transition.

"Well, I know a bus for senior citizens comes to your place," she said. "A lot of the residents use it. And there are cabs." She was eager to come to her mother's rescue, to fix the problem, yet she felt like she was doing a feeble doggy paddle when a firm breaststroke was in order.

"That bus doesn't run on my schedule. Everybody here complains about it. You have to go when the bus comes." She spoke as if Erin were a total idiot not to realize such a thing. "And I don't think there even are taxicabs anymore."

She could tell her mother was frightened. *I would be, too, if my independence were being threatened.* "There are still cabs, Mom," she blurted.

"Well, they're expensive. I can't afford a cab."

Her mom couldn't afford a cab, but here she was saying she would go ahead and fix a clunker whose rear wheel wells were rusting out, and whose interior roof was starting to look like birds had taken up residence. Erin watched as a neighbor got into her SUV with her youngest daughter dressed in a tutu and remembered being a child herself and her mom driving her to dance lessons. She couldn't imagine not being able to just get up and go somewhere when you wanted to.

"Well, Mom, I'm sure this must be really upsetting."

"It certainly is upsetting."

"I'm just concerned about you. What if you were to get into a worse accident? I mean, look what happened with the cake." The words flew out of Erin's mouth before she could stop them. She braced for a rock slide.

"Well, Erin, why don't you and your brother just take me out to pasture and shoot me then?"

"Mother ..."

"If I can't drive, I might just as well be dead."

27

Should she even attempt to do damage control? Erin decided to try.

"You've worked so hard all your life, Mom. Most people are retired and enjoying themselves at your age. Maybe you should just have some fun."

"How in the world can I have fun if I don't have a car?"

She was in a deep, thick jungle. She had no further answers and wasn't sure her mother wanted any just yet.

She had planned to finish her curriculum vitae by the end of the week, but when Sandy called from the Easton Area Public Library's Marx Room, Erin dropped everything. The CV would just have to wait.

"Wherever did you find this?" She looked up from the 18th-century document bearing a firm though faded signature at the bottom right— "Peter Kichline." The looping "P" and the strong "K" were a window into his soul, a man with flair and potency.

"I bought it at a barn sale a few years ago," the owner, an older man, said. "Sandy told me about you last week when I was in here, and I offered to show you since he's your ancestor."

Howard Clarke may have been stumpy, bald, and generally past his prime, but to Erin he was red carpet ready. "That's so very nice of you. I can't thank you enough."

"It's my pleasure." He leaned back and examined her. "So, how are you related to the Colonel?"

Erin savored Clarke's obvious admiration, as well as the small crowd the centuries-old document had drawn around the table. "He's my six-times great-grandfather."

"Sweet."

"This writing is hard to make out." She started taking pictures of the yellowed paper covering almost the length of one desk. "What exactly is this?"

"It's a deed from 1766," Clarke said, "for a tract of land on the outskirts of Easton."

"I'm familiar with the early layout of the town," Sandy said, "and I think this property was close to his milling operations."

"What's this, Mr. Clarke?" Erin pointed to a clump of paper hanging from the bottom by a narrow and heavily faded blue ribbon. She was careful not to touch the document, although no one was using white gloves like they often did in episodes of "Who Do You Think You Are." Clarke had obviously treated the record with great care, even to the point of storing it in a leather case resembling a quiver for arrows.

"It's a wax seal, which would have made the document legal, something like what a notary public does now, but with more panache." He smiled at Erin. "That's actually his personal seal."

"So, this is wax?"

"Yes, but at this point in time it looks like crumpled paper. If the seal were in better condition, you could see the actual design."

Ever since she'd laid eyes on the deed, Erin had wanted it for herself. This was part of her many times great-grandfather's personal possessions and owning the record would give her a deeper sense of connectedness to him. She didn't know how attached Howard Clarke was to the document, or even if he'd just shown her because he was being nice. *Oh well, nothing ventured, nothing gained as Jim used to say. I might as well try.* "I can't thank you enough for showing this to me, Mr. Clarke. I'm just wondering, well, if you'd ever be willing to sell this to me."

He inhaled slowly, his light brown eyes roaming over the historic deed. "I'm very fond of this. I can see why you would be as well, and I think someday I'd be willing to put it back in the hands of the Colonel's family. I hope you'll understand that for now, I just want to enjoy it a little longer."

"I do understand." She handed him a business card containing her personal information. "Please contact me any time. It's been just wonderful to meet you and to see this."

She was about to leave the Marx Room when Sandy stopped her. "Erin, before you leave, I just wanted to suggest you go to the Sigal Museum for more information about Peter Kichline. Have you been there yet?"

"Just briefly. I've been meaning to go for a longer visit, but I was finishing my doctoral dissertation, then I had the defense."

Sandy smiled. "And are you 'Doctor' now?"

"Yes, actually I am."

"Congratulations! What did you write about?"

"Have you ever heard of Samuel Miles?"

"The name is very familiar."

"He was my husband's six-times great-grandfather and one of Philadelphia's 18th-century political leaders. I wrote about his role in the Presidential election of 1796. During the Revolution, Samuel Miles was at the Battle of Long Island, just like my Grandfather Peter. I've been wondering for a long time if they might have known each other. Because my studies were so precise and locked into deadlines, I haven't had a chance to really look into the possibility."

"What a fascinating prospect," Sandy said. "I know they have items related to Peter Kichline at the Sigal, some of them from the Revolution, so maybe you can begin your search there." She wrote a name on a piece of scrap paper she kept on her desk and handed the note to Erin. "Call this number and ask for Leslie Sueter. Tell her I suggested you call. She's a whiz at finding information about people."

"Thanks so much, Sandy. You're pretty good yourself!"

She stopped by to see Audrey briefly before heading back to Lansdale, wondering if her mom would be at home or at work since her part-time hours shifted from morning to afternoon. Erin could've just called, but after grabbing a hot dog at Jimmy's in Union Square—the window help had grimaced when Erin requested whipped cream and chocolate sauce instead of ketchup or mustard—she decided just to drive up the hill to her mom's apartment. Besides, gas was cheaper in New Jersey, plus she didn't have to pump it herself. After filling the tank, Erin arrived at her mom's building. When she got out, she saw Audrey's car in the residents' lot looking like a junkyard reject. She wondered what kind of mood her mother would be in.

"Erin!" She turned in the direction of the voice. There was her mom sitting on one of the benches talking to a woman in Sag Harbor pants and a "PHS Stateliners Wrestling" tee shirt. A poodle lay at her feet. Erin walked over to them and hugged Audrey.

"I didn't know you were coming! It's a good thing I worked this morning, or I would've missed you. Peggy, this is my daughter, Erin. She lives in Lansdowne."

"Lansdale."

"Oh, right, I keep forgetting."

"Well, I'm glad to meet you, Erin. I'm going to take Nelson for a walk now." She got up. "Youß enjoy your visit with your mom. It's such a nice day."

"It was nice meeting you too."

"She's new here," Audrey said. "Sit down, Erin. What brings you here?"

"I was in Easton at the library and thought I'd stop over here before I head back home." She looked at her watch. "I only have a half hour."

"What were you at the library for?"

She told Audrey about the deed.

"That must've been amazing to see. I wish I could see things like that again."

Erin waited a moment. "So, you worked this morning."

"I sure did."

"Um, I saw the car."

"It looks pretty beat up but drives okay. I don't think I'll get it fixed."

Her mother was still driving, even after the accident.

"All I really need it for is work and to go to the grocery store and CVS. I don't go far. I think I'll start working in the morning, but not too early. If I leave here around nine, the light is good for me. The sun doesn't get in my eyes, and then I can go home by one, before I have to deal with the school buses. Of course, when it rains, I have a harder time seeing, but overall I'm doing just fine." She smiled at her only daughter who, for the moment, was speechless.

CHAPTER FOUR

On this mid-March day, he couldn't tell whether winter was coming or going. The cold, steady drizzle was enough to make old limbs ache. He warmed himself at a fire in the log schoolhouse with six elders from the Reformed and Lutheran congregations, discussing plans for a union church. Due to a maddening shortage of funds, the original strategy to erect a dedicated house of worship on the adjacent property had stalled like a stubborn mare.

"I still say we should take subscriptions." Christian Gress folded his arms across his ample chest and rocked back in the chair. "How else can we afford to build?"

Michael Butz spoke up. "Mr. Gress's idea could work, but I think donations might be just as good. I don't think most people will like the idea of being assigned regular amounts."

Gress frowned. "I'm afraid you misunderstand me, Mr. Butz. We wouldn't be assigning amounts—each member will give as he is able, a pledge from his own heart, on his own terms."

Butz pursed his lips, his fingers working his dark beard. "Would everyone in the church know who was giving what? I don't go for that. It reminds me too much of the Scribes and the Pharisees doing everything to be seen by men."

"I think we could keep who gave what between the elders."

Peter watched the back and forth exchange, studying the faces of these earnest men.

"If you'll recall," Jacob Pfeiffer said, "when we took up a collection for the first school house twenty years ago, we published the names of those who gave."

"Published where?" Butz was never one to back down. "There wasn't a newspaper."

"Well, I mean everyone in town knew who had contributed to the schoolhouse fund."

"I think this is a different situation," Butz said. "This is for a church, for a sacred purpose. I think we should all give without sounding a trumpet."

Elder Garrett Moore said his piece. "We would then need to depend solely on regular gifts, but giving tends to fluctuate with the seasons."

"People in Easton are generous."

"Yes, Mr. Butz, they are, but for a capital project such as the one we're undertaking, a more concerted effort is required." Moore tented his thick hands, gently rocking his chin against them. "We need a good bit of money up front to get this building started, not dribs and drabs here and there, and we must get going soon. Not having a church to worship in when we've been a village for over twenty years just isn't right."

The other men nodded in agreement, except for Peter, who tended to weigh all sides of an argument before speaking.

"We also need to remember the need for a good organ," Moore said. When the others muttered their consent, he gave a satisfied smile. "I would like to engage Mr. David Tannenberg for the work."

"How much for everything then?" Butz asked.

Moore spoke as he wrote "What Current Commodities Cost." He muttered, scribbling, "Wood and all that pertains to it—carpenter and joiners—walls—organ and paint." He fell silent as he added up the numbers, his quill scratching against the paper. Then he motioned toward what he'd written. "Judging by these plans, I'd say at the very least a thousand pounds, but more likely upwards of fifteen hundred."

The crackling and sparking of logs in the fireplace filled in a silent space.

"Where are we going to get that much money?" Butz asked, his voice low. "Even if people give regularly, by subscription or freewill offerings, I can't see us raising that much." After a moment he added, "Perhaps by enlisting members to help construct the church, we can keep costs down." The men started buzzing, and he raised his voice. "No matter how we do this, Easton is a growing village and the county seat, and we require a dedicated church building—with an organ."

"The problem with volunteer labor, Mr. Butz, is what happens when men can't or won't keep their end of the bargain," Moore said. "Sometimes this happens because of accidents and illness. Just think of poor Mr. Krontz who lost his life when he slipped in his field and struck his head against a rock. Then there was Mr. Anderson who drowned a while back when his horse threw him into the Lehigh River at flood stage."

The men gaped at the gruesome parade of tragedy. Peter's mind stirred, running through the numbers as well as the issues related to financing the project, trying to solve the problem. He was, after all, good at solving problems.

A few moments later, Elias Shook had his say. "Do you know what I think?" He didn't wait for an answer. "I think we need a benefactor, someone with enough means to help us."

"Yes, but who in Easton is wealthy enough to give the kind of money required?" Michael Butz asked. "Certainly not Mr. Hart. He has money, but why would a Jew fund a church?"

He spread his hands and lifted them.

A grin spread across Garrett Moore's expansive face. "Well, Mr. Butz, fortunately Mr. Hart isn't the only, or the wealthiest, man in town."

Peter felt every eye in the room look in his direction.

After supper, Catherine and Peter walked down Northampton Street toward the new church building site, her hand entwined in his arm. Then they'd go to the Delaware River to watch the annual spring greening commencing from shore to shore. As they reached the courthouse, Catherine said, "I could almost smell spring yesterday. There was just such a freshness in the air." She sniffed a few times and frowned. "Now all I smell are pigs and sheep."

Easton may have added houses and businesses in the last several years, and the courthouse now boasted a steeple, lending a greater air of dignity to the county seat, but one thing remained the same—an abundance of pig pens still fronted the street. When livestock took their daily bath in the pond at the Great Square, an unholy ruckus often erupted, making life especially interesting when courts were in session. "Mr. Smith, I find you guilty"—snort squeak grunt—"of trespassing on the property of Mr. Fielding with an intent to steal his prized chicken"—grunt snort squeak—"and I sentence you to a day in the stocks." Then there would follow a chorus of squealing, as if Anthony Esser, the butcher, were slaughtering a frightened pig.

No one was more upset about the situation than Ziba Wiggins, the venerable keeper of the courthouse who'd helped built the place nearly a decade ago and stayed on to make sure no one abused it. "Either I go or the pigs go," he'd often say, but when the pigs didn't depart, neither did he. Ziba's hope they'd someday be banned sprang eternal.

Peter didn't mind the animals' presence as much as Ziba or Catherine did. In fact, seeing pigs and sheep in the center of town reminded him of his distant boyhood in Germany where village and farm life often converged.

He teased his wife. "Aren't we not more sophisticated than the Wyoming Valley?" "Humph." She tossed back her head.

In the near distance, he heard the delectable sound of cowbells. The small herds were heading home to the north and west of town along Ferry Street, and Peter pictured the women tending them lining the cows up for the evening milking. Passing several villagers and greeting them, he and Catherine turned down Julianna Street a block or so from the courthouse where the new church would be built.

"This is such a nice piece of land for the new church," she said.

"I like the central location at the heart of Easton."

After walking around the site, they continued on their path to the river and got as far as the Bachmann Publick House when Catherine's gait slowed to a crawl, her limping more pronounced. Peter stopped altogether and gazing at her, noticed color draining from her normally pink cheeks. "Are you alright, dear?" He tried to keep his alarm from showing, but where the health of his spouses was concerned, he was understandably jumpy.

"I'm fine, just a trifle queasy."

Her cheeks weren't only pale, they looked almost hollow, and dark circles spread under her eyes. Was she getting enough to eat? Was she sleeping enough? "Perhaps we shouldn't go as far as the river," he said.

She didn't argue. "Maybe another time."

"I can get the carriage if you need to ride."

"Oh, no, not at all. I'll be fine. Let's just head back. I'm a little tired is all."

He tried to swallow fear rising like bile in his stomach, fear of Catherine's not being alright, fear she might not outlive him after all.

"Papa, are you okay?" Susannah rode next to Peter atop her tricolored horse on their way to visit one of his best customers, a Moravian farmer in Hanover Township.

He looked over and down at her, taking a moment to register her effort at conversation. Since they'd set out from Easton fifteen minutes earlier, he'd only spoken two sentences about the muddy conditions after a few days of hard rains. Still, he was happy for his daughter's pleasant company. Peter had been hoping to bring Catherine along, but she said she wasn't up to the dozen or so mile trip. In fact, she'd barely touched her breakfast and had risen from the table in such a hurry she'd knocked over a vase of wildflowers Frau Hamster had put near her mistress. For a second, Peter wondered if he'd heard his wife mutter an oath in German, but he quickly dismissed the thought. Catherine had never kept company with oaths and couldn't abide their use by other people. And why, for pity's sake, was Frau Hamster scowling at him as if he'd done something wrong?

"Frau Hamster, in the future I would advise you to bring a more pleasant expression to my table," he'd told her. Judging by her raised eyebrows and respectful curtsey, she'd understood the message.

Clearly, Catherine wasn't her usual self. When he'd asked her before breakfast if she knew where there might be a clean pair of woolen hose, her eyes had flashed. She'd barked, "Why don't you ask Frau Hamster?" Just as quickly, she'd smiled and apologized.

"Papa?"

"Uh, yes, Susannah, you were saying?" He cleared his throat and his mind of the prior images, feeling the up and down motion of his horse underneath him. He willed his focus on the blossoming young woman beside him, who daily seemed to bear more of a striking resemblance to her departed mother.

"I asked if you were okay."

"Why, yes, I'm fine. Why do you ask?"

The sound of their horses' hooves clomped against the soggy dirt road. "You seem distracted."

How much should he say? Susannah wasn't a child anymore, something becoming more evident by the day as she left girlhood and dolls from Meyer Hart's store behind. "I suppose I am, a little." He smiled in her direction.

"You can tell me, if you like, I mean why you're distracted, but I'm pretty sure I already know."

His eyebrows rose. When had she become so self-assured? "You do?"

She gave a small laugh. "I know you very well, Papa. I can read you like one of your leather-bound books."

Her lightheartedness filled him with a kind of ease, and he answered in a semi-teasing tone, "You can, can you? And what, may I ask, am I thinking?"

"You're concerned about Mother Catherine."

Dread scattered his cheerfulness to the light winds he felt on his face under the brim of his hat. "A little, yes."

"I know she's been tired and a little grumpy lately."

"Well, yes, I suppose she has been."

Susannah added, "And a little sick to her stomach."

He stared at her, not seeing a half dozen deer bounding past them on the right, disappearing with the stamping of brush into the woods. "I hardly know what to say."

"Men usually don't, Papa."

He frowned, feeling grumpy. "Men usually don't what?"

"Understand what happens to women. You just go about your own business."

"Susannah, would you please make your point more directly?"

"Why, of course, Papa. There's nothing to worry about concerning Mother Catherine's health. She's going to be fine, you know."

He tilted his head to one side. "How do you happen to know this?"

"Like I said, women know more than men." She paused. "That is, they know when a lady is expecting."

"Expecting?" He let the word, seep into his consciousness. Thirty seconds later the light came on. "Catherine is expecting a child?"

"Yes, Papa."

He mentally brushed away the confusion filling his mind like so many cobwebs. "Has she told you this?" He didn't add, "Why hasn't she told me?"

"I didn't have to be told." She wore smugness like a cloak.

Catherine was expecting. Catherine was expecting! Of course, she was. Had he been such a dolt he hadn't read the early signs of pregnancy and him a father several times over? He wanted to abandon their trek and rush straight back to Easton and hold her in his arms and tell her how happy he was for her, for them. A new baby! Right now, he wouldn't consider the dangers—what had happened to his sweet Anna as she struggled to bring new life into the world. Not now, not when relief filled him.

He stood at the door of the Konk farmhouse preparing to leave, enjoying these last words with Wilhelm, yet wanting to get home to Catherine. The men had discussed Peter Jr.'s wedding, plans for Easton's new church building and spring's early arrival.

"Now that young Peter has gone into fulling, are you pleased with the way the mills are running?" Wilhelm asked.

"I am. Jacob and Andrew work well together. Jacob has a head for numbers and is very organized with accounts, and Andrew keeps the mill operating smoothly."

"How's the new indentured servant working for you?"

Peter nodded, watching Bruna Konk bustling in the background with her daughter, looking as if they were gathering food to send back to Easton with him. He hoped they realized he hadn't brought the wagon. "Peter Horeback is doing well. He's a loyal, hard worker, a lot like Hans Schmidt has always been."

"Ah, now, there is a good man for you," Wilhelm said. "How is he faring with his new family? Didn't he marry an Indian?"

"Yes, he did. They and their three children enjoy good health." He paused. "Of course, once I retire in a couple weeks I plan to get my hands in once again."

"You've served our fair county well these many years."

Peter gave a slight bow. "I thank you."

"I should thank you." He rummaged around in his pants pockets, making them bulge with his chubby fists until he produced some money for Peter.

"What's this?" He looked from the currency to his friend's face.

"You overpaid me for my last shipment of oats."

"Are you sure?"

"Quite sure, my friend." Wilhelm smiled.

"Thank you, then, but I assure you, this isn't necessary."

"Oh, but we Moravians strive for honesty in all our dealings, especially with friends."

Peter smiled back. "You are a good man."

Bruna hustled over to him bearing a full-to-bursting sack. "Here is leetle something for you and Frau Kichline." She handed the package to Peter, who realized a man of smaller, lighter stature would have surely sunk under the weight.

"Frau Konk, did you put the entire contents of your kitchen in here?"

Her laughter came easily. *"Nein! Es gibt zwiebel, brot, keske, und kase."*

He bowed from the waist, thankful for the gifts of pickled cabbage, bread, cookies, and cheese. *"Danke so sehr."*

"Bitte."

"Mama knows how much Susannah enjoys our Moravian *keske*," their daughter Elise said.

Peter stared at the girl for a moment and realized Susannah wasn't with her. Why was that? Hadn't she come to spend time with Elise? "Uh, yes, Susannah does like the cookies very much. Speaking of my *tochter*, where might she be?" He looked about him.

A grin spread across Elise's face as she nodded her head toward the open door. Leaning against a fence near the barn stood Susannah and Hans, each of them looking as if they'd swallowed the very sun. Peter disliked what he was seeing, disliked it intensely. *She's just a child. She should be in the house with Elise discussing needlework.* Sure, Hans was as upstanding as his father, but Susannah was only ten. No, wait a minute, Twelve. No, he had that wrong. No matter how many times he did the mental calculating, Susannah still came up fourteen.

CHAPTER FIVE

Dear Dr. Miles,

My name is Connie Pierce, and I'm a volunteer at the Jane Moyer Library at the Sigal Museum. I'm also a DAR, George Taylor Chapter, and we met last Heritage Day when you and your son stopped by the Parson-Taylor House. I was very happy when your email to the library and Leslie Sueter got forwarded to me! I'm also pleased Sandy from the Marx Room referred you to us because we do indeed have a lot of primary source information about your ancestor, Colonel Peter Kichline. (I know there are multiple spellings of his last name, but I prefer this one. Judging from your email, you do as well!) I would love to shepherd you through some of the documents we have. If you give me a date and time to come in, I'll make sure I pull everything I can find. Just give me about three days' notice. The library is open Wednesday through Friday from ten a.m. to two-thirty p.m. or by appointment. I look forward to hearing from you and seeing you very soon.

Yours,

Connie Pierce

With school about to close for the summer, there was no time to waste. Erin checked her schedule and answered the email immediately. Her search for a teaching position would just have to wait. Again.

She arrived at the Sigal Museum promptly at ten o'clock on Friday armed with a newly minted membership card from the Northampton County Historical Society, which worked in tandem with the Sigal and the Jane Moyer Library. She also carried a fresh notebook, camera, and plenty of cash to make copies. She took the elevator to the third floor and proceeded to the library's main room, which featured well-designed wooden tables, a few rows of book shelves and a counter toward the back where an attendant waited to be of service. A red-headed teenager sat at a table toward the far side of the spacious room with a stack of open books to her left, typing furiously on an iPad, apparently in the throes of a term paper. A bald man stood at the copy machine and smiled at Erin as she entered the room. She was not only surprised to find people here so early, but on glancing around, she didn't see as many books and stacks as she expected. When she stepped up to the counter, however, Erin noticed there were many bookshelves behind the attendant. Their location suddenly made sense—this was no ordinary library, but a repository of Northampton County history, and as such, housed rare and delicate items.

The twenty-something attendant, whose badge identified him as Michael Thatcher, looked up from texting on his phone. "Hi. Can I help you?"

"Yes, I'm Erin Miles, and I have an appointment with Connie Pierce."

A woman appeared from a side door. "Dr. Miles! How good to see you again." She came over and shook Erin's hand. "I'm glad you were able to come so quickly. I have so much to show you."

Erin hadn't anticipated being addressed so formally, but she couldn't say she was displeased. She liked being called *doctor*. "I'm happy to be here. This is a wonderful library."

"Thanks. We think so."

She studied the woman's face and remembered how she'd instantly liked her the summer before when they'd met briefly. Connie was somewhere in her late forties, Erin guessed, a little shorter than herself, trim, with deep-red hair cut stylishly short. Although she was dressed simply in a short-sleeved sweater and slacks, she looked impeccable.

"We have a lot to show you today."

Erin wondered who "we" were. "Are you okay with my taking notes and photos? I know some research libraries discourage those."

"I don't have a problem with either. I'll just gather the documents and be right with you." Connie motioned to a table on the right side of the room. "Have a seat."

Erin hung her purse over the side of a chair as Michael the attendant used a loud electric pencil sharpener. She withdrew her notebook and the Villanova pen her doctoral advisor had given her, along with her camera. Five minutes later, Connie appeared with a short stack of folders and a tall, blond man, who smiled in Erin's direction. Her brain clicked into gear, conjuring up his name just as Connie began introducing them.

"This is Paul Bassett, a local historian who volunteers in the library. Paul, I'd like you to meet Dr. Erin Miles."

He reached out a hand for her to shake, and Erin once again noted its dissonant roughness for a man who embodied a preppy vibe. He didn't strike her as someone who worked with his hands, so why the calluses? "Doctor, is it now?" he asked.

"Hello, Paul. It's nice to see you again, and yes, I received my doctorate a few weeks ago."

"Well, congratulations, Doc!"

When he smiled, his blue eyes crinkled, and Erin had the same feeling she'd had upon first meeting him the year before—that he reminded her of someone. She started wondering who, but then Connie interrupted her thoughts.

"You've met?" She looked from one to the other.

"Twice," Paul said, but he didn't elaborate.

Connie's dark eyes squinted, and she looked puzzled. "I didn't know."

"We met when I was doing research at the Marx Room last year," Erin said.

"Then we bumped into each other at Heritage Day."

"Oh, well, how nice." Connie smiled.

Paul addressed Erin. "When I found out you were coming today, I made sure to be here. I'm deeply interested in your ancestor and wanted to see what Connie could round up from the files."

Erin felt slightly dizzy, as if she'd just stepped off a carousel. She was happy to see Paul, but something about him made her uneasy—what she couldn't quite put her finger on. She turned to Connie, trying to right herself. "It looks like you have a number of things to show me."

"Indeed, I do, Dr. Miles."

"Please call me Erin."

Connie grinned. "Okay, Erin." She opened a folder and began removing documents weathered to a crisp antique brown. A few were encased in protective plastic slips.

"Will I need gloves to handle these?" Their fragility almost frightened Erin. She harbored a flashing image of her touching one, only to see the document dissolve into papered dust.

"That won't be necessary. The most delicate ones are already protected." Connie took a seat to Erin's right, and Paul sat in the chair to her left. Erin thought he smelled like the sheets her grandmother used to line dry on warm summer days.

"Are there any pictures of Colonel Kichline?" There was no mistaking Erin's eagerness.

Connie tilted her head. "Well, yes and no, at least nothing original. I've looked for a portrait, figuring there might be one since he was so prominent in Easton and Northampton County history, but I haven't been able to find one, not yet anyway. I think if he'd lived long enough, there would definitely have been a portrait since he was Easton's first Chief Burgess."

Erin was disappointed. To see what Grandfather Peter looked like was Erin's Holy Grail, but Connie had said something about there being some sort of image. *I wonder what she meant.* She knew from prior research Peter Kichline was something like six-feet-two-inches tall and had a commanding presence. Sometimes she stared at her Uncle Thomas's photograph, which had been taken the year before he died, since he was the one male in her immediate family with connections to both Peter and Charles Kichline. Thomas might have looked something like them. Her uncle had also stretched to six feet, what little hair he had left on the sides was light and sandy, and he'd had dark blue eyes. Somehow, she never imagined Grandfather Peter sporting the billiard ball look, though. Uncle Thomas also looked perpetually up to something—kind of a male Mona Lisa—and Erin wondered if Peter Kichline had looked at life the same puckish way.

Connie's voice interrupted her musing. "This first document I'll show you is a letter written to Colonel Kichline while he was a prisoner of war."

The curator slid the piece in a plastic sleeve gently in Erin's direction. As she picked it up, she tried to decipher the looping handwriting of another era, as well as the signature. "This is pretty hard to read." Erin squinted at the document until she made out and read aloud, "'Your wife and family are well. Remember their love to you and all your friends have join with me in our best respects to you, wishing we may see you soon.' The wording sounds awkward." She moved the document to catch more light, but concluded, "I'm afraid I can't make out the rest." She handed the paper back to Connie, hoping she'd be more successful.

"Over the years, I've become pretty good at reading 18th-century handwriting. Let's see, then, the signature line appears to say, 'Your affectionate friend, Herman,' hmmm, looks like 'Schingerer.' I don't recognize that name, do you, Paul?" She moved the document across the desk to him.

Paul telescoped the paper back and forth a few times, and Erin figured he must be over forty. She remembered her eye doctor's comment when she turned that corner. "Most people over forty deal with myopia and will need reading glasses."

"Could be Schingner. I'm not sure." Paul handed the document back to Erin. "The date is clearly December 19, 1776, though."

"He'd been a prisoner of the British since August," she said, "and he wasn't exchanged until February of the following year."

Paul pressed his lips together. "What a tough time for him."

Erin had an intimate glimpse into her ancestor's situation as a prisoner. *What must his family have gone through with him away, not knowing if he'd ever be coming home?*

Connie presented another manuscript. "This next document isn't very old at all. Actually, it's a typewritten account of a letter written by Colonel Robert Hooper testifying to Colonel Kichline's character after being released by the British."

As Erin read, she learned of Grandfather Peter's having been "intimately acquainted" with Hooper, who also was his "near neighbor." *I wonder where he lived. I'd love to be able to go there and know he'd been in the same spot, too. His house was most likely along Northampton Street since he and Margaretta had come so early in Easton's history when most of the buildings were along the main thoroughfare.* As she continued reading, one sentence seemed to shout at her, and she read the words aloud. "'He has in confidence often mentioned to me the cruel treatment he and his officers received when prisoners.'"

For a long moment she, Connie, and Paul kept silence. Then Paul spoke. "I've done some research on American prisoners of war after the Battle of Long Island, and I can tell you the ones who were sent to prison ships usually didn't come out alive or in their right minds. The conditions were brutal, and the British had no pity. They wanted to end what they considered a lawless rebellion, and this was one way to accomplish their objective."

Erin's throat felt as if she'd swallowed a ping pong ball. "Do you think Peter was on such a ship?"

Paul closed his eyes and shook his head. "He was an officer, so he probably was treated better, though 'better' is certainly relative. He likely was kept in a house or other building with his fellow officers. Still, he would've relied on support from home to keep him alive since the British weren't going to provide more than the bare minimum of food, clothing, and shelter."

"He certainly made a great sacrifice for our country." Connie's tone was low, reverent.

Erin wanted to say something about Colonel Miles, to find out if Paul knew anything about a possible connection between him and her Grandfather Peter, but she was too eager to see the rest of the documents to go in that direction. She tucked away the thought for future reference.

Connie presented another document, a March 1777 letter written by Captain John Arndt. "What's this one?" Erin asked.

Paul was looking over her shoulder. "Essentially, it's a statement saying the Colonel had returned to Easton in February and had remained loyal to the Patriot Cause. This is Arndt's sworn testimony that Peter Kichline voluntarily took an Oath of Allegiance and Fidelity on, let's see, on March 3, 1777." Paul grinned at Erin. "He didn't waste any time! You might even say this was his way of thumbing his nose at the British."

She cocked her head, looking at Paul. "What do you mean?"

Paul turned to the curator. "Connie, do you have the document he signed upon his release?"

"Yes, just give me a minute to find it." She looked through the pile, quickly locating the item. "Here you go." She placed the faded paper before Erin.

"What this means is he's promising not to take up arms against the King again," Paul said.

Erin read the letter, which had been witnessed by the infamous Loyalist commandant of prisoners, Joshua Loring Jr., whose wife had become General William Howe's mistress. While connecting her Grandfather Peter to those historically noteworthy people was fascinating, what really got Erin's attention was seeing her relative's signature again, the one bearing a confident, rounded "P" and the surname "Kachlein." *Another window into his spirit.* "Where did all these original documents come from?" she asked.

"Various places," Connie said. "Most were given to the historical society decades ago by family members who wanted them to be preserved for the public record, and some were found in places like people's attics in long-forgotten boxes."

She wondered aloud whether there were any Kichline family Bibles or diaries.

"I haven't seen any, but we have many archives that haven't been opened in years. It's possible there's something there."

"Oh, it would be so wonderful if you could find other things, not that these aren't special," Erin hastened to add. "I'm thrilled with what you're showing me. I feel like I'm on my own personal episode of 'Who Do You Think You Are!' And you're both taking so much of your time to do this."

Paul smiled at her. "Believe me, I may be enjoying this as much as you are."

"I can say the same for myself. I love connecting people to their ancestors. My job is always more exciting when I'm helping someone discover their ancestry."

For the next hour and a half, Erin reviewed one document after another, including an *Easton Express* article about Peter from the nation's Bicentennial in 1976. The piece featured drawings of him from the French and Indian War, as a Revolutionary War Soldier, and then one of his face. She felt an adrenaline rush. "Do you think this is really what he looked like?" she asked Paul and Connie. In a way, she hoped not because her many times great-grandfather had been portrayed with a narrow face and pointy nose, wearing an almost dainty expression, hardly the look of a robust sheriff and military commander. She'd pictured him to be considerably more vigorous—more of a man's man.

"Somehow, I doubt it," Connie said.

"The article was written by William Weiss and James Wright," Paul said. "I've come across Wright's name a lot. I think he used to write for the paper about local history."

"That's what I know about him, too," Connie said.

"Maybe we could ask him!" Erin almost shouted.

"I'm afraid he died a while back," Paul said.

"Oh, what a shame." Erin felt like one of her son's popped water balloons.

"Yes, but don't worry," Connie said, "I'll keep looking for a portrait or something."

The final document she showed Erin was a carefully preserved copy of Peter Kichline's Last Will and Testament, a lengthy missive written in tight script. Erin knew in order to give the will justice, she'd have to make a good copy and transcribe it at home when she had a longer stretch of time. She couldn't wait.

"If you like, I'll try to read some of the will for you now," Connie said. When Erin nodded her head, her new friend began, "In the Name of God Amen; I Peter Kachlein of Easton in the County of Northampton in the State of Pennsylvania, Esquire, being advanced in years and visited with bodily infirmities, but of sound and well disposing mind, memory, and understanding thanks be given unto God, for this and all his other Favors conferred upon me in this life ..."

Erin's mind wandered, mulling over those strong and certain words, echoing her ancestor's faith and gratitude for a life well lived. She found herself loving him more than ever for bequeathing such a legacy to her—to all his descendants.

"Oh, this is funny," Connie said a few minutes later. "Listen to this, 'And I do give and desire unto Catherine, my dearly beloved wife the sum of One Hundred and Fifty Pounds Lawful money of Pennsylvania, my best Bed—Bedspread and all Furniture thereto and one cow of her own choice to be paid and Delivered unto her within Ten days after my decease.'"

Erin laughed out loud. "How funny about the cow and the bedspread! I can just picture a soulful looking beast being led to Catherine Kichline by a sturdy rope tied around its neck, bearing a carefully folded bedspread."

Connie wiped her eyes with a tissue as she laughed. When she regained some composure, she said, "This gets funnier. The will goes on to say during her widowhood she's going to receive a yearly stipend from proceeds from the family crops and 'three cords of good firewood to be delivered to her dwelling house in Easton (and nowhere else) by my son Peter.' In other words, the Colonel will see to it that Catherine is taken care of, but if she remarries, the gravy train stops!"

Erin laughed again. She was looking at yet another part of her ancestor's character, and she liked what she was seeing. Yes, there was something winsome about him, just like there had been about her Uncle Thomas.

She said her thanks and goodbyes to Connie, sharing a hug with the woman who'd enjoyed the morning as much as Erin, sprinkled with sincere promises of keeping in touch. Paul rode the elevator with her, and Erin decided to ask her question about Colonel Miles and Peter Kichline.

"Have you heard about Colonel Samuel Miles? I'd like to find out if they knew each other since they were both at the Battle of Brooklyn, and they were both prisoners of war afterward."

"Maybe I can help out. I love that kind of research, and since I live right here, I have access to these wonderful libraries."

"Oh, would you?"

"It would be my pleasure." He paused as they got off on the main floor where a class of noisy first graders jostled each other as they waited to tour the museum. "Here you go." He reached into a pocket and produced a business card. "Do you have one?"

"Yes, I do." Erin pulled one out of her purse's side pocket. "This is old, but my contact information is the same."

He took the card and placed it in his pocket. "I'll be in touch."

"Thank you so much for today. I won't forget this any time soon."

Paul grinned at her. "Neither will I."

CHAPTER SIX

He stood by a front window protected from slashing rain and a howling wind so loud the very Furies appeared to have been unleashed. He'd planned to take his copy of *The Pennsylvania Gazette* to the courthouse, a tradition he'd established back in Easton's early days when he first started making the paper available to patrons at the tavern he and Margaretta had run. He believed a well-informed people made better, more responsible citizens. He gave up the business to become Northampton County's Sheriff, the first time around, but he continued taking *The Gazette* to the Eckerts when they bought the tavern. When the courthouse opened eight years ago, Peter gave the newspaper a wider distribution there, although Ziba Wiggins guarded *The Gazette* as if it were the Magna Carta. He found himself smiling. *Funny how the two places have converged—Frau Eckert is now Mrs. Ziba Wiggins. One way or the other, I'm still contributing the paper to both establishments.*

Not even the intrepid keeper of the courthouse could expect Peter to go out on a day suited more to water fowl than human beings. The malicious March weather reminded him how happy he was to retire in just a few days. After two, three-year terms, he was eager to lay the mantel of Sheriff about the neck of Henry Fullert so he could tend to his own family and his own "castle." He'd had his fill of chasing criminals up and down Northampton

County's hills and dales to its remotest edges near the New York border. His memories drifted back to January 1771 when he and two deputies had taken a posse into the Susquehanna River hinterlands to root out the murderous Paxton Boys. He could still recall the damp coldness creeping into his bones. He'd been successful in ridding the Pennsylvania frontier of Paxton's ruffians, but not before Peter's fine deputy Nathan Ogden lay dead. A persistent ache in his left elbow served as a souvenir of the mission, as well as a reminder he was no longer a young man, something he tended to forget on warmer days.

His wife's soft steps and gentle scent, like a lily of the valley, alerted him to her presence, and he turned to see her radiant face, grateful the morning sickness had passed after just a few weeks. He smiled at the memory of her hearty breakfast: a piece of sausage the size of his flintlock pistol, half a loaf of rye bread slathered with fresh butter, and a bowl of applesauce. Her appetite had raised Andrew, Jacob, and Susannah's eyebrows before they'd scattered off to the mills and school bundled in layers. "Hello, my dear." He held out his hand to her and when she received it, he felt the smallness—and the chill. "Your hand is cold. Are you cold? Should I stoke the fire? Do you need another shawl?"

Catherine laughed. "I'm just fine, Peter, although I do rather like the warmth of your hand." She glanced out the six-paned window at the lamentations of wind and rain. "Did I catch you day-dreaming?"

"A little. I'm mostly waiting for a break in this storm to take the paper down to the courthouse. I'm sure no one will be there just now anyway."

"I think you're nice to share your paper with everyone." She stood closer to him. "You're always giving to others."

He felt the warmth of her body along his right side and held her against himself. "You know what my mother taught me." He waited for her to follow his lead and they both recited, "To whom much is given is much required." Their laughter echoed in the room.

She tilted her head and looked in his blue eyes. "There are people who give but complain about the giving afterward, or who give mostly to call attention to themselves. You, on the other hand, go about your good works quietly."

His voice was soft. "As it should be."

Out of the blue, a large, dark blur swooped before them outside, filling the window. They both jumped. A moment later, the apparition was banging on the door. Peter gently led his wife to the love seat and, on high alert, strode to the door where he discovered his friend, Robert Traill, standing there dripping from top to bottom.

"Robert! Come in." He stepped aside to give his sturdy friend entrance as Frau Hamster barreled down the hall.

"Thank you, my friend." Traill removed his sodden hat, which the housekeeper accepted wordlessly. She stood waiting while he removed an enormous wool overcoat, which lent to the entryway an odor of wet sheep. The housekeeper stepped back to hang the hat and cloak on wooden pegs and turned to the sheriff.

"Please bring our visitor a cup of tea," Peter said, watching as she gave an all-business nod and turned on her heels. "Come inside and sit by the fire, Robert." He led Traill by the arm into the parlor where Catherine greeted him.

"Good morning, Mr. Traill. It's a pleasure to see you, although I regret you had to endure such conditions to get here."

Traill bowed. "The pleasure is all mine, Mrs. Kichline. I deeply regret spreading this dampness throughout your home."

"I hadn't noticed."

Peter took his place at the side of the fireplace, watching his friend rub his hands together before its cheering heat. Everything about Traill— hands, face, even his ears, seemed pale, as if a giant cloth had erased his usual ruddiness. He'd never seen his friend so out of sorts.

"I'm pleased to see you, too, but I wonder if all can be well if you've come to visit on such a day."

"I appreciate your concern. I am on a rather urgent mission." Traill's r's rolled with more gusto this morning, a testimony to his Scottish heritage.

"I trust you aren't getting cold feet, Mr. Traill?" Catherine teased her husband's friend.

He grinned and shook his head. "I assure you cold feet are not in play at the moment, not from the frigid weather or for any other reason."

"Good. Elizabeth is not only my dearest friend, but she'll make you the very best wife."

"I know. I don't half deserve her. That's why I'm here, however—about the wedding."

"Is something wrong?" Peter asked.

"I'm afraid so." Traill reached into a pocket of his waist coat and produced a crumpled envelope. "I just received word that Reverend Hanlon won't be able to officiate on Thursday."

Peter frowned. "What happened?"

"He's been preaching to the Presbyterians throughout northern Sussex County and came down with a heavy cold. Phoebe has gone to be with him and wrote this letter on his behalf." He tapped the envelope with the back of his right hand.

"Oh, what a shame. I hope he'll soon be well," Catherine said.

"As do I."

"His illness does leave you and Elizabeth in a tough spot, though." Peter pulled his chin, considering what he could do about the situation.

"Does Elizabeth know?" Catherine asked.

"I haven't told her yet. She's so happy I don't want to dampen her spirits."

"Perhaps one of the Moravian ministers could do the ceremony."

"That thought crossed my mind as well, Mrs. Kichline, although I was hoping for a Presbyterian wedding." He momentarily gazed out the window.

"How could the son of a Presbyterian minister want anything else?" she said.

"Aye, and the grandson of one as well."

Peter's eyes brightened, as if the sun had just broken through. "Yesterday afternoon, I was talking to Mr. Duffburd at the ferry, and he told me Reverend White had just come across from New Jersey."

The gloom lifted like a fog from Traill's face. "He's in the area, then?"

"I think Duffburd said he was heading up toward Nazareth to preach to the Presbyterians around the Drylands."

Catherine said, "I like him. He's such a quiet, pleasant man."

"Except when he's in the pulpit of course," Peter said. He remembered the times White had preached in Easton, and the minister's voice had carried clear across the Delaware into New Jersey.

"How do we find him?" Traill asked. "The wedding is two days from now."

"Don't worry," Peter said. "I'll get him for you."

While serving as sheriff across many years, he'd come to know pretty much everyone's business in Northampton County, which is how he knew Reverend White always stayed at the Sign of the Plough, the Lefevres' tavern. Five miles north of Easton, on the edge of the hinterlands, scattered settlers looked forward to itinerant preaching like a spring rain after the first planting. While the prospect of bringing the pastor to Robert Traill's rescue brought joy to his heart, Peter couldn't deny his stomach also celebrated the anticipation of a plate filed with Frau Lefevre's crispy trout and one or two of her acclaimed apple dumplings. Both she and her husband were getting along in years—well into their seventies by now—but they remained hale, if not entirely hearty, and managed to keep their beloved public house operating.

He arrived soaking wet, hating to drag his drenched overcoat, hat, and boots into their immaculate establishment, but Frau Lefevre wasn't having any of his protests as she reached for the soggy garments. "Ach! Do not let's say another word, Sheriff. Let me have that *mantel*, and I'll dry it for you." She practically wrestled the coat off despite her only coming up to his chest. "Go you by the fire, *ja*, and I'll get you a nice *grog*."

Peter smiled at her mix of English and German, pleased she never entirely discarded her native tongue. As for himself, living in America over thirty years, he'd never fully dropped his accent either, although he spoke the King's English with perfect enunciation. "You better mind her, Sheriff." John Lefevre spoke around his pipe stem, his upper lip curled in amusement. "As you know, my wife is a force to be reckoned with."

"Indeed, she is!" Peter felt five pounds' lighter without the drenched garment and followed his old friend to the fireplace where logs spit and blazed. He spread his chapped hands before the heat.

"I can't imagine you coming here on a day like this for a social call, Sheriff, though I'm always pleased to see you." Lefevre pulled two chairs up to the fire, and the men sat, appearing to be the only ones in the tavern.

"You are correct, my friend. I take it you're aware of Robert Traill's impending marriage?"

"That I am." The gray head nodded. "It's this week, isn't it?"

"Yes. He came to see me a little while ago with some unhappy news— Reverend Hanlon was scheduled to perform the ceremony, but he's taken ill and can't come. I heard Mr. White is back in the area and figured you'd know where I could find him."

Peter heard footsteps descending on the stairs and looked up. "You have found me, Sheriff Kichline."

"Reverend White!" He jumped up, and when the pastor came over to Peter, they shook hands. White certainly lived up to his name. He wore a white suit of clothes, white riding boots, and even his hair was white, lending an air of age and authority. However, his skin was completely unwrinkled, and Peter believed him to be in his early thirties. Only the placid green eyes provided relief from the cascade of white. "Oh, but I'm happy to see you, sir. You're the very reason I've come today."

Lefevre pulled up another chair, urging the men toward the fire as he and his wife scrambled in the background to prepare food and drink.

"The matter must be urgent, Sheriff." White leaned forward. He repeated the news about the Reverend Hanlon's illness and Robert Traill's preference for a Presbyterian minister. "Might you be able to do the ceremony this Thursday?" He reminded himself of Susannah when she asked him for a new dress or permission to go on an outing with friends at the Point.

White gazed into the fire as if he were considering the request. Finally, he said, "Yes, I'll be able to manage a wedding in Easton and still make my weekend preaching commitments."

"Thank you, Mr. White. Thank you very much." Peter inhaled deeply, enjoying the relief flowing through him.

Lefevre reappeared. "Before you two leave for Easton, I insist you take some nourishment. Perhaps the rain will let up by then as well." He looked toward the windows, which appeared to be weeping.

Peter wasn't about to argue. Settling in, he asked the pastor, "How have you been since we last saw each other?"

"Quite well, thank you." White sat back and crossed his legs. "I've been preaching right about where Pastor Hanlon is now—in upper Sussex County. In fact, he came to relieve me so I could visit my flocks here in the

61

Drylands, then make my way up toward the New York border."

"Have you encountered any particular difficulties in your circuit riding? You are, after all, in some rugged territory."

White nodded and smiled. "There's been nothing the Almighty hasn't been able to handle. As long as I fix my eyes on him, I do well." He gazed at Peter. "What about yourself? I understand you married recently."

"You heard correctly. My dear Anna died a year ago, and I have been blessed to once again find myself wed to a young woman of deep faith and upstanding character."

"May this be a long and blessed union." White paused then smiled. "I understand another change is in order as well."

Peter raised his eyebrow. "About the time I join Mr. Traill to his lady in holy matrimony, you will be stepping aside as Sheriff of Northampton County." Peter grinned as he realized sheriffs weren't the only people who knew everyone else's business.

The Traills' parlor swarmed with Eastonians exclaiming over tables covered with damask cloths and platters of meats, vegetables, breads, cakes, pies, and cookies. Peter watched as his namesake greeted the bride and groom near the fireplace, but when Peter Jr. and his own wife turned toward him, he blanched at the sight of her. For a confusing moment, he saw the face of his Anna, and time took on the oddest aspect, as if this weren't March 9, 1774, but a few years earlier, and somehow, Anna was here talking to his son. He shook his head to clear the muddle. Sarah Doll, now Kichline, looked so much like her deceased sister—except for the variation in height—Anna had been shorter.

Ziba Wiggins provided comic relief as he came up to Peter, his cravat bearing a sauce stain the size of a crab apple—and about the same color.

"So, Sheriff, are you looking forward to retirement?"

"Yes, I certainly am."

"Please don't make yourself scarce at the courthouse." He looked down at his shoes. "I would be missing you, that I would."

Peter clamped a hand on the aging man's shoulder and felt its leanness. "You shall still get my copy of *The Gazette*, and I'll visit you at least once a week beside that, Mr. Wiggins."

Some of his friends, George Taylor, Robert Levers, and Lewis Gordon, stood in the hallway near the door. Peter tilted his head to one side when he saw them talking among themselves while looking at him directly. When Taylor saw Peter gazing back, he raised his right hand and motioned him to come.

"Please excuse me, Mr. Wiggins."

"Of course, Sheriff. Oh, I just thought of something. Can I still call you 'Sheriff' after this?"

"I think that particular honor should be addressed to Mr. Fullert. 'Mr. Kichline' will do just fine."

"That'll take some getting used to."

"Yes, I suppose it will for me as well. Good day, Mr. Wiggins." Peter headed toward the gathering of men, briefly greeting the blacksmith and his wife, who stood in his path to the door.

"There you are, Sheriff," Taylor said. "We need to speak to you."

The distinguished gentleman was holding a document of some sort. "Yes, of course, Mr. Taylor." He nodded toward the others. "Mr. Levers. Mr. Gordon."

Levers spoke up, placing his hands on his hips, feet astride. "You know that retirement you've been looking forward to, Mr. Kichline?"

"Why, yes. Yes, of course. What about my retirement?" Peter's left calf tingled.

"You'll need to put it off a bit longer, I'm afraid. Governor Penn has just appointed you a Justice of the Courts of Common Pleas and Quarter Sessions."

CHAPTER SEVEN

She stepped out of the Sigal Museum onto Northampton Street taking personally the words of former slave Harriet Tubman after crossing the Mason-Dixon Line to freedom—"there was such a wonder over everything." Easton shimmered, as if Tinker Bell had just sprinkled fairy dust all over the city. The Soldiers and Sailors shrine could have competed with the Washington Monument itself in its nobility. Clunky LANTA vans conveying riders gleamed like a Marine's dress shoes, and the huge statues of Crayola Crayons in the Circle seemed to have emerged from the very hands of a Renaissance sculptor. First UCC's slender steeple was as stately as if gracing the National Cathedral. Even the Dollar Store where Woolworth's used to be seemed more venerable than cheesy. Because of Peter Kichline and Erin's connection to him, she felt as if she were wearing gold taffeta instead of a sweater and khakis. A verse from the Psalms came to mind—"The lines are fallen unto me in pleasant places; yea, I have a goodly heritage." She savored the words' sweetness like the lime green lollipops she used to purchase at the Carmelcorn Shop.

Arriving at her minivan, she slid in and turned the key in the ignition. Just then, she noticed the time on the meter had expired and consulted her dashboard clock—12:15. Her stomach felt like an empty storage container, and she briefly considered crossing the bridge to see her mom and having lunch with her. Against everyone's advice and better judgment, Audrey was still working and probably would be at her post. Her mother insisted she was still perfectly capable of driving, which struck terror into Erin's heart, causing her to force horrific images of her mother's mangled Toyota, piercing sirens, and fire trucks from her mind. Not wanting her bubble of wonder to burst, she decided against seeing Audrey or her dad today. She was getting to know Easton on her own terms.

She could feed the meter and eat downtown at the yogurt café, Public Market, or one of the restaurants, or she could drive over to Spring Garden Street to Colonial Pizza. She'd always loved how they put the cheese on the bottom and the sauce on top. At that moment on the radio, she heard familiar introductory piano notes, and reaching back into her mental playlist, immediately identified the coffee-grounds voice of Rod Stewart and his ballad, "Have I Told You Lately?" Erin cranked up the volume as memories took her back to 1993 and her senior year at Lafayette— to a Zeta Psi graduation party. There she'd slow danced to the song with Barry Cavigliota, a biology major from Allentown. He'd taken her to the Lafayette-Lehigh football game and accompanied her to hear Clarence Thomas when he came to campus, but he'd never turned out to be more than a passing ship in her life. She recalled him whispering in her ear while Stewart crooned, "I'm going to miss you. Let's stay in touch." Like so many college friendships, however, this one had gone the way of her grandfather's Buick. Although she and Barry had savored only a brief connection, their relationship was a pleasant bookmark in the pages of her memories.

She knew where she wanted to have lunch.

Erin backed out of her parking spot, circled the monument and headed down South Third Street past the church, through a couple lights and up College Avenue's steep incline, which provided a panoramic view of Easton.

Erin turned left onto McCartney Street, then onto Pardee Drive where she parked at one of the residences' lots because the Quad was closed to traffic. She guessed spring semester classes might be over by now, but remained hopeful she could get a bite to eat at the Farinon Center. A breeze wafted through her medium-length hair, which Erin pushed out of her eyes as she ascended the steps. Two men in dickies were mopping the entry way and cleaning the glass doors while a hefty woman pushed an industrial-sized steam cleaner in the lobby.

"We're closed until three o'clock," the smaller of the two men shouted above the din.

"Oh, okay. Thanks." Erin went back outside. There was always the Wawa over on Cattell Street, but although her stomach was growling, she didn't want to leave her old haunts just yet. She walked in front of Pardee Hall and laughed at her memory of the tour she'd taken of the college as part of the admission process. The guide, a dead-serious sophomore, had told her, "This is Pardee Hall, the oldest building on campus," and Erin had joked, "Is this where you have all the parties?" The boy had shot a withering look at her. "We'll stand in the twilight's glow in front of old Pardee," she sang to herself, "in all the world no other sight, so fair, so dear to me." The words of her alma mater slipped back as easily as if she sang them every day. Walking toward her from the opposite direction came a medium-built man wearing khakis, a bright yellow polo shirt, and a pleasant smile. She couldn't help but grin back. Then she noticed a look of recognition in his eyes, and his step quickened in her direction.

"Can it be? Is that you, Erin Pelleriti Miles?"

Her mouth dropped open. "Dr. Weinreich?"

"In person!" He covered the brief distance between them in two steps and hugged her, nearly cutting off her circulation. "Oh, it's good to see you! How are you?"

"Very well, and you? You look wonderful!"

"Why, thank you for that. I'm afraid I am getting old, though." He pointed to the top of his head where his once-receding hairline had made the journey to points north.

"You'll never get old," she said, but she couldn't help but notice deepening lines around his mouth and eyes. Without his once-signature beard, however, he managed to look a fit and youthful—what would he be now—sixty-something?

"Posh! As for you, young lady, you have imbibed from youth's very fountain."

She felt herself blush and gave a small bow. "Many thanks."

"May I wish you congratulations on getting your doctorate?"

"Thank you."

"I'm so sorry Bev and I couldn't come to your party, but we were very touched by your invitation. We were away with the grandkids that weekend."

"So your note said. I hope you had fun."

"Three days at Great Wolf Lodge nearly sent us to Manor Care, but we'd do it all over again." He rubbed his backside. "No more waterslides for Gramps, though. So, Doctor Miles, what are you doing on the hill today?"

She smiled at the recognition of her new title and eagerly told him what she'd been up to. "I've been doing some family research at the Sigal Museum. Last year, I discovered my six-times great-grandfather was all over the place in Easton history—one of its first settlers, Northampton County Sheriff, a judge, and Colonel of the Northampton County Flying Camp, known for its performance at the Battle of Brooklyn."

He put his hands on his hips. "You don't say. How exciting to find all that out!"

"Oh, it is! I never thought my mother's side went back that far, but that branch of our family got here in 1742."

He checked his watch. "Say, have you had lunch yet? I just finished turning the last of my grades in, and I'm ready for a bite."

"I just went over to Farinon for something, but it's closed."

Herman Weinreich pursed his lips, staring unseeingly while he thought. "I'll bet the Starbucks inside the library is open. Let's go there. My treat."

"Why, thank you."

They walked toward the building just ahead to the right and inside found the coffee shop open with a smattering of patrons sipping beverages at the tables. She and her former favorite professor ordered, waited for their food and drinks, then took a table near the window overlooking the Quad.

"What a very strange combination." Weinreich frowned at Erin's yogurt parfait which she'd sprinkled with peppered kale chips.

She laughed. "Believe me, this is tame. I'm known for my culinary confusion."

"I'll just stick with my turkey and cheddar, thank you very much. So, how's your family?"

"Doing well. My parents are pretty good—still living across the river— and Ethan is just finishing fourth grade now."

He lifted his hands. "They grow so fast. I know it's a cliché, but how else to put it? And how is that handsome husband of yours?"

Erin dropped her spoon, which clattered to the floor. She bent over to pick it up, straining against tears. Straightening, she looked in her former professor's dark chocolate eyes. "I guess you didn't know. Jim died a little over a year ago."

Herman Weinreich's sandwich fell onto his plate. "Oh, I'm so sorry." He put his hand over hers. "I didn't know."

"I must have forgotten to tell you. After it happened, I wasn't operating on all cylinders."

"Was his passing sudden?" He'd always had an expressive face, which sadness now covered like a shroud.

"Yes. He was diagnosed with a fast-spreading liver cancer, and he passed away less than three months later."

"Oh, what a shame! How has Ethan taken it?"

"He had an understandably rough time, especially at school—acting up in class, bursting into tears over missing assignments, or when he didn't score a goal in soccer." She studied a hangnail on her right pinkie. "This year he's been more even-keeled emotionally, but we still miss Jim something fierce."

"He was so young—you are so young." He sipped his coffee, the sandwich apparently forgotten. "I'm proud of you for finishing your doctorate under those circumstances."

"Thank you." She let out a small puff of air.

"Wasn't your dissertation about your husband's ancestor?"

"Yes, Samuel Miles. You remember!"

"Of course, I remember." After a few moments, he asked the dreaded question. "So, what happens next?"

"To be honest, I don't know. Last year, I'd hoped to get a full-time position at Hatfield where, as you know, I taught as an adjunct for ten years. But I was all-but-dissertation, and they hired someone who had the doctorate in hand."

"Tough break."

"I've been working on my CV since graduating, and I plan to look for a teaching position."

"American history?"

"Yes."

"What period—Colonial?"

"Basically, yes—up to the Constitution. I like 20th century as well and have taught classes on that period."

He frowned and gazed at the ceiling. "You and I need to stay in touch."

The phone rang as she pressed the last button on the dryer. Her sort of aunt, who also happened to be her mother's next-door neighbor, was calling. "Aunt Fran. How are you?"

"I'm fine, Erin, and you?"

"Pretty well, thanks. What's up?"

"Well, I'm afraid your mom has done it again."

A prickle of fear traveled up the back of her neck. "Done what?"

"She had another fender bender this morning."

Erin went to the family room and sank down, Toby at her side. "What happened?"

"She insists on going to work when she should be retired, you know, but nobody can tell her anything."

She sighed. "I know."

"Well, she said the rain made it hard for her to see, and she bumped into another car in the parking lot. She barely missed hitting a toddler who'd broken away from his mother."

"Oh, dear God." Acid churned in her stomach, then rose toward her throat.

"You and your brother need to do something."

Erin sat up straighter. "You know how she is, Aunt Fran."

"Indeed, I do, but someone has to talk some sense into her before she kills herself—or someone else."

Erin spent the next hour talking to Allen, neither of them reaching a satisfactory conclusion.

Her Grandmother Owen would not be pleased, not in the least, as Erin slumped over her keyboard, her shoulders taking on the appearance of a dowager hump. Days of searching for a new teaching position had come to this—a four-year liberal arts college in Siloam Springs, Arkansas. Arkansas, where she knew not one person and had no connections whatsoever. According to the school's website, "Ours is a cosmopolitan campus with small-town charm, located just one hour from Dallas and some of the nation's best shopping." Where she presently lived there was a major downtown as well as malls only minutes away. She shuddered. Teaching English Comp to freshmen would be better than colonial American history in such a place.

Erin didn't want to teach English Comp, and she didn't want to be an adjunct professor at Villanova or anywhere else. She'd earned her doctorate for Pete's sake. If only the job market for history professors wasn't as stuffed as last year's Thanksgiving turkey.

She looked over her shoulder at a photo of Jim she'd taken on their last vacation in Washington, DC, as tears spilled down her cheeks, tears which came less frequently now but still appeared when she found herself especially missing her husband. *What would he be telling me about getting a job? Would he want me to keep searching for a full-time position, or wouldn't he mind if I kept doing adjunct? With adjunct, I do have more flexibility with my schedule so I can spend more time with Ethan, but there's no job security and no benefits. How long will the insurance money last? Will I need to work full time? What if I don't find a teaching job—would I need to teach high school instead? I really don't want to do that, and I don't even have teaching credentials, but what else am I trained for? What if I have to work somewhere I hate so I don't lose this house?* Erin's chest tightened and her breathing quickened.

What had happened to her simple, predictable life—the one she'd built so carefully? A life so different than the one she'd known as a child when she couldn't count on living in one place for more than a couple of years— when her mother could no longer afford the rent? In those years, she never knew if her father was in or out of her life, and even when he was in, Audrey didn't hold back her hatred of him. Erin yearned for Jim and the safety she'd always felt with him emotionally, physically, spiritually, and yes, even financially. *Why did he have to die? Why can't Ethan have his good father to guide him?*

"I can't do this," Erin said, rising from the desk chair. She wandered into the kitchen where she pulled out a half gallon of peanut butter ice cream and a jar of poblanos. Toby looked up at her with that certain bassett look of his, which she answered with her best Sly Stallone imitation—"What?"

Before she could eat her concoction, however, the phone rang. She padded down the hall to where she'd left the cell on her desk. *Sigal Museum* read the caller ID. She cleared her throat before answering.

"Hello. This is Erin."

"Hi, Erin. It's Connie Pierce from the Jane Moyer Library. How are you?"

"Doing well." She half expected lightning to strike for telling such a blatant falsehood, but by the same token she had felt better at the sound of Connie's soothing voice.

"Paul and I found something in a box from, oh, about 1910, and we'd like to show it to you."

Her anxiety morphed into excitement. "Is it a portrait?"

"I'm afraid not, though I'm not giving up on finding one." Connie paused. "Do you want me to tell you, or do you want to be surprised?"

"I'll take the surprise." She needed something happy in her life.

"When are you coming to Easton again?"

Today was Friday, and Ethan's last Little League game of the season had been the weekend before. "How about tomorrow? Will you be there?"

"I will, between ten and two."

"I'll see you at ten."

CHAPTER EIGHT

He winced as his morning tea trailed unpleasantly all the way down his throat. He'd expected the deep boldness of the usual English blend and instead had had an experience something like ingesting half of their kitchen garden, including the dirt.

"What is this?" He plunked down the cup into its saucer and pushed them to a safer distance, then hastily buttered a piece of bread and swallowed half the warm slice to banish the repulsive taste.

"I believe the proper name is 'Liberty Tea,'" Catherine said.

Susannah lifted her hand to her mouth as if to conceal her mirth.

Catherine gamely took her own taste of the brew and made a face ugly enough to scare a small child in broad daylight.

"Liberty Tea," he repeated. "So, the effects of the Boston Tea Party have at last reached Easton."

Catherine nodded her head. "There isn't a drop of pure British tea to be had in the village." Peter let out a small puff of air and looked at the windows where sunlight contended with rain.

"When tea shipments to Philadelphia were turned back several weeks ago, our supplies started dwindling."

He was glad his wife kept up with the news, and he smiled at her in spite of the lingering bitterness in his gullet. He quickly lost no time eating the second half of his rye bread.

"I instructed Frau Hamster to buy a little extra from Mr. Hart before all the tea was gone," she said. "Then, I decided we didn't need any British tea after all."

Peter frowned. "I don't understand."

"You see, Papa," Susannah said, "a lot of people didn't even want the tea Mr. Hart had. The ladies of Easton told him since the people of Boston are going without so much more than just tea—you know because the British closed their ports—the least we can do is stop drinking the tea we have in a show of support."

So, both my wife and daughter have become patriots. He smiled to himself. "What, then, is this concoction?" He wrinkled his nose as he pointed to the offending cup.

As if on cue, the housekeeper showed up, her hands folded on the front of her apron. *"Dies ist Basilikum Tee."*

"Basilikum Tee?" he repeated. "This tea is made of basil?" He raised his eyebrows.

Ja, mein Herr, gefällt es Ihnen?"

She looked so pleased with her efforts he couldn't bring himself to tell her what he really thought. Only because he was sitting and she was standing was he able to look straight into her eyes. He smiled at Frau Hamster, which produced a similar reaction in her, revealing her nearly toothless condition. "This tea is quite robust," he said as honestly as he could without hurting her feelings. Perhaps for the time being, he'd switch to coffee.

Before stopping at Meyer Hart's store for a supply of horehound drops,

Peter went to the grist mill to see Andrew and Jacob. The coolness he felt inside contrasted with the bright warmth finally settling upon this late-May day. Hans Schmidt was in the process of bagging grain, and the sturdy man, now sporting a gray head of hair, paused to wave and call out, "*Guten morgen!*"

"*Guten morgen, Herr Schmidt. Wie geht es dir?*" He spoke loud enough to be heard over the grinding.

"*Mir geht es gut, danke.*"

Peter was never quite sure which language Hans would use since his English remained unsteady. Nevertheless, the man valiantly continued teaching his Lenni-Lenape wife his own version of English, along with his native German. Their children were known to speak in all three languages at once, a veritable Babel.

Andrew was wiping grit from his hands with a handkerchief and walked up to his father to greet him.

"Ah, good morning, son." Peter shook Andrew's hand, proud of the young man nearly as tall as himself with a deepening chest and the sinewy arms of a man for whom work was no stranger. "How are you this fine day?"

"Very well, Papa. You just missed Wilhelm Konk. He placed a big order for himself and then four other farmers."

"Excellent work! He's a good customer, and you and Jacob are doing a fine job running both mills. I was hoping to have more time to give you myself, but now with being a justice of the peace and overseeing the church building ..." Peter looked around. "Where is your brother?"

"He went to help Peter Horeback at the sawmill. They've had a lot of work with the church—not just making lumber, but putting up the building, and as you know, more cabins are constructed this time of year." Andrew gave a short laugh. "I don't know why I'm telling you when you already know all these things."

Peter clapped his son's solid shoulder. "Just be sure to keep up with your books."

Andrew gestured toward a desk containing three volumes. "I am, Father."

"Good."

"How is Catherine this morning? I didn't get to see her before I left the house. In fact, I haven't seen much of her these past few weeks." His question was heavy with unspoken meaning.

"She's very well, thanks be to God." He found himself praying silently, *May Catherine and the baby continue to experience good health.* He didn't want his frequent fears about losing her to dim her happiness about becoming a mother.

He and his second son spoke for several minutes about the overall condition of the millstones, and when and how Andrew planned to clean them. Then Peter walked across the bridge he'd constructed years ago to the site of his sawmill where Jacob and Peter Horeback were outside cutting pine boards. *I've been fortunate in my choice of indentured servants, first Hans and now Horeback, although he only has a year left.*

When Jacob saw his father standing there, he signaled with his hand to Horeback, and they stopped their work.

"Hello, Father!"

"Hello, Jacob." Peter nodded toward the servant. "Horeback. I see you're busy filling orders."

"We were hard at it before the church construction started, but now our work has tripled."

Jacob wiped his arm across his sweaty brow, which was darker than either Andrew or Peter Junior's—more like his father's side of the family. Peter remembered his own father, who died when Peter was just shy of six years old, as a stocky man with hair the color of a raven and vibrant green eyes.

"Do you need extra help, son?"

"We could use another man."

Horeback gave a smile and nodded.

"I'll see what I can do to help you. Perhaps young Peter wouldn't mind lending a hand?"

"I think he's pretty busy with his own business, but I can ask." Jacob reached for a dipper of water and drank the contents in three gulps.

"Tell me about your orders."

"Well, there's the church and then, what is it, Horeback, do we have orders for three or four cabins?"

"Five," the servant said, moving his right arm across his own forehead.

Peter nodded and exhaled. "You do need more help. Of course, I can pitch in. I have some work to do in town, but I'll be back this afternoon. My other duties come in cycles, so I'm free just now."

"Thanks, Father. We'd appreciate your help."

"Uh, sir, before you go, may I have a word?" Horeback removed his hat and approached slowly, his chin dipping. Despite his shortness, he was a powerhouse of a man, almost as wide as he was tall with an unusually large head, a thatch of dark brown hair and almost no neck to speak of.

"Of course. What's on your mind?" Peter stepped aside from his son in case Horeback wanted to discuss something personal.

"Well, sir, you know that Old Pig Drover who comes through here?"

"Yes, of course. What about him?"

In broken English he explained, "I saw him in the field just outside the village two days ago when Mr. Kichline and I were delivering an order. He looked cold and just, well, broken down, and there's been so much rain lately. I was wondering." He twisted his hat into a tight cylinder until it looked something like Frau Hamster's dish towels on wash day. "I was wondering if you'd object to my having him stay with me in the mill house while he's in these parts."

Peter smiled at Horeback. "Young man, I think yours is an excellent idea. I've been concerned for him myself lately. If you think he needs medical attention, I'll get Dr. Gray."

"*Vielen dank.*"

"*Gern geschehen.*"

He tipped his hat to a small group of women and children standing near the church construction site. "Good day."

"Good day, Sheriff," they said in unison. One of the women, who held a rather large baby, giggled. "Forgive us. You're not sheriff anymore."

He grinned. "Sometimes, I forget myself."

A little girl he guessed to be about ten spoke up. "I think they're digging all the way to China!"

"The hole is deep, but still, China is a very long way from Easton." Once again, he tipped his cap, gave a slight bow and continued walking to Hart's store. As he approached the steps, he saw Robert Bell exit the establishment, letting out a foul-scented breath. Peter took a step back.

"If I were you, Sheriff, I'd hold onto my wallet."

He wondered if the townspeople would ever stop referring to him as sheriff. Before he could ask what Bell meant, the man stalked off down Northampton Street, most likely to the Bachmann Publick House. Peter proceeded inside the store, which smelled of molasses and tobacco, where he saw Robert Levers having an animated conversation with the proprietor, his son, and Robert Traill. Three female customers stood on the other side of the store holding what appeared to be buttons and thread up to the light streaming from a window.

"Collecting funds is the least we can do for them," he heard Levers say in his booming voice. "Boycotting tea is just a start." His expression sparked at the sight of Peter. "Good day, sir!"

He bowed his head. "Good day, gentlemen."

"We're just discussing the actions we should be taking to help the good people of Boston, who are being squeezed into starvation by British tyranny." Levers highlighted his remarks by making a fist.

"You mean you are talking," Traill said with a frown. "We haven't had much of a chance to get a word in edgewise."

Levers bowed. "My humble apologies, Mr. Traill." He turned to Peter. "What do you think of the poor Bostonians being treated worse than heathen by the British?"

"The closing of their ports has resulted in a good deal of suffering." He stood next to Traill, facing Levers.

"Yes, indeed. Poor innocents suffering hunger and other deprivations! And we, British subjects. More like British slaves, I'd say." Levers placed his hands on his hips. "I say we must do something about this outrage! If we were the ones suffering, we would need the help of others." He was practically shouting. "We also need to send a message to the British that the American colonies won't take such abuse. So many of our numbers came to America to avoid tyranny and here come other tyrants, stalking us yet again."

A woman dressed in bright yellow came toward them, appearing to shrink with every step. "Excuse me, Mr. Hart. I, I'd like to buy this if you don't mind."

"Indeed! Please excuse this group of unwashed rowdies monopolizing the place today." Hart took the woman's money, handed back two coins and returned to the male conversation. "What do you suggest, Mr. Levers?"

He hooked his thumbs inside his waistcoat, as if he were about to deliver a great speech. "I propose we take up a collection for the relief of Boston. I will personally deliver the funds."

"That could be dangerous work, and you do have a wife and children to consider," Traill said. "While many share our sentiments, there are those in the county still very loyal to the king."

"I consider, sir, my greatest duty to them is to protect their freedoms."

Peter recalled the story his mother had told many times on the long ocean crossing to America. Johann Andreas, his father, had decided to settle in Germany rather than Switzerland because educational opportunities were better near Heidelberg. "And now we are leaving Germany because the wars our nation fights are endless, and we suffer without hope of relief," she had told him all those years ago. "I don't want my sons fighting for kings and dukes and people who rule us with rods of iron. God intends people to live in peace."

"You can count me in," Peter heard himself tell Levers.

"What's wrong, Peter dear? You look pale." Catherine touched his right forearm gently as he looked up at her from the new edition of *The Pennsylvania Gazette*. They were alone, lingering over lunch while the young people finished their school day.

"Listen to this." He pointed to the front page and began reading aloud, "The Virginia Assembly has called for a Continental Congress to 'consult upon the present unhappy state of the Colonies.' The meeting is to be held in Philadelphia at Carpenter's Hall as soon as individual colonies can choose and send delegates."

She carefully stirred her tea, although what little sugar she had put into the cup had already dissolved. "Do you think you'll be called upon to go?"

He looked up from the paper. "Somehow, I think more distinguished delegates will be chosen, perhaps by the Pennsylvania Assembly."

"I have a feeling you'll be involved in some way before this conflict is over." She sipped her tea then said, "You do have a way of being at the center of things."

They smiled at each other, then he sighed. "This friction between the colonies and Britain has the potential to impact millions of lives across many generations." He picked up the paper and continued reading.

CHAPTER NINE

Ethan was squinting at a brown-edged, three-by-five card on Connie Pierce's desk top. "What are they?" he asked.

Erin peered over her son's head for a better look, and seeing a caption in dark handwriting, read aloud "Colonel Kachline's Cuff Buttons." She glanced at Connie. "These are my Grandfather Peter's?" She knew she was stating the obvious, but she felt so elated by the sight of the buttons—she couldn't think of anything else to say just then.

Connie nodded, her smile taking up half her face. "They sure are."

"What's a cuff button?" Ethan asked.

Sitting on the edge of the expansive desk, Paul Bassett fielded the question. "They're sort of like cufflinks on the bottom of your sleeves."

"My dad had cufflinks, didn't he, Mom?" Ethan looked up at her.

"Yes, he did." Erin's throat felt like she'd just swallowed an over-sized vitamin. She had to distract herself. She turned toward Connie, uncertain as to who knew more about the cuff buttons, her or Paul. "What exactly are they made of? I'm guessing brass because they're so tarnished."

"Brass is possible, but they might also be silver or pewter."

Erin longed to handle them, to make physical contact with something Peter Kichline had worn, the closest she might ever get to him physically this side of heaven.

Connie seemed to have read her mind. "Would you like to hold them?"

Erin clapped her right hand to her chest. "May I?"

"Of course. Just give me a moment to remove them from the card." In less than a minute, Connie handed the buttons to her.

"Can I hold them, too?" Ethan asked.

"Yes, hon, after I do." Erin felt the roughness of the antique metal against her hands and rubbed her forefinger lightly over the raised engraving on the front, trying to figure out the design. She held them up to the light for a better look. "The pattern looks kind of floral, but then there are lines making the design more intricate."

"I've had some difficulty trying to figure that out myself," Paul said, his arms folded across his chest. With a navy-blue cotton sweater draped around his shoulders, the arms tied across the front, Erin thought he looked preppier than ever. For some reason, her heart skipped one beat, then another, and jostled by her swirling emotions, she focused her attention back on the buttons.

Ethan screwed up the corners of his mouth. "They look like flowers to me. I'd never wear flowers."

Melissa had come along with them, and she laughed and tousled the boy's hair. "Those aren't pretty flowers but more like symbols, and I'll bet all the colonial men wore them." She looked at Paul, and Erin noticed something like approval in her friend's blue eyes. "Isn't that true?"

"Oh, yes, I'd have to agree," he said.

Connie spoke up while Erin gingerly handed the objects to Melissa for inspection. "I'm familiar with 18th-century buttons, but I've never seen this particular design before. There appears to be a kind of thistle, but the metal is so worn I can't be sure."

"Since your ancestor was a man of means, Erin, he probably had these custom-made, rather than off the counter," Paul said.

Melissa handed the buttons back to Erin. "Where exactly did these come from?"

Connie and Paul exchanged glances, then she spoke. "We found them in a box that hadn't been opened in decades. Because you've recently been researching Colonel Kichline, when I saw his name, I snatched them right up to show you. We have a lot of items needing to be archived, so I've been looking for anything related to him." She paused. "Do you know anything about the Easton Library's history?"

She frowned. "The public library?"

"Yes."

Erin wondered why Connie would ask such a question now. "I know the building dates back to the early 1900s, and there used to be a cemetery there."

"You're right. When the library was built with Carnegie money, the graves on site had to be removed—at least as many as could be identified."

Melissa crinkled up her nose. "How macabre! Why in the world did the city build there?"

"The cemetery had long since been abandoned and wasn't in good repair, and many people believed that piece of land was the best remaining spot in Easton to put the library," Connie explained. "As far as Paul and I can tell, the person who dug up the Colonel's grave to relocate his remains found these cuff buttons. Knowing how important he had been, the guy turned them over to the historical society."

As the news sank in, Erin cringed, Melissa coughed, and Ethan exclaimed, "Cool!"

"Do you mean," Erin said, "these came from his, uh, remains?" She couldn't quite stomach the thought and immediately slammed the door on her fertile imagination.

"I'm afraid so," Paul said, but Erin detected a trace of a smile.

Melissa spoke up. "The strangest thing my family ever did in terms of burial was when my grandmother asked to have a Phillie Phanatic doll put inside her casket. She adored the Phillies, although my grandfather couldn't stomach them. He liked the A's, starting from when they were in Philadelphia, but then he followed them all around the country as the team moved."

Melissa looked from Connie to Paul to Erin, her face reddening. "Sorry. I get off on bunny trails sometimes."

Erin got out her cellphone to take photos of the cuff buttons from different angles, using varying degrees of light to get the best effect. How she wished she could take these home with her, but Peter Kichline wasn't just part of her family, he was part of local history. Nor was she the only Kichline ancestor. The buttons needed to stay exactly where they were.

Erin and Melissa treated Ethan to pizza at the Crayola Experience's dining area. Erin topped her slice with a crumbled fudge brownie and mustard. Afterward, they spent the rest of the day touring the venue's three floors, which pulsed with the riotous energy of three busloads of elementary school children.

Erin raised her voice above the din. "I'm so glad you decided to come, Melissa. I love this place, but Ethan tends to take his time here, like with those canal boats." She pointed in her son's direction.

"I think this is his fourth time in line to run the boats through the locks. What a cool display!"

"Yes, and here we are, able to talk like grown-ups while he has the time of his life." She grinned. "Maybe shout is more like it."

"I'm happy to be here," Melissa said. "I just love Easton! I haven't been up here in years since Ryan was small and we brought him. Crayola was nothing like this back then, nice but much smaller. Also, your connection to local history thrills me to my toes. Seeing those cuff buttons—well, what a find!"

"I know. I still can't believe I actually held something that belonged to my Grandfather Peter."

"Connie is so nice."

"She is."

"And Paul … well, he's really nice too." Melissa gave Erin a sideways look.

"He's really interested in Kichline history."

Melissa opened her mouth as if she were about to say something but decided not to.

"Does he remind you of anyone? He does to me, but I can't figure out who."

"Sure. He looks just like Mike Farrell from *M*A*S*H*."

"That's who it is!" Erin clapped her palm to her forehead. "He really does, doesn't he?"

A toddler wearing only a diaper—just barely—streaked past them chortling with delight while his mother ran after him in hot pursuit. "Get back here, Liam!" Someone who appeared to be the father stood nearby recording the scene with his cellphone.

Erin and Melissa burst out laughing as the mother finally caught the child and scooped him up while the diaper slipped all the way off.

"Oh, my!" Melissa reached into her purse and pulled out a tissue, wiping her eyes. "Oh, I remember those days." Then, she just as abruptly sighed. "Sometimes I really miss them."

Erin's levity screeched to a halt, a sudden cloudburst falling upon her spirit. She missed those days, too, not just because Ethan was growing up so fast, but because Jim wasn't there to see their son's boyhood unfold.

They stood outside the Crayola Experience deciding what to do next.

"Your mom and dad live nearby, don't they?" Melissa asked.

"They're right across the river."

"I haven't seen your mom since the party. Maybe we should pay her a visit."

"Really? You'd do that?"

"Sure! I like your mom. She says what she thinks, and she's so, well, energetic for a woman her age."

"When do you have to be home?"

Melissa waved her hand like she was swatting a gnat. "Not for hours. When Tim takes Ryan golfing, they're out all day."

Erin considered the possibility of a visit while mentally replaying her Aunt Fran's recent phone call begging Erin to do something about Audrey's refusal to stop driving. *Maybe we should go. Having Melissa there would be a kind of safety buffer.* She was about to tell her best friend they could stop by for a brief visit when Erin noticed a man walk up to Ethan, who was standing a few yards away holding a Crayola bag filled with souvenirs. Her mama bear instincts kicked in, and she walked closer to let the man know Ethan wasn't alone.

"I see you've been to Crayola." The man pointed to the bag. "Did you enjoy yourself?"

Ethan nodded, looking as if he wasn't sure he should be speaking to the guy. Then he said, "I really like the canal boats."

"Those are my favorites, too."

Erin took note of the man's crisp gray suit, white shirt, and striped-silk tie. He appeared to be in his fifties, or maybe early sixties, and he sported a stylish pair of horn-rimmed glasses. He seemed friendly and normal enough, but was he harmless? She drew closer, seeing Ethan's somewhat bowed head and hunched shoulders. He knew all about "stranger danger."

"Are you this fine young man's mother?"

"Yes, I am." She put her hand on Ethan's right shoulder, and looking directly at the man's smiling face, had an "aha" moment. "Why, you're Mayor Panto!"

"That I am." He reached out his hand to her, and she shook it.

"I'm Erin Miles, and this is my son. Ethan, this is Mayor Sal Panto."

"Wow!" Now he was smiling, reaching out to shake the official's hand. "I'll bet he'd like to know about your ancestor."

"What about your ancestor?" Panto asked.

"Tell him, Ethan."

The boy's face flushed, and he almost burrowed his face into her chest as if he were four years old. "You tell him, Mom," he muttered.

She decided not to force him. "Well, my six-times great-grandfather was Colonel Peter Kichline, who commanded Northampton County's Flying Camp in the Revolutionary War. He was also a sheriff, and a judge, and Easton's first Chief Burgess."

Panto drew himself back as if startled. "Well, then, my boy, you practically own this town!"

"You get Melissa a nice glass of iced tea, Erin," her mother said.

Melissa was sitting on a couch as petite as Audrey herself while Ethan played with a wooden set of coasters that, for some reason, had fascinated him since early childhood. Audrey sat in her recliner while Erin tried to make sense of her mother's jumble of glasses. Most of them looked slightly filmy as she chose first one, then another in an effort to find four clean, matching ones. When her effort ended in futility, she settled on three of the same pattern, though different sizes, and an old Welch's jelly glass bearing images of Ewoks from *Return of the Jedi*.

"So, you went to the Crayola. How did you like it, Ethan?"

"I liked the canal boats, Grandma."

"And you went, too, Melissa. Well, I haven't been there in ages."

Erin felt her mother's guilt arrow hit its mark in her spirit as she peered into the refrigerator, finding three open cartons of iced tea—one dated February 5. She discreetly poured the contents down the drain.

"Oh, Audrey, we also saw your ancestor's cuff buttons," Melissa said.

"My whose what's?"

"Colonel Kichline's cuff buttons."

Melissa told the story while Erin looked for ice. When she located two plastic trays under three opened containers of Turkey Hill coffee ice cream, she decided not to use ice this time. Tan byproducts of the frozen dessert had leaked all over the top of the trays and spilled onto the bottom of the freezer. She wanted to join the story about Grandfather Peter, but Melissa was telling the adventure so well, Erin hung back. When she distributed the cold drinks, her mother was saying, "I'm not getting out as much as I used to. I have the macula, you know."

"Yes, I know. That must be very hard on you." Melissa sipped the tea then put her glass on one of the coasters Ethan handed to her. "You're still working, though, aren't you?"

Audrey let out a sigh. "I told them yesterday I wasn't going to be able to work any longer."

Erin felt a jolt in her chest. "You're going to retire, then?"

"It's time, Erin. I've had too many near-misses with the car." Audrey looked down at her feet. "I don't know what I'm going to do with myself, though. I've been working since I was fourteen years old. Plus, what will I do about doctor's appointments and groceries and the drug store?"

Erin threw her mom a life preserver. "I'm sure Allen and I can help, Mom."

She looked up, brightening. "I guess you'll have to."

Melissa glanced at Erin, who was tempted to either break into a gale of laughter or head for the piney hills.

CHAPTER TEN
Late June 1775

"I assure you, gentlemen of Northampton County, Boston's troubles have become our own." George Taylor waved a gnat from his perspiring face. "Mr. Edmonds, perhaps you'd like to tell us what happened at the Provincial Assembly a few days ago."

William Edmonds rose and bowed to the county's leading men, cutting an elegant figure in his crimson waistcoat and black silk cravat. Apparently, he'd purchased the clothing in Philadelphia—at least Peter had never seen them on Edmonds before this. The speaker placed his hands on his hips, feet astride. "My friends and fellow patriots, I found myself in the midst of some eight thousand like-minded people gathered in the city to discuss the encroachment of British policies on the rights of her American colonists."

Jacob Arndt interrupted. "That's quite a large number, Mr. Edmonds. Surely not that many delegates presided?"

"You are correct, Mr. Arndt. The masses were quite vocal, however, about their dissatisfaction with recent British actions and I assure you, we delegates listened. The people were also in full support of our taking up a collection to assist our fellow brethren in Boston, whose harbors have been closed until they pay for the destroyed tea."

The men filling the courthouse exchanged glances of approval.

"We were emboldened in our meetings by the actions of other colonists in refusing British ships laden with tea at their ports in favor of creating our own, home-grown beverages."

Arndt elbowed Peter and whispered, "Is Frau Hamster still making her basil tea?"

Peter nodded and grinned. "Though lately she's been experimenting with dandelions."

His friend winced, his cheeks stretching south while his eyes went north. "Let's encourage our housekeepers to try brewing mint for a change."

Edmonds glanced at Peter and Arndt as if they were errant schoolboys, cleared his throat and continued. "A few days ago, I had the honor of serving on a committee to correspond with Pennsylvania's other ten counties, as well as the dozen other colonies, to make plans for the convening of a Continental Congress. It is time, gentlemen, we speak with one voice to let the British know we must be represented in Parliament, or the Crown must suffer the consequences. The words of Mr. James Otis from a decade ago continue ringing in our ears today, but with greater urgency—'No taxation without representation—"

"—is tyranny!'" several of the men shouted in unison. Others broke out into comments and whispers about the idea of such a congress.

"Are you on it?"

"Are we breaking away from Great Britain?"

"When will the Congress be?"

"Will the meetings be in Philadelphia?"

"Does this mean war?"

Edmonds raised his hands in a gesture to quiet them. "If you please! The Congress will meet this September in Philadelphia with delegates from each colony. In the meantime, gentlemen of Northampton County, we have been called upon to select, in addition to myself, three more delegates to attend a convention of Pennsylvania's counties to meet on July 15 at Carpenters' Hall in Philadelphia. We will be deciding as a body what recommendations we have for the Continental Congress and the actions we wish the Pennsylvania Assembly to take in preparing for that gathering."

Thirty minutes later, Robert Levers read the results of the balloting. "The three delegates accompanying Mr. Edmonds will be, in alphabetical order: Mr. Jacob Arndt, Mr. Peter Kichline, and Mr. John Okely."

He felt the clapping of hands on his back, thinking he wasn't entirely surprised at being chosen for the task. *I'm just glad this is happening now and not in October when the baby is due.*

As committed as he was to the public weal, nothing would keep him from his wife's presence when that day came.

"Peter, do be careful this morning." Catherine stood beside him near the front door as he prepared to assist Andrew and Jacob at the mills. Orders had picked up at both his businesses, but especially the sawmill. "That cut on your hand could've been so much worse. Don't you think you should rest today? You went from the Courts of Quarter Sessions to the mills and haven't had a chance to pause for a breath."

"I wouldn't let a simple cut stop me. Besides, I'm the one who should be concerned." He frowned.

"Whatever do you mean?" Her light brown eyes sparked.

He didn't want to argue. He'd never been one for bickering, not with Margaretta, Anna, or any of his children. Peter found the very idea as distasteful as Frau Hamster's dandelion tea, which he'd found worse than her original basil concoction. He looked at Catherine's expanding waistline, then in her eyes where he thought he detected her own desire for peace. "I don't want you doing more than you should. You have Frau Hamster, and Susannah is a good helper. If you need more assistance, I'll gladly get another woman for you."

"I enjoy baking and shopping and keeping our home."

"Fine. Just promise me two things—don't lift anything heavier than a small sack of grain, and when you get tired or overly warm, especially in this heat, you'll sit down and rest right away."

"You really do worry too much." Her lips curled at the corners.

"I have reason to."

She tilted her head to the right as she cupped his cheek with her hand. "I am not Anna. I am Catherine. Remember, your dear Margaretta delivered healthy babies four times. Childbirth doesn't always end in sorrow."

He closed his eyes and took a deep breath. She was right, of course. He just wished he hadn't overheard Frau Eckert—that was, Frau Wiggins—the other day. He'd stopped by the tavern to see her and Ziba and when he left, Peter overhead her say, "I just hope this wife makes it through. She's so delicate." He'd clenched his fists, fighting an inner battle. Just because Catherine limped a little didn't mean she was fragile, for Pete's sake. He'd seen her heft a large bag of flour without breaking into a sweat. Besides that, he refused to be like Satan, who came to steal, kill, and destroy. He wasn't going to steal her joy over the baby—not with God as his helper.

"You're deep in thought, husband."

He smiled down at her. "I'm very happy about this baby, and I won't steal your joy." When she opened her mouth, he raised his right index finger to indicate he wasn't finished. "Just promise me about the lifting and resting."

"I promise." She laughed. "I love you so."

He kissed her hand, which was easier for him than saying what came out of his mouth next. "And I love you." Catherine was much more vocal about her emotions than either Margaretta or Anna had been, and while he sometimes felt uncomfortable saying what he himself felt, he did find such words reassuring. He wasn't about to rob this dear woman of her forthrightness either.

Both jumped nearly out of their skin when the front door burst open like a cannon shot. Two men covered in dirt and debris carried a third, whose head hung limply, his mouth open either in sleep or death. Peter couldn't tell which.

"What is this?" he shouted.

"Father, there's been an accident at the sawmill." The voice was Jacob's. He and Catherine led the trio, trailing debris, into the parlor.

"Peter Horeback is with me too." Then Jacob nodded toward the unconscious man lying on the sofa, pieces of wood clinging to what remained of gray hair and forming a sort of halo on the cushion. "This is the Old Pig Drover."

Catherine clapped her hand to her mouth. "What happened?"

Peter knelt by the man's head and placed his fingers on the dirty neck to see if there was a pulse. Finding the Old Pig Drover's heart still beating, he breathed slightly easier, though his own pulse throbbed in his ears.

"He was staying on the second floor of the mill house. Apparently, all the rain we've had recently weakened the roof, and the floorboards had begun to rot," Jacob said.

"I'll get water and a cloth." Catherine gathered her skirts and headed toward the kitchen.

"Have Frau Hamster bring the water," Peter called after her. He helped his son and Horeback unbutton the old man's familiar waistcoat, which had seen far better days a very long time ago. "Were you not aware of the leaking, Mr. Horeback?"

"*Es tut mir sehr leid!*" Although he'd been learning English at a fast clip, whenever the young German got emotional, he used his native tongue.

Peter could tell Horeback was sorry for neglecting the roof by the way his hands trembled. "When was the last time you were on the second floor?" he asked in German.

"*Ein monat.*"

"Well, a lot can happen in a month." He guessed the servant didn't have much need to venture to the second floor when he lived on the first, especially since there'd been so much work at the mill occupying his time. Peter told himself to calm down. Horeback wasn't at fault here. They needed to get the Old Pig Drover cleaned up and get the doctor.

Susannah came into the room along with her stepmother and Frau Hamster, who bore a large basin of water. "They told me what happened, Papa." She bent over to see the Old Pig Drover. "How can I help?"

"Go find Dr. Gray. Tell him we have an emergency."

"I'll be right back." She raced toward the door and disappeared onto Northampton Street.

Dr. Gray's presence filled the parlor, although he was slight of build and looked little more than a boy himself. He sported thinning, reddish-blond hair, with pale, freckled skin and a brogue second only to that of Robert Traill. In less than ten minutes, he concluded, "The left leg is broken below the knee and a swelling at his temple indicates he was struck—probably by a heavy piece of wood."

Frau Hamster handed him a cup of tea as they sat by the patient. Gray took a sip and blanched. "Liberty Tea." He set the china cup and saucer on a nearby table.

"What should we do, Doctor?" Catherine asked. "When do you think he'll wake up?"

"Keep him quiet. As for waking up …" He shrugged. "That would be anyone's guess. This is an old man, and he doesn't seem to be in the best of health to begin with."

Peter wondered if Gray might be expecting the Old Pig Drover not to survive the accident.

"What is this fellow's name?"

Peter lifted his hands. "All anyone knows him by is 'The Old Pig Drover.'"

"I've never heard him called anything else," Susannah said.

Peter asked his indentured servant in German if the old man had provided another name since they'd been living together, but Horeback just closed his eyes and moved his head back and forth. "*Nein. Gerade Das Alte Schwein Treiber.*"

Gray sniffed and smiled. "I find German such a picturesque language. Somehow, without even knowing the tongue, I can understand what this fellow just said—that there is no other name except Old Pig Drover." After a pause he asked, "So, where does our friend live?"

"Everywhere and nowhere," Peter said. "He gathers shoats from village to village, then drives them to market in neighboring towns and cities. Usually he sleeps in fields, but my servant here suggested since we'd been having such hard rains, the fellow could stay at my sawmill house. I gave my permission, not wanting the fellow to be out in the harsh elements."

"What about now? He's certainly in no condition to be outside or look after himself."

"He's welcome to stay in our room," Jacob said. "We have plenty of space. If Andrew objects, I can always move up to the third floor."

"Thank you, son. If you'll recall, I'm going to be leaving in a few days' time for the Provincial Convention in Philadelphia. Can you handle a needy house guest in my absence?"

"I can help take care of him," Susannah said. "That way Mother Catherine won't have to go up and down stairs too much."

"I'll be just fine, Susannah, but thank you," Catherine said.

"That's settled then." Peter considered something else. "Where are his pigs?"

"He had about a dozen in the hills behind the mill," Jacob told him. "I don't mind looking after them. Horeback can help."

Peter wondered how this situation was going to resolve, thankful he had a loving family. He couldn't help but wonder what kind of family the Old Pig Drover had come from and if there were any who'd want to know what had happened to him.

He finished the noon meal at City Tavern, satiated with salmagundi, corn chowder, and a handful of delectable sweet potato biscuits. He hoped he could describe them well enough to Catherine and Frau Hamster so they could somehow replicate the chewy, lightly sweet flavor. He noticed John Arndt had put three of the leftover biscuits in his handkerchief when they left the table to pay their bill.

"Please don't tell my wife, but those are the finest biscuits I have ever tasted."

Peter grinned. "I won't tell, if you won't tell."

They enjoyed a chuckle as they pressed through the crowd of men occupying the tavern's first floor.

"Do you think we should wait for John and William?" Arndt looked over his shoulder for their companions.

Peter used his height to full advantage as he craned to look above the heads of the patrons. "I don't see them. Perhaps they've left and will catch up with us at Carpenters' Hall."

The hot sun blazed on their heads and shoulders as they exited the tavern's relative coolness onto Second Street. As Peter's eyes adjusted to the brightness, the figure of a woman walking north on the other side struck him as familiar.

Arndt followed his friend's look. "What is it, Peter?"

"I just saw someone, a woman, who looks familiar." With a laugh, he added, "She reminds me of my former servant, Greta, who married a Captain Hough about ten years ago."

"I don't remember her very well."

"They moved to the west after their marriage, but her father has stayed on in Easton."

"Isn't he the one who married an Indian?"

Peter nodded. "The last I heard, Greta and her husband had moved to Philadelphia."

"Well, that could've been her then, but my friend," he took up his pocket watch and pointed it in Peter's direction, "we'll be late for the afternoon session if we don't hurry."

"Yes, of course." If that had been Greta, maybe he'd catch up with her another time. He'd like to see how she and her family were doing since they never came to Easton anymore.

On the following morning, July 21, Peter marched two-by-two with the other Northampton County representatives, as well as delegates from all over Pennsylvania. They were headed to the State House where august lawmakers awaited the men clad in heavy leather breeches and wool socks, even in this heat. The men, arms crossed over ample chests, remained mute as delegate Thomas Willing, an influential Philadelphian and no fan of independence, read the Convention's Resolves and Instructions.

"We also desire to remain loyal subjects of King George III and to maintain harmony with Great Britain, but we believe firmly that colonists are entitled to the same rights and liberties as citizens of England." He ended with "a resolve to call a congress of delegates from every colony."

Then he put down his arms to his sides and waited for a response. The Assembly just sat there staring at the delegates with what appeared to be disdain or disregard. Following the awkward silence, the counties' delegates departed.

The next morning, behind closed doors, the Assemblymen acquiesced to the idea of a Continental Congress, but they insisted on appointing their own delegates without consulting the Provincial Convention. When news of this reached the delegates, most of them congregating at City Tavern, Peter felt grim. *Sooner or later, they will have to listen to the will of the people.*

CHAPTER ELEVEN

Erin checked her email one last time before leaving home to drive to her mother's, pleased with the way she and her brother had agreed to take turns helping Audrey. They figured every other week would work fine as long as their mom stocked up, which would take some convincing. Audrey had never been one for stocking up. *Hmm, I wonder who Pat Larris is.* She stopped to read the message.

Dear Erin, I volunteer at the Sigal Museum, and Connie Pierce just told me about your connection to Colonel Kichline. Congratulations! He was an amazing man, and Easton is proud to call him "native son." I'm the history coordinator for Easton Heritage Day, and I'm wondering if you and your son would like to march in the parade this July. We'd love to feature the Colonel's descendants in our lineup. Do you have colonial outfits? If not, I'm guessing we might have something you can borrow. Please let me know. Yours, Pat Larris.

Erin's calves tingled at the thought of marching in the parade with Ethan, both of them paying homage to their Grandfather Peter. She recalled the fun they'd had in last year's Collegeville-Trappe Memorial Day Parade with the Valley Forge DAR and Children of the American Revolution. Their only disappointment had come from having to wear red, white, and blue tee shirts instead of colonial attire like most of their group.

Erin recalled one of the DAR ladies, Mary Bennett, telling her, "If you ever need a colonial dress or uniform, let me know. I've made them for a number of our members." Erin decided to email her as soon as she got back from her mom's and, of course, after she looked through the latest edition of the *Chronicle of Higher Education*, due out later today with updates on teaching positions.

While she turned off lights and put Toby in his crate—her mother-in-law would look in on him at lunch time—Erin did some mental calculating. *If I get to Phillipsburg by nine-thirty and finish by noon, I'll grab some lunch on the way back and still have time to email Mary Bennett and look at the new job postings before Ethan gets home. Not that there'll be any new ones, at least in places other than Timbuktu.* Getting in the minivan and turning on the radio for a traffic report, she pushed aside her discouragement. Something was bound to open up—wasn't it?

"How many stores?" Erin felt sweat trickle down her back in her mother's overheated apartment. She was happy to be able to help Audrey make the transition from car-less to depending on others to get around, but she hadn't bargained on running a cross-country race through P'burg and half of Easton.

"Well, I have to go to CVS, and I have to go to P'burg Pharmacy, and I need stamps, and I have to go to the bank, and then there's groceries at Hinelines."

"Mom, I'm curious. Why do you need two pharmacies?" As she waited for an answer, Erin noticed her mother had colored her hair again, managing to look very much like a seventy-something version of Anne of Green Gables.

Audrey grabbed her purse and stuffed a wad of tissues on the top.

"CVS has two prescriptions waiting for me, but they don't have the kind of toothpaste I like."

"What kind is that?" Erin couldn't imagine CVS not having any kind of toothpaste under the sun.

"I've looked there already." Audrey spoke as if her daughter were too thick for words.

Big inhale. "Okay, we can get stamps at CVS, and when you check out there or at Hinelines, you can get cash back so we don't need to go to the post office or the bank."

"I know this is a lot of trouble for you, Erin, but I don't like this any better than you do. I hate not working, and not being able to get around how and when I want to is no picnic for me either."

"You're no trouble, Mom." She gave Audrey a reassuring hug. "I'm glad to help, and so is Allen. Right now, I'm just trying to organize our time together."

"Oh, I know you are. Don't mind me." Audrey perked up. "I've been thinking about my car. You know, selling it. Would you help me? It's vintage. I think I could get at least a couple thousand dollars for it."

Erin coughed into her sleeve. Her mom would be lucky to get a thousand pennies for that clunker. "Let me check the Kelly Blue Book to see what the car's worth." She already figured she knew, but her mom might take the news better coming from a third party.

They finished running errands by one o'clock, and Audrey offered to buy her daughter lunch.

"That's really nice of you, Mom, but I need to head back," Erin told her. "I have some things I want to do before Ethan gets home from school."

"I'm sorry everything took so long."

"That wasn't your fault." Waiting in line a half hour while one pharmacist took care of both the drive-through and six customers had left Erin shying away from the free blood pressure device near the check out.

"So, Allen will take me next week, right?"

Erin was edging her way to the door of Audrey's apartment, trying not to appear in too much of a hurry. "He'll come in two weeks."

"What if I need something in the meantime?"

"The idea is to try to get everything when each of us takes you, but if you really need something in the meantime, I'm sure one of your friends here could help you out."

She frowned. "I don't like to ask anyone. Now, what do I do about doctor's appointments?"

Erin was halfway out the door. "Allen and I will take turns. Mom, you're going to be all right. We'll make sure. Please don't worry."

She gave her mom one last hug and hurried past her Aunt Fran's door. She loved her relative but needed to get going. On the way out of P'burg, she stopped at the Burger King drive-through for a veggie burger and Coke. Juggling the overly full sandwich bursting with ketchup-sodden lettuce and tomatoes, she headed across the toll bridge to Easton. As she reached the Route 33 exit and was finishing the burger, she heard her ring tone, "Someone's Knockin' at the Door." She found her phone on the console underneath the Burger King bag, a pocket pack of tissues, two sticks of bubble gum, and three pencils. Erin saw "Allen" on the caller ID and tapped "answer" and "speakerphone," smearing ketchup on her device. "Hey, Allen."

"Hi, Erin. How are you?"

She thought his voice sounded as if it were being dragged through a mud puddle. "I'm good."

"How's Ethan?"

"Just fine. I'm heading home now after taking Mom shopping."

"Oh, that's right. You were going to take her today. How did that go?"

"Pretty well." She successfully fought an urge to whine about how many stores her mom had initially wanted to go to and how Erin had talked her down from that cliff.

"Where are you now?"

"I just pulled off 22 onto 33."

"So, you're still in Easton?"

She wondered what was going on. "Yes, why?"

"Well, Dad just called me from Easton Hospital."

Her scalp prickled. "Is he okay?"

"He is, but Bridget had a stroke."

"Oh, my! Are you there?"

"No, I'm at work. I can't get over there until about five."

"I'll just turn around at William Penn Highway and head back." She paused. "Why not Warren Hospital?"

"Apparently, they were shopping in the Circle, and when Bridget collapsed, the Easton squad took her."

"Okay. Well, I'll go right over there. I need to call my mother-in-law to make sure she's there when Ethan gets home from school."

"Thanks for going, Erin. I'm sure Dad'll appreciate it."

She turned onto William Penn Highway and back toward the hospital on Northampton Street. After she found parking in the lot, she reached for her phone and called Pat Miles, who answered on the second ring.

"Well, hello, Erin, I just came back from your house. Toby and I went for a nice long walk."

"Thanks. I'll bet he loved that. Listen, I'm calling from Easton Hospital. I was on my way home when my brother called to tell me my, uh, stepmother, had a stroke."

"Oh, I'm sorry to hear that! How serious is her condition?"

"I don't know. I just reached the parking lot and wanted to call and see if you or Al could be there when Ethan gets home and stay with him until I can get there. Do you have other plans?"

"Of course, we can help, hon. Don't give us another thought. Just go to your dad and Bridget. We'll take care of everything down here. Do you want us to tell Ethan?"

"Yes, that would be okay. You're the best, Mom."

"The feeling is mutual, Erin. Give your dad our best wishes. Tell him we'll be praying."

"Thanks." When she hung up, she paused for another moment to do the same.

She found her dad in the ER sitting on a plastic chair, looking blankly at a wall holding a waste container for used syringes.

"Dad."

He looked over and gave her a sad, semi-smile. "Erin." He rose and received her with a hug and a kiss on her cheek. "How did you know we were here?"

"Allen called me."

"I didn't want to bother you. You've had enough to deal with."

She realized she hadn't stepped foot in a hospital since Jim's illness and pushed aside the memories. "I was with Mom this morning, taking her shopping. She's given up driving, and Allen and I are going to take turns helping."

"I didn't know that." He pursed his lips. "I guess her eyes are pretty bad. Allen told me about her accidents."

She wondered where Bridget was. "What happened, Dad?"

"We went over Easton to that Quadrant Book Mart. Then, we decided to stop at the Dollar Store. Bridget wanted to buy some birthday cards and when she started looking, she told me she felt dizzy. The next thing I knew, she keeled right over. I thought she'd dropped dead."

Erin was only slightly taken aback by her dad's blunt assessment. He was just that way.

"Somebody called the ambulance, and they brought her here."

"Was she conscious?"

"Her eyes were rolling back in her head." He took a deep breath. "The squad got here real fast, and I got here a few minutes later. They don't let you ride with the patient, you know." He wasn't making eye contact.

"Where is she now?"

"They're running all kinds of tests. She was in pretty bad shape."

"How long have you been here?"

"About an hour. Allen said he'll be here later. You didn't have to come. Who will take care of Ethan?"

"I called my mother-in-law. She and Al will stay with him until I get home."

"That's good. They're real nice people." He looked away again, toward the hallway. "Thanks for coming,"

She touched his arm as the loudspeaker sputtered overhead, a summons for what sounded like "doctorpearsandoats," but couldn't possibly be.

A thin, balding man in a lab coat appeared. "Mr. Pelleriti? I'm Dr. Vaughn, one of the neurologists on staff."

Tony shook his hand. "This is my daughter, Erin Miles."

Vaughn nodded in her direction without looking at her. "We've run some preliminary tests on Bridget, and we're going to put her in intensive care after we run a more comprehensive CT scan. At this point, we're assessing the damage from the stroke."

"How bad is it?" Tony asked.

Erin drew closer to his side.

"I'm afraid her condition isn't good. Her vital signs are weak." He paused. "Has she been complaining lately of any discomfort?"

Although Tony shook his head, Erin thought he looked more like he was thinking hard than disagreeing. "She did say she felt dizzy this morning, but then she seemed fine."

"Did she look okay? Was there any drooping of her mouth, for example?"

"I didn't see anything different."

The doctor nodded. "Maybe you'd like to go to the waiting room since she won't be coming back here after the tests. I'll come and get you when we have more information."

After finding seats near the water cooler, with a TV talk show blaring in the background, Tony said, "I have a bad feeling about this."

So did Erin

She stood next to her father and brother at Bridget's casket receiving friends and family members, wearing a pleasant but subdued smile. Erin felt strange standing there when she'd never known any of Bridget's friends, let alone her brother or cousins. "Hello, thank you for coming," she told a woman Tony identified as a neighbor.

"I'm sorry for your loss," the stout woman told Erin. "Bridget was a special lady. She was always baking something and sharing it with me." She dabbed at tears with a well-used pink tissue.

"Thank you."

Allen leaned over and whispered to her. "Do you know any of these people?"

"No, but they sure are being nice."

He drew a little closer. "Wouldn't Mom have a fit if she saw us here?"

Erin nodded. She watched Ethan standing on the other side of his grandfather, shaking hands like a little man, all dressed up in khakis, a navy-blue sport coat, and clip-on tie. She hadn't been sure about his coming to a funeral, but when she gave him the option of staying with his Miles grandparents, he told her, "I'm going, Mom. Grandpa needs me." He didn't seem bothered by the casket. Interestingly, she wasn't either. She hadn't known Bridget all that well, and the woman had had a long life. Not like Jim. Tears sprang to her eyes, and she quickly wiped them away as Bridget's brother patted her on the arm.

As the luncheon for family and friends at Riley's Family Restaurant was coming to a close, Allen asked, "How are you going to get home, Dad? I can take you, but I'll have to leave in a few minutes since Tanya and I have to get back to work."

Erin spoke up. "I can take him home, Allen. Ethan and I aren't in a hurry." She'd never thought of her dad as vulnerable until just now. Since he'd just lost his wife of over thirty years, she hated to see him go home to an empty apartment. She'd stay with him for a few hours at least. Ethan would like the chance to hang out with his grandfather.

An hour into the visit, while her son set up a word game on the kitchen table, Tony suddenly told Erin, "I'd like you to go through Bridget's clothes and jewelry and see if there's anything you want."

Erin opened her mouth to say that wasn't necessary, but her dad kept talking.

"Then I'll see if her cousins or sister-in-law or Tanya would like anything. The rest, I'll donate to The Salvation Army." When she hesitated, he urged her. "Go ahead. She had the dresser with the mirror, and her clothes are in the closet. I always used the guest-room closet for my stuff. Take your time. Ethan and I have a game to play."

Thus dismissed, Erin ventured into the inner sanctum of her dad and stepmother's life, feeling out of place. The shades were drawn, so she lifted them halfway to admit natural light and turned on the overhead fixture. The room with its faux-quilt and oak furniture bore testimony to a then-middle-aged couple who'd wed in the eighties. Sniffing, she thought she detected a hint of Bengay ointment. Her dad's fishing gear occupied one corner of the room next to Bridget's worn Deerfoam slippers. She opened the closet door, half expecting an alarm to go off, but when nothing happened, she half-heartedly shuffled through the woman's clothes, thankful to be two dress sizes larger, not to mention a few inches taller, than Bridget. None of the clothes suited Erin's style and the shoes were too small. Turning to the dresser, she figured she'd better come away with something or risk hurting her dad's feelings. Since nothing would fit, she decided to take a crocheted shawl and two cotton handkerchiefs. Just as she was about to close the drawer, Erin felt something jamming the top part, so she jiggled until two stiff envelopes came loose. Pushing them down flat, she gasped when she saw her own handwriting, recognizing the two Mother's Day cards she'd sent. Bridget had tied them with a pink ribbon and when Erin looked a little closer, she saw a red heart drawn on the front of the first one next to a smiley face.

CHAPTER TWELVE

Before leaving for the mill, Jacob asked to speak with his father alone in the parlor. "I hate to say anything, but we haven't had any payments from the church for lumber."

Peter frowned as he searched his third son's earnest face. "For how long?"

"Two months. I haven't told you until now because sometimes we've had to wait before, but the money always came within a week or two of due dates."

Peter thought back to the last meeting of the elders, how they'd stayed with their original decision to take subscriptions. Apparently, people weren't keeping up with their payments or there hadn't been enough subscriptions to begin with. Maybe he should have a discreet discussion with Christian Gress about the situation. "Thanks for letting me know, Jacob. Don't say anything to anyone else until I get back to you."

"I've tried, Herr Kichline, but most people who gave once with the best intentions have found it hard to give again. Many are rendering services as they're able, including blacksmithing from your brother-in-law, Frederick.

Then there was that collection for the people of Boston." Christian Gress shrugged as they sat in his Ferry Street home. "Our people are generous, but there's just so much they have to give. I'm afraid we do need a large gift after all."

Peter had had a hunch this was the case. "Mr. Gress, I would like to loan the amount needed for the church's construction, free of interest. The church can pay me back within a reasonable period."

Gress shot up as if someone had lit a fire underneath him. "Oh! My! That is wonderful, Herr Kichline!" He took a deep breath, as if to slow himself down. "May I share this news?"

"Let's keep this to ourselves until the next elders' meeting which is, I believe, in two days." He grinned. "Do you think you can do that?"

"Na sicher!"

When Gress walked his guest to the door a few minutes later, he paused and slapped his hand to his forehead. "I almost forgot to share some good news."

Peter waited, feeling the sun's warmth filter into the house. "What might that be?"

"Herr Hart told me he would like to donate a cask of nails for our church."

"Herr Hart?"

"Yes, Meyer Hart, the Jew."

Peter thought aloud. "What an amazing gesture. Nails are difficult to come by, and expensive. Did he say why?"

Gress nodded. "He believes houses of worship are important, and he wants Easton to have a proper church."

"Well, then, we must find some way to show our appreciation."

Meyer Hart was his usual courtly self. "I see the church building is finally progressing, Herr Kichline."

"And that not in small measure due to your generosity." Peter bowed his head in respect and gratitude.

Hart sniffed and shrugged his shoulders. "What is a nail to a church building?"

"An entire cask of nails, may I add? Perhaps you aren't aware the Lord Jesus said even a cup of cold water given to honor him would not go unrewarded."

Instead of responding to those words, Hart asked, "When do you think the church will be ready for services?"

Someone opened the door to the mercantile,—a cluster of bright red leaves skittered across the floor.

"We'd hoped to begin worship next spring, but the building has been coming along rather slower than expected."

The proprietor's faded blue eyes twinkled as he leaned across the counter. "And how is your dear wife coming along? She will bring you a son or daughter soon, I believe."

"We think the child will come by the end of October, and she's quite well, thank you, although she chafes at my insistence she do very little."

He raised his grizzled, unruly, eyebrows. "Perhaps you treat her too cautiously?"

"Perhaps, but ..."

"Listen, my friend, you don't have to worry about this one."

Peter gazed at the man he'd known since Easton's beginnings and found a kind of knowledge in Hart's expression. "But how do ...?"

"Sometimes one just knows these things." The proprietor patted his heart. "Like you, I pray, and I have a sense all will be well."

He wanted to respond, but he couldn't speak around the thickness in his throat.

Another breeze signified the opening of the door to a customer, but when Peter turned toward the entry, he saw Sheriff Henry Fullert looking in his direction. Peter nodded his head and waited for the stocky fellow to come to him.

"Good day, Sheriff." Peter extended his hand.

"Good day to you." Fullert removed his hat and shook his predecessor's hand. "Mr. Hart."

"Sheriff."

"I wonder if I might have a word, Mr. Kichline. Of course, I don't mean to interrupt the two of you."

"We were just finishing. I bid you good day, Mr. Hart."

"And a very good day to you, Herr Kichline."

Fullert led Peter to a quiet corner of the store. "Do you still have the Old Pig Drover at your house?"

Peter pressed his lips together and shook his head. "Not any longer. His leg has mended and he's regaining his strength, so he's back with my indentured servant."

"I'm glad he's still in Easton because I need to speak with him. First, I wonder if we could go someplace more private." He tilted his head toward the door.

Peter walked with the sheriff the short distance down the street to the Bachmann where they took a seat at a corner table, their backs turned away from other patrons to discourage anyone from joining them.

Fullert leaned on his beefy arms. "What do you know about the man?"

Peter thought he smelled of burnt wood and sweat, as if he'd been camping in the woods.

"Not much, I'm afraid. I've known him for several years, since he started moving through the area collecting shoats to take to market."

"You've never had a personal conversation with him?" The sheriff frowned.

"I guess that depends on what you mean by personal. He only ever talked about his pigs or told jokes." The last one the Old Pig Drover had shared with him the day before yesterday brought a flush to Peter's face.

"He lived under your roof for weeks. Didn't he ever talk about where he came from?"

Peter narrowed his eyes. "Henry, I assure you if anyone could get information out of a man, it would be my wife and daughter. Even given their persuasive skills, they couldn't get him to open up about himself."

"I'm sorry for putting you on the spot," Fullert said, lifting his hands. "This man has kept his secret amazingly well and for a very long time."

Peter furrowed his brows. "What secret are you talking about?"

The sheriff leaned back in his chair and gazed around the room. "There's someone I'd like you to meet. I believe he's nearby, so can you stay here while I go get him?"

"Certainly."

Peter watched as Fullert scraped the chair against the floorboards and marched down the hall to the front door. He wondered what was going on, having been curious about the Old Pig Drover since he'd started coming through Easton years ago. The man, however, always acted and spoke as if the only life he'd ever known was in the open fields, driving pigs to various markets. Since he'd never posed a threat, Peter had chosen to let him be.

Fullert returned a few minutes later with a man who appeared to be in his thirties with thinning brown hair, green eyes and a ruddy complexion. Something like sadness and hope gave him the enigmatic look of a Renaissance portrait. Although his clothes were dusty, presumably from travel, Peter could tell they were well-cut and of a good quality. He rose as they approached him.

"Mr. Kichline, I'd like to present Mr. Matthew Forker."

"Mr. Forker." Peter shook the man's proffered hand.

"Mr. Kichline has served as sheriff twice, most recently until early this year."

"I'm happy to meet you, sir."

"The pleasure is mine." Peter's curiosity was aroused—the man had spoken with a Southern accent.

The men took their seats, and after Forker disinterestedly ordered an ale, the new sheriff threw down his gauntlet. "Mr. Forker thinks the Old Pig Drover might be his father."

Peter inclined his head back. "I see. What makes you think so, Mr. Forker?"

"I've been searching for my father on and off for the past five years. Earlier this spring, I ventured north after having no success in South Carolina where we're from or any of the other southern colonies. In Philadelphia, I heard stories about a so-called Old Pig Drover, which seized my attention because of the mystery surrounding the man. On the off chance I might be on to something, I began traveling to communities he'd visited, which is why I've come to Easton. Mr. Fullert told me the man had an accident a while back and had recuperated at your home."

"Yes, that's correct." Peter tented his hands. "I'm happy to say he's made a full recovery."

Forker bit his lower lip. "Is he still in Easton?"

"Yes, he's here and for the time being living with my indentured servant at my sawmill."

He exhaled sharply. "That's a relief."

"How old would your father be now?" Peter asked.

"Sixty-four. I'm thirty-two, and my father was my age when I was born."

Peter looked up at the ceiling beams. "I'd say our Pig Drover is about the same age."

"I was twelve when he left home quite abruptly, and my memory of him has faded over the years, but my mother tells me he looked more like me than my two brothers." Forker sipped his ale while swatting a fly buzzing around his head. Then he laughed. "Another thing about my father—he used to tell rather bawdy jokes, which drove my proper mother to distraction."

Peter gave a short laugh, signaling recognition. "Ah, yes, our dear Pig Drover is known for such jesting, is he not, Sheriff Fullert?"

"He is indeed, Mr. Kichline. My good wife won't allow me to repeat his jokes in our home."

When the men's laughter dwindled, Peter spoke. "You say your father left home, but do you know why?"

He nodded. "After moving to South Carolina from somewhere in New Jersey as a young man, he became a successful merchant, and we lived well—not exactly high, but well. Then he invested all our savings to establish an inn with a neighbor, which seemed a sure bet to Father. However, his partner ran away with the money and spread vicious rumors. A few weeks later, Father simply disappeared. My mother was frantic, and my brothers and I did everything we could to find him, while keeping the store going. At first, we couldn't pay our creditors because business had slackened off so much, but when people saw how we struggled, and how the blackguard had cheated others in the community before heading west, they came back. Then we were able to make a go of the shop."

"Judging from appearances, you're a successful man." Peter glanced meaningfully at Forker's clothes.

"Yes, I suppose I am, sir. More importantly I have a fine wife and four children, but there's still a good deal missing in my life."

"Your relationship with your father?" he guessed.

Forker nodded. "For years, I've wanted to find him, hoping he was still alive, to tell him all is forgiven, and we want him to come home." He stopped when his voice caught. After sipping the ale, he spoke again. "My older brothers discouraged me. They'd never forgiven him, you see. Since my oldest brother died and the other moved further south, however, I felt free to search for our father with my mother's blessing."

Peter had no reason to believe this man wasn't sincere, but he hesitated to take Forker straight to the mill house, believing the shock of seeing his son might be too much for the Old Pig Drover. "If you will kindly bear with me, Mr. Forker, I'd like to ease the way for you to see the man you believe is your father. I just don't want him to be unduly surprised, especially since he's just recovered from the accident."

Forker nodded, closing his eyes. "I completely understand, Mr. Kichline. Sheriff Fullert told me all about the mishap. Thank you very much for taking good care of him. I'll be staying here at the Bachmann, and I won't try to see him until I hear from you again."

He found the Old Pig Drover outside tending to his herd, looking as he always did, except for a fresh stoop in his shoulders. Seeing Peter, the man waved his right hand and smiled. "If it isn't the sheriff! I was hoping you'd be comin' along afore I head out. Say, did you hear the one about the feller who out-did the very prophet Elijah?"

Actually, Peter had heard the joke from a tavern patron some weeks ago. He interrupted the old man so he didn't have to endure the story again. "Yes, in fact, I have."

The old man worked his lips and eyes into a frown. "Well, then ..."

"Your shoats are looking healthy."

"Aye, and I have yer Mr. Horeback and the Masters Kichline to thank fer their condition. I am grateful from the bottom of this black heart of mine, for all ye've done fer me."

Peter gave a slight bow. "I believe in looking out for one another."

"It occurs ter me ye've gone way above any call of duty in my case."

He smiled. "I've enjoyed having you under my roof—or roofs as it were."

"Ye won't have me in yer hair much longer, Sheriff."

He cocked his head to one side. "Where are you going?"

"I'll be takin' off soon's I gather me few belongings—likely tomorrow or next day. It's time I drive me shoats to market one last time afore winter sets in."

Peter spoke slowly, with his clearest enunciation. "You may want to reconsider, Mr. Forker."

The Old Pig Drover squinted, moving his head forward. "What's that ye called me?"

"Mr. Forker."

"If ye'll be excusin' me . . ." He sat on a pile of lumber, looking confused.. "But why did ye call me by that name?"

Peter sat next to him. "That is your name, my friend, is it not?"

"That it would be, but one I aint' be hearin' for many years." He looked up at Peter. "How?"

"From your son."

"My son?" The Old Pig Drover's voice was hoarse. "My son is here?" He looked around, his eyes darting into the woods, the creek, to the village just beyond. "Which son?"

"Matthew. He's been searching a long time for you." *Take it slowly. Let him absorb this information. No doubt hearing his name, and his son's, is a shock.*

"I'd like to see my son." He wiped at his misty eyes with his sleeve.

"And he'd very much like to see you."

"Papa, I really think you should leave the house," Susannah said. "You're boring a hole in the floor."

Peter tried to stop pacing, but his feet wouldn't heed his brain, as if they were two completely different entities. A moan from upstairs brought forth much raking of his hair with his hands. He was having trouble holding himself together as he battled fear. *Be pleased, oh Lord, to deliver my wife and child from every evil and myself from this infernal dread.*

"She's going to be fine, Papa." Susannah pressed her hand against his right forearm. "Doctor Gray says so, and the birth is on time and progressing normally." She spoke like she was the parent and her stalwart father, the child. "And Phoebe is with her too, and Mrs. Traill."

"When did Phoebe arrive? I seem to forget."

"She and Reverend Hanlon came two days ago. She's a good midwife. Honestly, Papa, Mother Catherine and the baby will be fine." She suddenly stood taller, hands on her hips. "Which is more than I can say for you. You must go to Mr. Traill's. I promise to come for you as soon as the baby arrives."

He looked down at his slim daughter. "Alright, then. If you promise." He walked to the hallway for his hat, straining to hear any noises from upstairs.

Susannah came over. "Before you go, Papa—you might want to comb your hair."

He'd fallen asleep in his friend's cozy parlor, lulled by a good fire, a fine meal he'd barely tasted, tree branches swaying outside the window, utter fatigue, and the effects of a glass of port. Darkness filled Northampton Street when his daughter slipped next to him, kneeling beside the wing chair.

"Papa." When he didn't respond, she once again uttered, "Papa."

He jerked awake, sitting up so quickly he nearly knocked himself over, and Susannah with him. "You've brought news?" *Pull yourself together, man!*

"Yes."

She was smiling. She. Was. Smiling.

"Is Catherine alright? And the baby?"

"They are both well, Papa. Baby Elizabeth came into this world not a half hour ago."

"A girl?" His face and body tingled, aglow with wonder.

"Yes, Papa. You have a fine daughter and I, a new baby sister."

"You mean 'another fine daughter.'" The sun rose on his countenance. "Thanks be to God!"

CHAPTER THIRTEEN

They arrived at the Bachmann Publick House to the tune of fifers coordinating their piercing strains. Revolutionary and Civil War reenactors, along with a unit representing World War II, highlighted the event's importance. Erin stepped into the protective shade of a slender tree hoping she didn't do an impersonation of the Wicked Witch of the West and melt straight into the sidewalk in her linen gown. She tried not to long for shorts and a tee shirt, focusing instead on how special she felt in her 18th-century apparel. She glanced at Ethan, whose sweat-streaked bangs pressed against his forehead under the weight of a tricorn hat. Fortunately, Mary Bennett had stitched both a winter and a summer coat for him, so he didn't have to deal with the oppressiveness of wool on this hot day in July.

At least there was no rain in the forecast, and the breeze tickling her face did feel good. The wide straw hat kept the sun off her face as well. She couldn't help but think about her Grandfather Peter and what his men had gone through in the Revolutionary War, suffering through intense heat at the Battle of Brooklyn, then either getting killed or being imprisoned under totally inhumane conditions. Erin stood straighter, feeling a welcome cracking in her lower back. If they could go through such ordeals, she could surely march one block to the "Great Square" and stand for fifteen minutes to hear the Declaration of Independence read aloud.

Her eyes searched through the parade participants for her high school friend Sean O'Malley and his group of reenactors and spotted them standing several feet away on the corner of Second and Northampton Streets. Apparently, Ethan was on the same wavelength.

"Mom, there are those guys from last year, the ones we met at the church, you know, the guys with the cannon!"

"I know. I see them, too."

"Can I go over to them?"

"Well, I guess s—'

"Is this Erin Miles?"

She turned toward the voice and saw a woman carrying a clipboard and walkie talkie, which were in anachronistic contrast to her 18th-century dress. "Hello! Yes, I'm Erin."

"Nice to meet you. I'm Pat Larris."

"I'm glad to meet you too. This is my son, Ethan."

"We're all so pleased you could come and be in the parade." Pat's floral skirt caught the summer breeze as she took a step back and smiled. "How stunning you both are! You look exactly like a period soldier, young man, and you, Erin, are amazing. Where did you get that gorgeous gown?" She gave Erin a thorough once-over.

"A friend from my DAR chapter made my dress. She also did Ethan's uniform."

"Aren't you lucky to have someone like her around!"

"You look nice, too, Pat."

"Thanks." She ruffled her skirt as she said, "These are from good ole James Townsend and Son."

Erin laughed. "I bought my hat and purse from them and Ethan's socks and shoes."

She was momentarily distracted by the presence of a dignified-looking man bearing a large scroll and a walking stick—the guy who portrayed Robert Levers, reader of the Declaration of Independence back in 1776.

"Hello, Bill. Are you ready to lead us?" Pat asked him.

He bowed formally. "As ever, madam." His eyes turned to Erin. "And just who is this vision of loveliness?"

Erin felt her cheeks redden.

"This is Erin Miles, and her son, uh, Evan?"

"My name is Ethan," he corrected her.

"Yes, of course, Ethan. Erin and Ethan, this is Mr. Robert Levers, who'll be reading the Declaration in just a few minutes. Mr. Levers, you may be interested to know these people are direct descendants of Colonel Peter Kichline of Northampton County's Flying Camp."

"Levers" tucked his chin and looked at them. "Well, then, madam and young sir, I tip my hat to you both." He removed his tricorn and swept the hat past the front of himself as he bowed. Erin curtsied but felt so awkward that embarrassment swept over her.

"I want to find those soldiers," Ethan said, apparently unimpressed by the exchange.

Pat Larris came to the rescue. "I'm going over there next. Come along with me."

Erin turned to the reenactor. "Nice to meet you, Mr. Levers."

"I assure you, the pleasure was all mine." He bowed again.

He really gets into his role! I remember him from last year, and he was so authentic.

As she, Ethan, and Pat approached the group of soldiers, she saw Sean glance in their direction and break into a big smile. "Well, there's my young friend and his beautiful mother!" He shook hands with Ethan and bowed toward Erin. "You look wonderful." He leaned forward and kissed her cheek under the bonnet. "My wife is going to be jealous of your dress."

Erin laughed. "Is she here?"

"She's organizing the children who're doing the Pageant of Easton." He looked down at Ethan. "Young man, would you like to march with us today?"

"Would I ever!" Ethan burst into a super-wide grin.

"Ah, that might be a slight problem." Pat consulted her clipboard. "You see, I have Ethan and Erin coming right after the fife and drum corps, just behind Robert Levers."

"You do?" Erin wondered why they were right up front.

"You're the Colonel's family! You'll be marching about where he did, to honor him."

Her jaw went slack with wonder.

"I have an idea," Sean said. "We're right behind them. How about if Ethan leads us?"

"You mean it?"

Someone was going to have to tether this boy to the sidewalk so he didn't shoot straight into the air.

"Sure. After all, you are a Kichline."

"That's settled then," Pat said. "Excuse me. I have to get moving." She climbed the Bachmann's stairs and called out. "May I have your attention, everyone? Attention, please! We're about to line up for the parade, then we'll be leaving for the Great Square in about five minutes. Let's begin with the fifers, drummers, and flag bearers lining up right at the intersection here by the police barricade." She pointed to the right spot as she descended the stairs. Then, standing behind the first group, she called out, "Robert Levers!" He came and took his place behind the musicians. "Alright, next we have the Kichline family!"

"That's us," Erin whispered to Ethan, who looked over his shoulder at Sean.

"Proctors Militia!"

128

As the men stepped in line, Sean handed Ethan a gun. "We found an extra one for you to carry."

"Wow! Thanks!"

Although he nearly sank under the rifle's weight, Ethan manned up and carried the weapon on his shoulder like the other reenactors. For at least the thousandth time since last spring, Erin found herself regretful. *I wish Jim could see this.* Before she could start sniffling, though, the roll call continued, distracting her, and a few minutes later, the parade commenced with the fifers filling the humid midday with sharp notes. She followed close behind them, past the barricades through dense crowds lining the sidewalks on both sides of Northampton Street. Children waved American flags, adults took pictures with cellphones. A man with newspaper credentials flapping around his neck walked backward ahead of them, snapping photos as they marched ever forward.

"I have a declaration!" the man portraying Levers cried out, lifting the parchment and tapping it with his cane. "An important declaration!"

My Grandfather Peter walked this same route toward the courthouse on this day so long ago, leading his troops—I'm literally walking in his footsteps! Tears filled her eyes, and she squeezed them tightly for a moment to stop the flow. She'd always been a sucker for anything patriotic, and this fanfare was about her colonial American family.

When the parade reached the Circle—or Great Square as it was known in the 18th century—she smiled at the crowds, resisting the urge to wave because this was, after all, serious business. The colonies were about to break away from Great Britain! The marchers hung a left, rounding the Soldiers and Sailors Monument, past the Crayola Experience, on to North Third Street where the stage with its 18th-century Easton backdrop stood. Levers mounted the steps, and Pat signaled to the fifers and drummers to flank the left side while Erin, Ethan, and the regiment stood to the right. Hundreds of people surrounded the platform, and as Levers began his speech, Erin gazed into the tented area. There she saw the welcome faces of Melissa and her husband, along with Pat and Al Miles and Erin's mother, whom they'd picked up and brought with them. She smiled as Melissa nudged Audrey and pointed toward Erin and Ethan. Audrey waved, and Erin nodded, feeling suddenly more contented than at any time since Jim's death.

Levers dramatically intoned, "We hold these truths to be self-evident ..." Erin looked up at the old buildings, the Detwiler on the left, then down South Third at the slim spire of First Church, following the line all the way up toward College Hill and her alma mater. *I wonder what was going through Grandfather Peter's mind as he stood in this place all those years ago. When he pledged his life, his fortune, and his sacred honor, he had no idea what lay ahead. Neither did his wife, Catherine.* She suddenly realized something startling about that day. Catherine had been seven months pregnant! He wasn't the only one making sacrifices. She sighed. *My roots go deep in this place. I so belong here.*

"That was amazing, Erin!" Melissa hugged her so hard Erin's bonnet popped off. "Oops! Sorry!"

"No problem." She repositioned the hat then embraced her in-laws.

"I've never seen anything quite like that parade and speech before," Al said. "Seeing all those soldiers really brings to life the debt we owe them for our freedoms."

Pat added her own commentary. "You were incredible, and our Ethan did a wonderful job. You really look like you belong in the 18th century."

Audrey stepped forward and placed her hands on Erin's cheeks. "You bring so much honor to our family. And here we are, standing by my old church where I came when I was a girl." She let go and looked around her. "I haven't been to Heritage Day in ages. I just wish I could see everything better."

"We should go into their fellowship hall, which is air-conditioned by the way. They have cold drinks and snacks. The woman I told you about from last year might just be there." Erin was hoping she was so her mom could reconnect with someone from her youth.

"What woman?" Audrey asked.

"I think her name was Beverly. She said she knew you when you went to church there."

"Oh, yes, you did mention her, and I remember. I'd love to go in." She sighed. "I just can't believe we're here."

"Let's go find ..." She was about to say "Ethan" when he came bounding over to his family, grinning so hard his energy could be measured in kilowatts.

"There's our little man!" Al said.

Many hugs and exclamations later, they were walking across the church lawn when Connie Pierce came puffing up. "Erin! I was hoping to see you. Thanks so much for being with us today."

"The honor was all mine. I'd love for you to meet my family." She smiled at Melissa, and they shook hands, having met before.

"This is your family?"

"Yes. Everyone, this is Connie Pierce, my DAR friend who works at the Sigal Museum and showed me my ancestor's papers and cuff buttons. Connie, this is my mother, Audrey Pelleriti."

"Hello, Mrs. Pelleriti. Your family was a great addition to the parade."

Audrey held onto Connie's hand as she said, "I'm so proud of them. You know, I grew up here, and I never knew about our family history."

"You didn't?" Connie placed her hand over her heart.

"And this was my church. My father used to bring us kids here every Sunday."

Erin hated to interrupt her mother's obvious enjoyment of the moment, but there were other people in their party. "And these are my mother and father-in-law, Pat and Al Miles."

"Nice to meet you, Mr. and Mrs. Miles."

The fifers and drummers played impromptu melodies quietly in the background as Heritage Day visitors wandered over to them. Some listened, others asked questions.

They shook hands and said, "Same here," and "The pleasure is mine."

"Finally, this is Melissa's husband, Tim. We were just about to go inside and cool off."

Connie's ruddy complexion divulged her own discomfort. "What a great idea! Listen, Erin, my husband and I always host a cookout for Sigal people and other Heritage Day volunteers. It's between the parade to the riverfront and the evening concerts and fireworks. We'd love for you to come." She paused. "In fact, all of you are welcome."

Pat glanced at her husband. "We appreciate the offer, but we need to be getting back in an hour or so."

"We do, too," Tim echoed. "But, thanks."

Ethan put on his "But, Mom" look. "All I want to do is go to Crayola. You know we get in free today if we're wearing costumes."

Erin weighed the options. She hadn't been planning to stay for the concerts or fireworks or even the afternoon parade, for that matter. "We're going to Crayola after we wander around first," she told Ethan.

"How long will that take?"

"Maybe an hour."

He tugged on her purse and leaned close to her ear. "Mom, I don't want to go to a picnic."

Erin could always tell when her son had had enough activity, and she didn't want to push him.

Al spoke up. "How about if we take Ethan home after Crayola, and you stay for the picnic and whatever else is going on here? Have yourself a good time."

"Yeah, Mom, that would be great!" Ethan bounced up and down as if he were on a trampoline.

"I might be late getting home."

"He can spend the night with us. Right, Champ?" Al nudged his grandson's shoulder.

"Yeah, Mom, please? Please?"

"What's happening?" Audrey asked, her brow puckering. Her eyes weren't the only thing going.

"I've been invited to a picnic with some of the people from Heritage Day," Erin said, trying not to broadcast to the world news of her activities.

"A picnic? I can't go to a picnic."

"Uh, I'm planning to go, Mom."

"What about Ethan?"

"He's going home with Al and Pat."

"Oh, okay. Well, what about my groceries? Didn't you say you had my groceries delivered to you or something? I didn't quite get all you were trying to tell me."

Erin had figured getting a grocery delivery was the only way she could manage to do her mother's shopping and participate in Heritage Day at the same time. "Yes, Mom, I did, and they're in my minivan."

Audrey looked as if she'd just seen an aardvark levitating above the church. "The ice cream, too? It'll melt in this heat!"

"All the cold stuff is in coolers." She touched her mother's arm, feeling the warmth of its loose skin, and pulled her a few steps away from Connie.

"I'm sorry, Erin, I don't mean to be a bother. I hate being dependent on you and Allen, but without my car ..."

"Don't worry, Mom, you're not a bother. I'm glad I can help. So, about today—after we walk around some and do Crayola, I'll drive you home and unload your groceries. Then, I'll take a shower at your place and change my clothes. I have extras in the car."

"Oh, okay. I just hope I'm not stopping you from doing what you want."

"No, you're not." Erin slid back into the main group, smiling. "Well, we're all good to go, then. Connie, thanks for the invitation—I'll be happy to come. Would you like me to bring anything?"

"Just bring yourself, Erin. I'm so glad you'll be there. Oh, and my address—do you have anything to write it down on?"

"I do." Melissa rummaged in her purse and pulled out an ATM receipt and a bank pen for Erin to use.

"Okay. We're at 195 High Street, on the Hill. Our house is a white Victorian with the usual gingerbread and a big porch."

Before Erin wrote the address down and slipped the note into her small bag, she said, "High Street? My Aunt Jane lived on High Street when I was growing up, but I forget the address. The front part faced the river, and the view from her porch was spectacular."

"That's about where I live, too. What did her house look like?"

"White clapboard with black shutters and a really nice porch."

"I think I know the house, which is just down the street from mine and still very pretty."

"She hasn't lived there since the early nineties." She paused. "Thanks so much for inviting me."

"And thank you for coming! I'll be there from two-thirty on, so just come any time after that."

Erin noticed a look of something like satisfaction pass between her in-laws. She was feeling pretty good herself.

CHAPTER FOURTEEN

He paused in the doorway to their bedroom staring at a scene worthy of a Flemish master—his beautiful wife with her dark brown hair haloed by the backdrop of a glowing fire nursing their two-month-old daughter, Elizabeth. The look of tenderness and contentment on Catherine's resplendent face was almost too intimate for him to view. Yet, he could not pull himself away. She looked up just then and smiled at him, both wordless. He pushed down an urge to go to her, to kiss her lips and press her sweet head against his chest, not wanting to interrupt mother and child. Instead, he closed his eyes and bowed, and upon straightening, received her blown kiss like a benediction.

"God bless you today," she whispered.

Having her support meant so much to him—who knew where current events were heading? He went downstairs, to his hat and coat hanging in the hallway, and as he put them on still in a state of hushed reverence, Frau Hamster trundled over to him. She looked way up, seemingly eager to be of service.

"Ich denke, wir Schnee haben warden," she said, handing him woolen gloves.

"Ja, glaube ich auch." When he walked outside, he could almost feel the weight of the leaden sky pressing down on him. By the sharp clearness in the atmosphere, he knew instinctively Frau Hamster was correct—snow was on the way, likely soon.

All was calm along Northampton Street as villagers ambled toward the shops for their daily bread and other needs in a kind of hush, bearing expectancy about what? The anticipated snow? Christmas in just four days? The business about to be conducted at the courthouse? He tipped his hat three times to women who greeted him and nodded at the shoemaker, baker, and Anthony Esser, the butcher whose brassy personality had mellowed to a dull patina. He made his way to the courthouse where Ziba Wiggins greeted him as if they were meeting at a funeral. In a way, they were experiencing a death—that of British rule over the colonies.

"Ah, good day to you, Mister Kichline."

Peter nodded. "And to you, Mr. Wiggins. How is your good wife today?"

"She's keeping well, thank you." He paused, looking toward the main room where men stood in clusters of twos and threes.

He consulted his pocket watch. "I trust I'm not late."

"No, sir. Everyone else is plenty early, however. May I take your coat?"

Peter shrugged off the outer layer, feeling the garment slide into Wiggins's hands. Straightening his waistcoat, he strode into the courtroom where heads began turning in his direction, and he nodded his welcome solemnly. This was no time for lightness. Indeed, the pending proceedings were as heavy as the leaden December sky.

Robert Traill broke away from a conversation with three men from the surrounding townships and walked over to Peter. "Good day, friend. Are you ready?"

"Indeed I am, Mr. Traill. This is a momentous day." Peter breathed in deeply, feeling his chest expand, looking about the swarming room filled with some of Northampton County's finest men, those willing to put their

136

lives on the line for a principle. Not for the first time that morning, he prayed silently to be a good and faithful servant of the Almighty.

"May I suggest we begin in ten or fifteen minutes, once everyone has arrived?"

"Yes, Mr. Traill, I think that's a good idea." He looked in his friend's green eyes. "Are we still of the same mind in this?" They'd spoken two nights ago in the Kichline parlor about the American colonies' relationship with Great Britain and seemed to be in agreement. They had exchanged thoughts and ideas, iron sharpening iron.

"Indeed, I am, sir. I have rarely been as certain of anything as I am of the path we're about to take." He paused, placing his hands at his hips. "And you?"

Peter nodded. "The same."

"Mister Kichline! Good morning to you, sir." George Taylor interrupted the two men, managing to look dapper in his somewhat outdated frock coat. He might have kept up with the times politically, but where menswear was concerned, he was about a decade behind.

Peter bowed. "Good day, Mister Taylor. How does your lady?"

"Mrs. Taylor enjoys good health. And your dear wife and child?"

"She is also well, as is little Elizabeth." Although the words sounded casual in his ears, Peter spoke them out of the depths of a grateful heart. No sooner had he begun to relax about his family's health, however, then the winds of political change blew to gale force.

A short man with large round eyes joined them, and Taylor asked, "Have you met Mr. Krause from Weisenberg?"

"No, sir, I have not had the pleasure." Peter extended his hand.

"I assure you the pleasure is mine, sir." Krause bowed over their handshake. "I am your humble servant."

Lewis Gordon walked up to them, purpose written in every line of his face. "Good day, sirs. I think we should get the proceedings underway."

"Yes, Mr. Gordon, let's begin." Peter excused himself and went to the front of the room, to the bench where he stood before the men whose conversations ebbed as they began to face forward. "Gentlemen, if you would please, find a seat so we may begin." He looked at Robert Traill. "Mr. Traill, will you please take the minutes?"

"Yes, indeed, I'll be happy to do so."

Peter waved toward a chair at his right, and Traill filled the seat with his bulk as the other men sat near friends old and new. Then he began. "Gentlemen, as you know, a convention of delegates from each of Pennsylvania's counties met last July in Philadelphia, including Mr. Edmonds, Mr. Okely, Mr. Arndt, and myself from Northampton. We passed resolutions stating our allegiance to King George and our desire to return to a state of harmony with our mother country. However, we also insisted the colonies are entitled to the same rights and liberties as all other Englishmen. In addition, we endorsed a calling together of delegates from all thirteen colonies, which culminated in the First Continental Congress of September and October just past.

"In the meantime, our friends in the Virginia Assembly appointed a Committee of Safety and recommended the formation of similar Committees throughout the colonies. That is why we are here today, to appoint men from every township in our good county to serve in this capacity."

His steady, deep voice carried not only the bass notes of his German accent but more weight than usual. Judging from their eye contact, they were holding on to his every word. He chose them carefully.

"Our purpose is to oversee the safety and security of our county as we steadily march toward cutting our ties with Great Britain, ties made looser by its resistance to our measured and justifiable requests and conditions. Should the King refuse to pay heed to us, we must have in place a body of dependable and upright men to govern our affairs. They will keep watch over and act upon events dealing with the public welfare, including the creation of a militia and to provide for the local defense. Rather than act on our own accord, Northampton will stay in touch with other Pennsylvania counties. We'll try to quell any violence, even as we are charged with the task of dealing with dissenters." He certainly wasn't looking forward to the latter.

"At this time, we need to appoint such men, as well as a standing Committee of Correspondence. You've been chosen by freemen in your townships to represent them on the county level, and I trust each of you will live up to their good measure of you. You haven't been chosen because you are better or more important than any other man, or in order to have more privileges and rights than others. Rather, you have been entrusted with a sacred duty—to keep the peace of our county, and our commonwealth. You've been chosen, my friends, to serve with all your might according to God's ways and in His strength." He took a sip of water from a glass Ziba Wiggins had placed there for his use.

"As members of the Committee, your responsibility will be to muster men from your townships regularly and to train our county's men in the art of war should we come to that unhappy state of affairs. As a body and as individuals, we are to follow the dictates of the Continental Congress. This includes the order for all free men to have arms and ammunition and that no powder be used except when the need is urgent. We simply must not allow our ammunition to run dry or our arms to be lacking. To that end, only members of this Committee can give permission to sell or dispose of arms or ammunition in Northampton County." He looked over at his friend. "Mr. Traill, do you have the names of the men who've come to represent the townships so we may take a roll call?"

"Yes, sir. Would you like me to read them?"

"Would you please? Gentlemen, when you hear your name, please rise to be recognized."

Traill put his quill down and stood. "These are the members of this Committee, chosen by their peers as upstanding and trustworthy men: from Easton, Lewis Gordon and Peter Kichline. From Forks, Jacob Arndt and Michael Messinger. From Williams, Melchior Hay. From Allen, George Taylor." He stopped to clear his throat. "From Bethlehem, John Okely. From Lower Saucon, Anthony Lerch."

A procession of names followed—men Peter knew, farmers, blacksmiths, carpenters, shoemakers, coopers, tavern keepers, whose wives and children he also knew. Men willing to defend their God-given rights, to turn the world right side up.

"From Upper Saucon, Jacob Morry and Henry Kooken. From Macungie, John Wetzel. From Upper Milford, Anthony Engleman."

Peter imagined the faces of their families, who also were being called upon to make their own brand of sacrifice.

"We have from Whitehall, John Griesemer. From Salisbury, David Deshler. From Plainfield, Casper Doll."

His old friend took his place among Northampton County's leaders, chin lifted, resolve sketched on every line of his countenance.

"From Mt. Bethel, Joseph Gaston. From Lehigh, Yost Driesbach. From Weisenberg, Daniel Krause. From Lynn, Thomas Everett. From Heidelberg, Michael Ohl."

Peter thought of his own wife and children, of their patriotism and faith, which he would be drawing upon himself in the coming crisis.

"From Lowhill, John Hartman. From Towamensing, Nicholas Kern. From Penn, George Gilbert. From Chestnut Hill, Abraham Smith. From Lower Smithfield, Nicholas Depui."

Traill cleared his throat as he came to the last of the names, those men still seated in this house of justice.

"Finally, we have from Delaware, Manual Gonsales, and from Upper Smithfield, Andrew Westbrook."

Peter looked around the room to find every man represented, standing as one, each looking determined to do whatever was necessary to secure the rights of his fellow man. He blinked hard. For a long moment, the room was silent except for their breathing and the sound of the fire in its hearth. At last, Peter spoke.

"Thank you, gentlemen, thank you so very much for your service. Now, if you would take your seats, we need to vote on a secretary to take the minutes of our meetings. We also need to elect members of a standing Committee of Correspondence, whose job will be to carry out Northampton County's daily affairs."

Lewis Gordon rose. "I move that Robert Traill become the secretary of this Committee."

"Mr. Gordon has moved that Robert Traill act as our secretary. Do I have a second?"

"I second the move," Henry Kooken said.

"Very well. All in favor say 'Aye.'"

A series of voices harmonized into one single "Aye."

"Are there any 'nays?'" Peter asked, then paused. "Seeing as there are none, the motion is carried unanimously to make Mr. Traill our secretary."

A half hour later, the six-man Northampton County Committee of Correspondence consisted of George Taylor, Lewis Gordon, Jacob Arndt, John Okely, Henry Kooken, and to no one's surprise, Peter Kichline. After the proceedings and lunch at the Bachmann, Peter walked up Northampton Street through a swirl of soft snow, enjoying a moment of peace. Such tranquility could prove to be elusive in the coming weeks. An old Latin phrase from his days at Heidelberg ran through his mind, *Alea iacta est*— "The Die is Cast."

"The service was crowded tonight," Peter Jr. mentioned. "Won't it be nice when we're in our new church next Christmas Eve? Still, I'm glad the school house was full. Do you think the new church will be ready by then, Father?"

Peter pressed his lips together and nodded, enjoying the cozy firelight in his parlor, the smell of evergreens in the windows and the warmth of glowing candles marking the birth of the Savior. "Yes, I think we will, hopefully well before Christmas. Construction has been delayed a few times, but I believe we're on course now."

"I've had a good year," Peter Jr. said. "My fulling trade has become prosperous, and Sarah and I enjoy good health. Perhaps by this time next year, we'll be welcoming more than a new church." His face matched the firelight, glow for glow.

Peter leaned forward. "Are you telling me ..."

The young man raised his hand in denial. "No, not yet, Father, but I have hopes."

"May they be fulfilled." He savored the thought of grandchildren even more than the piece of *hutzelbrot*—plum bread—Frau Hamster offered from a tray. He took a big bite, feeling completely content in his warm, safe home. The moment felt so serene—just the kind of life he'd been hoping for at the start of the year—he almost wished he could seize hold of time and somehow hold on, stopping the inexorable movement of men and nations. Unless King George learned the colonies were not errant children in need of a good thrashing and allowed them to be the adults they surely were, Peter knew the road ahead would be full of hazards. Still, he sat a little taller. He would never back down from doing what was right, or from protecting his family and his fellow citizens. Never.

CHAPTER FIFTEEN

She stood on Connie's porch gazing at the sweeping landscape featuring the Delaware and Lehigh Rivers, along with the town of Phillipsburg sprawling below College Hill.

I remember this view.

Memories flooded back—languid summer afternoons eating water ice from a truck that played "Three Blind Mice" while scouring her aunt's neighborhood in search of children with fistfuls of quarters; reading *The Babysitter's Club* series on the porch swing; watching *The Facts of Life* on her aunt and uncle's wide-screen TV, wishing she could live there too—where life's possibilities seemed as expansive as the panorama. Her favorite times back then came with nightfall as the twinkle from city lights shimmered on the water. Erin returned to the present, laughter reaching her from the backyard, and she wondered whether she should go out there and announce herself or just ring the doorbell. Before she could decide, Connie came out.

"There you are! Welcome, Erin."

"Thanks for inviting me." She took stock admiringly of the pink and green Lily Pulitzer sundress Connie filled so fetchingly and wondered if she were going to be hopelessly out of sync in her khaki shorts and polo shirt. Connie held the door open, and Erin walked into the coolness of a room with a late 19th-century fireplace, wood floors, and light-colored English cottage furniture. She heard someone moving around down the hall, opening and closing drawers.

"I hope I'm not underdressed, Connie."

"You look wonderful." She broke into a pert smile and beckoned Erin further inside as a little Bichon Frise padded up to them.

"At least I'm a lot cooler than I was in that gown, much as I loved wearing it."

"Heritage Day always seems to be a signal for Mother Nature to crank up the heat. I remember four years ago when the temperature hit a hundred degrees at noon. We all nearly fried like eggs on the sidewalks."

"And who is this?" Erin bent down to pet the pooch whose tail wagged fiercely enough to give the dog whiplash.

"This is Mandy. Do you have a dog?"

"I sure do, a bassett hound named Toby."

"I love bassetts!" She addressed her dog. "Now, Mandy, don't jump all over our guest."

The white dog sat and looked up at Connie.

"I'm impressed!"

"One of my lesser talents. Do come in. I'll introduce you."

Erin followed her hostess through a wall-papered dining room featuring French Provincial furniture against the backdrop of a Persian rug echoing the lavender and peppermint colors of the walls. The kitchen, smelling of vinegar and vanilla, was just as inviting with cream-colored cabinets, brown and white granite countertops and gleaming stainless-steel appliances. There was also a freestanding table featuring a drink station, then a sunroom which led to a patio where a dozen or so people stood holding drinks and plates. For a moment Erin froze, feeling needles-and-pins anxiety creeping into her temples. She probably didn't know anyone at this party except for Connie. She normally wasn't afraid of new social situations and enjoyed meeting strangers, but this was the first time she'd been at a non-family social gathering since Jim's death.

"Erin, I'd like you to meet my husband, Terry. Terry, this is Erin. She's originally from here, but she lives in, is it Lansdale? now." Erin nodded. "Her ancestor was Colonel Kichline."

Connie's husband stood a lanky six-foot-plus with dark brown hair and slate-colored eyes. A deep tan testified to a recent vacation or maybe just a good deal of yard work. Because he was wearing cargo shorts, a bright red Hawaiian shirt, and Birkenstocks, Erin felt more at ease with her own wardrobe.

"Glad to meet you, Erin. You must be a DAR then?" He put down a plate filled with what appeared to be marinating chicken to shake hands with her.

"Yes, I am, and I'm happy to meet you too."

"Can I get you a drink?" Connie waved toward the table with assorted bottles, cups, napkins, cut up fruit, and an ice bucket.

"Uh, sure."

"What's your pleasure?"

She could really use an iced tea but judging from the exotic array, wondered whether they had anything that pedestrian. She took a chance. "I'd love iced tea, if you have some."

"We sure do. Green or black? Sweetened or unsweetened?"

Erin laughed. "Now, I really am impressed."

"My wife is very serious about parties," Terry said.

"I'll say. Okay, then, green. Unsweetened. Extra ice."

"Lemon?"

"Never!" She felt her anxiety dissipate like morning mist and decided to stick with Connie until she warmed up to everyone else. She did, however, want to make sure she didn't cling or appear needy.

"Hey, Mom, Dad, I'm heading out with some friends to the concerts."

A miniature version of Terry had appeared, except this one was considerably younger and wore glasses and a well-tended goatee.

"And this would be Alex," Connie said. "Alex, my friend Erin."

Looking away from his mom's guest, he mumbled, "Hi. I'll see everyone later!" He picked up car keys from a wall rack and loped toward the front door.

"He's home for the summer from Lycoming College," Connie said.

Erin nodded as she accepted a plastic tumbler with a flag motif from her hostess.

"Come on out, and I'll introduce you to everyone. We'll be eating in about a half hour."

"More like ten minutes," Terry said.

"More like ten minutes, then!" Connie smiled and led Erin through a set of French doors onto a pavered patio with two glass-topped tables sporting purple umbrellas. Tiny red roses climbed a trellis on the side of an outdoor garage. Several partygoers looked in her direction, and one woman stepped forward.

"Hi! I believe we met at State Conference."

"Yes, I remember you." Erin was feeling more relaxed by the minute.

"I'm Kelly Howe, and this is my husband, Henry." She stuck out her hand.

"Erin Miles." She shook the smiling couple's hands, guessing they were in their late fifties.

"I didn't see you at the Parson-Taylor House today. I always volunteer there on Heritage Day," Kelly said.

"After the parade, we went to the Crayola Experience with my son."

"Maybe next year, then. He really should see the house. Did you know George Taylor signed the Declaration of Independence?"

"I did." Erin didn't feel like telling Kelly she was a historian and had come to know a fair amount of Easton's storied past. Not only that, but every school child in Easton and Phillipsburg knew about George Taylor.

"Which chapter are you with?"

"Valley Forge. I'm originally from the Easton area, and my family still lives up here."

"Her ancestor was Colonel Kichline," Connie said, as pleased as if he were her own.

"Oh!" Kelly flashed a huge grin.

"Hey, everyone, this is my friend, Erin Miles," Connie announced as if she were herding a group of elementary school children on a field trip.

Erin half expected her friend to disclose her pedigree and was relieved when she didn't. She almost laughed out loud when she noticed one of the men in the group wearing a tee shirt that read, "History Buff—I'd find you more interesting if you were dead."

"Well, look who's here!" Connie exclaimed.

Erin turned toward the open doors where Paul Bassett stood in his own version of her very own outfit—khakis, a navy-blue polo shirt, and Topsiders without socks. He was looking around the patio and when his gaze fell upon her, his eyes brightened. Erin was surprised when a tingling sensation started in her shoulders. Judging by the look on Paul's face as he walked over to her, she wouldn't have to rely on just the busy hostess for company.

Paul was staring at her plate. "If I may say so, that is one strange mishmash."

Erin laughed and shook her head. "What? You've never mixed coleslaw with ambrosia?"

He squinted while twisting his mouth into a kind of Popeye the Sailor Man grimace. "I was thinking more about how you dipped the chicken into the chocolate fondue, then mixed them up with shrimp."

"What can I say?" Erin spread her hands. "I'm creative with my food."

"That's for sure!" He took a man-sized bite of corn on the cob and when a kernel squirted out of his mouth onto her chicken, his face reddened. "Sorry about that."

"No problem." Erin flicked the piece off her plate onto the patio where the dog caught it in mid-fall, then looked up expectantly for more. "Maybe I should try adding corn to my mashup next time."

Paul laughed out loud. "C'mon, Erin, where did you learn to eat like that?"

She didn't mind the question since he seemed to be bantering rather than nagging. Some people truly became offended by her weird sense of taste—"food police" she called them.

"You know how some people rebel when they get to college and do all sorts of things they never were allowed to do at home?" When he nodded, she finished her point. "Well, I grew up in a Wonder Bread home with Jell-o salads and French toast fried in Crisco. We ate pasta with red sauce and meat and potatoes. My mother never even heard of Moo Goo Gai Pan or yogurt until I brought them home from college. I didn't exactly rebel against my white bread upbringing, but I moved away from that kind of food and became rather adventurous."

"At least your mother cooked, Erin. Mine actually scorched an army of tea kettles just trying to boil the water." He took another bite of the corn, butter dripping down his chin, which he wiped away with his red, white, and blue paper napkin.

"Who made your meals?"

"Dad was always too busy or not around, so I learned to fend for myself pretty quickly. We ate a lot of peanut butter sandwiches, also on Wonder Bread I might add, and went to restaurants most of the time."

Erin looked at the other people, their laughter and conversation mingling with a set of nearby wind chimes, creating a tranquilizing effect. She thought of Ethan and hoped he was also enjoying himself tonight.

"Where did you grow up?" she asked Paul. A fly started buzzing around her plate, and she swatted it with her napkin.

"Pretty much everywhere."

"Where is everywhere? I mean, where were you born?" She wanted to ask what year as well but controlled the urge.

"North Dakota. I was a military brat, and we moved a lot since my dad was a major. When the Army said, 'Jump,' we jumped. I even lived in Germany for a while."

"Sprichst du Deutsch?"

He smiled and held his right hand up with his thumb and forefinger a small distance apart. *"Ein bisschen."*

"I speak a little German myself." She paused. "So, is there any place you consider home?"

He smiled. "Easton."

She wanted to ask how he got here, but Paul got to the next question first.

"So, you grew up here, then?"

"Yes, and my parents, and their parents, and, well, you get the idea."

"All the way back to Colonel Kichline."

"All the way back to him," she said, grinning.

"By the way, you and Ethan looked great in the parade today. I hoped to catch up with you, but I was volunteering at the Bachmann and had to hurry back after the reading."

"We had a lot of fun dressing up, although I'm glad women today don't have to wear such elaborate clothing." She took a bite of her chicken and swallowed before asking, "Do you have any brothers or sisters?"

"Yes, a younger sister. She lives near Orlando with her husband and two sons, not too far from my parents. What about you?"

"I have an older brother who lives in Bethlehem—he manages the Hotel Bethlehem."

"Nice place. I've eaten there a few times. Your parents are still living, right?"

"Yes. In fact, my mother was at the parade with Melissa—you remember her from that day at the Sigal—and her husband, and my in-laws."

"Wasn't your dad able to come then?"

"No. My parents divorced when I was pretty young, and they don't really see each other." She didn't think this was a good time to delve into that morass.

"Did they remarry?"

"My dad did, but his second wife died recently."

They remained quiet for a few minutes, just enjoying each other's company.

"So, you moved away from here after college—Lafayette, right?" he asked.

"Right on both counts. I went to graduate school at Villanova where I met my husband, Jim. His family has a business in Lansdale, and after he graduated and we got married, we decided to stay close to them and raise a family." He didn't need to know about the two miscarriages before they got Ethan. Wanting to swim away from a rising tide of emotion, she moved toward calmer waters. "Where did you go to school?"

"As I mentioned, my family ended up living near Orlando, but I never wanted to stay there. Since I'd always loved history and wanted to be closer to where I could find a lot of it, I decided to go to Penn."

She was impressed. He must've been very smart to have gone there.

"How did you like Philadelphia?"

"Loved the city—so much so that I went to Temple for my law degree."

"Did you practice in Philadelphia afterward?" she asked.

He shook his head then, imitating Don Corleone in *The Godfather*, said "I got an offer I couldn't refuse." He cleared his throat as Erin chuckled. "The offer was in Manhattan, so there I went."

She wondered how long ago he had graduated but figured any information about his age would come at a natural pace, and she didn't want to push the process of getting to know him. He seemed to be around her own age, though, in his mid-forties. Erin couldn't deny her interest level was rising for this friendly, caring, smart man, but she was confused. How, she wondered, could she have been in tears earlier in the day missing Jim and now, be attracted to another man? Her emotions were starting to resemble one of her crazy food mash-ups.

She took a long drink of iced tea, then asked, "How did you find out about Easton?"

"I used to take day trips whenever my schedule allowed, which wasn't often because young attorneys work an unholy number of hours to establish themselves. Remember that book and movie *The Firm?*" When she nodded, he said, "Life was something like that. When I was twenty-seven, I met someone and wanted to get married, but she said she couldn't compete with the long hours I had to work. She needed a husband who'd be able to pay attention to her, so she found a CPA."

Not knowing what to say after receiving such a significant piece of his story, Erin reminded silent.

"After that I just worked and worked until I met Easton."

He'd spoken as if Easton were a person instead of a place.

"Whenever I could escape the grind, I'd drive an hour or so in different directions until one day, I found myself here. I had one of those love-at-first-sight experiences—I just felt like I belonged here." He smiled at her.

"And so you do!"

"I kept coming back, made some friends, then eventually decided to chuck the fast lane and follow my heart here."

"So, you left your firm behind?"

"Yes, although I still practice law here."

So, he was still working and not just writing local history books. "When did you move here?"

"Let's see." He looked up into the sky, still high and bright at seven o'clock. "I came nine years ago. I was forty and ready to settle down into a quieter life."

Aha! There was his age. "Are you happy here, then?" she asked.

He looked at her directly and smiled, reminding her more than ever of "B.J. Hunnicutt" from *M*A*S*H*. "Very much so."

At eight o'clock, everyone went to the riverfront for the fireworks except for Connie and Terry, Paul and Erin. "I prefer watching from the front porch," Connie said. "We have such a great view."

Terry added, "And I dislike the crowds and trying to find parking."

Erin looked at Paul. "I'd love to stay here, too. I have such happy memories of watching fireworks from my aunt's house just down the street."

"Staying sounds good to me," Paul said.

From her peripheral vision, Erin saw Connie elbow Terry, a gesture whose meaning wasn't lost on Erin. She wasn't sure how she felt about anyone regarding herself and Paul as any kind of couple and refused to go any further down that particular avenue. Just having a fun evening with an interesting, new—male—friend was enough.

She and Paul spent the next half hour collecting trash from the party, refrigerating leftovers and wiping down tables, much to their hosts' chagrin. Then they made their way to a wicker settee on the porch with stemless glasses of chilled Chianti and a plate of cheese, plump red grapes, and water crackers, which Erin placed on a glass-topped coffee table. An overhead fan swirled the warm air above their heads while pungent mosquito coils kept insects at bay. Being there felt so right, her childhood memories hugging her like Linus's blanket. She wondered if Jim would be okay with how much fun she was having and that she found Paul attractive.

Just as night fell, dazzling displays of light and noise boomed above the Delaware River, illuminating Riverfront Park, the water and the bridges. Other neighbors had joined them on the porch, all of them oohing and aahing. One of them hummed a loud, off-key rendition of "The 1812 Overture." Erin laughed to herself at the clichéd responses but considered how there really wasn't a more appropriate reaction to such loud brilliance.

When the fireworks ended, Erin thanked her hosts. "I've had a marvelous time. Thanks so much for inviting me."

"We're really glad you came." Connie moved closer for a hug.

"Come any time." Terry smiled but didn't embrace her.

"I'll walk you to your car," Paul said. As they left, Erin saw Connie's elbow slam into her husband's rib cage and resisted an urge to burst out laughing. She'd parked three houses away where the smell of honeysuckle scented the night air, and where they stood like two awkward teenagers.

"Uh, before you leave, I find myself wanting to know when I'll get to see you again," Paul said.

She gulped. "I'm up here a lot, especially since my mother stopped driving."

"I hope I'm not overstepping here, but …" A cricket chirped loudly. "Might you be open to going on a date? I'd be happy to come to Lansdale if you'd like."

She'd been anticipating words like these for most of the evening but now they'd been spoken, she hesitated. Then, in the back of her mind, she heard something Jim had said to her shortly before he died—"Someday, when the time comes, I hope you'll find someone new to pour your love into." At the time, she never thought such a day would come, and certainly not just a little over a year later. Still, there was no denying the fascination she felt for one of Easton's adopted sons and eligible bachelors. Maybe she could get to know Paul better—slowly of course. Naturally, she'd want to discuss this with Melissa, and Pat and Al. She wondered what they would say, what kind of advice they would offer. Most importantly, what would Ethan say? If he wasn't ready for his mom to date someone, then she wasn't ready either. She smiled to herself remembering something else Jim had said—"Of course, no one could ever replace me." Erin searched Paul's face, a study of sweet, hopeful patience under the streetlight casting him in soft tones.

"I'd like to go on a date, but can you give me a few days—I'm not sure how Ethan will feel about it."

He closed his eyes and nodded. "Take all the time you need. You've both been through a lot, and the last thing I want to do is pressure you." He smiled down at her. "You have my number. Just call me when you're ready."

CHAPTER SIXTEEN
Philadelphia, January 24, 1775

My dear Catherine,

I trust this letter finds you and the children in good health and spirits. I arrived in Philadelphia with the Northampton County delegation on the 22nd, having encountered one particularly snowy interval in Doylestown. Fortunately, the storm did not hinder our progress, and we were present for the first meeting of the Provincial Convention early yesterday. My good friends Misters Arndt, Taylor, and Oakley have found lodging at a boarding house just a block from Carpenters' Hall, but I have elected to stay with Mister Samuel Miles, whom I have known since the Indian troubles in the mid-1750s when he came to our good county's assistance. We met most recently when I was in Philadelphia last summer and were delighted to remake each other's acquaintance. He is a man of great faith and integrity and when we are together, I sense we are as iron sharpening iron. He has an especially attractive red brick home less than one mile from the Hall. His lovely wife and family are most engaging, and they are very eager to provide for my every need.

Although I stayed up late into the evening of my arrival talking to Mister Miles, I got up early for the meeting. Since then, I've been part of rather lengthy sessions that would have driven Frau Hamster to distraction because they were without regard to our earthly needs or appetites, so pressing is the business at hand. Indeed, when we finally convened for the midday meal, my stomach seemed rather confused, being used to that good woman's regularly timed fare. My favorite place to dine remains the City Tavern where the food is plentiful, tasty, and reasonably priced, and there is usually a fiddler or someone at the harpsichord to entertain us.

Shortly after my arrival, Mr. Gordon told me a rather astonishing thing. He saw our friend, Steven Forker—The Old Pig Drover—near his lodgings. Mr. Forker and his son had planned to leave Philadelphia for South Carolina in order to arrive home by Christmas, but the son became ill, and they ended up using a lot of their funds for medical assistance. Given their predicament, I paid a visit and have seen to their ability to stay in the city as long as necessary. Then they will leave for the South as soon as the weather clears.

I'm pleased to know how deeply interested you remain in these urgent affairs and will attempt to bring you up to date concerning our actions. You are sharing my work as you have done all along, which is a blessing to your grateful husband. At the heart of what this Convention is doing is the hope, not only of Pennsylvania's delegation, but those of other colonies, that we might be able to restore harmony with Great Britain. However, all of us are agreed and resolved that if the King disregards the Continental Congress's petition to redress our grievances, we will resist—we will defend America's rights and liberties, something I believe is going to happen. To that end, may I allude to the book of Nehemiah in which that Old

Testament Prophet *"prayed to God and posted a guard."* Likewise, we are praying for peace, yet preparing for war in case Providence should deem we undergo its rigors.

Among our grievances is our clear opposition to the slave trade and our desire for that execrable misery to end. Many Pennsylvanians have liberated their slaves, and even Virginia's Assembly has petitioned the King for permission to enact a law to prevent the further importation of slaves there. We are also making plans to set up various manufacturers to create and produce materials vital to a war effort including gun powder, iron, nails, steel making, glass, and fulling mills.

Knowing you stand beside me in supporting our rights as colonists buoys my spirit. I want our children and our children's children to live in peace and freedom from fear and tyranny.

While I do not know when our proceedings will terminate, I am hopeful we will need no more than a full week for our deliberations and to make recommendations. On the way home to dear Easton and to you, my beautiful wife, I plan to stop in Bedminster to visit my mother, stepfather, and brothers for a day or two. I will write again soon. Kiss our dearest Elizabeth and Susannah for their Papa, and greet my sons with my earnest devotion.

I Remain Your Loving Husband,

Peter

He needed to think his own thoughts, clear his brain of the constant musings and opinions of others. To that end, he slipped through the delegates clustered at the door and embarked on a solitary stroll in which winter's halfhearted sunlight was waning. Shadows around Carpenters'

Hall crept through bare tree limbs and swathed neighboring dwellings. He set out on a brisk pace to get his blood flowing, and like a homing pigeon, made a straight path for the river, the same one flowing past Easton, linking him to the place and people he held closest to his heart and missed so dearly. He nodded to those he passed on the hectic street quite out of habit. In Easton, he knew everyone and everyone knew him, but here he was just one more man in a city of thousands, moving past the steady clopping of horses and the bouncing of carriages along cobblestone streets William Penn had laid out in an orderly system and whose trees lent a placid, Eden-like note.

He stopped at a corner to wait for a horse and rider to pass and upon entering the street, encountered a trio of fashionable ladies whose high hairstyles, brocade gowns, and quality woolen coats broadcast their privileged station. As he tipped his hat, he didn't notice their admiring looks, but he did think one of them seemed strangely familiar. By her dress alone, he never would have concluded the woman was his formerly indentured servant, but her eternally startled look was a dead giveaway. Judging by the manner in which those brown eyes flared at the sight of him, Peter guessed Greta might have been much happier had she come upon a ghost. For a fraction of a second, he considered just walking away, but deep-rooted politeness and abject curiosity led him to greet his erstwhile housekeeper.

"Good day, ladies. And good day to you, G—Mrs. Hough." He quickly corrected himself, not wishing to call public attention to a past she most likely didn't care to broadcast. Maybe her new station was why she never came to Easton to visit her family.

Greta curtsied, but she didn't look at him. "Good day, Sheriff Kichline."

"I am pleased to see you looking so well."

"As are you." Still, the averted eyes.

She seemed to be ironing her words as if they were wrinkled linen. Perhaps, he thought, she'd been working to lose her German accent. He decided to step carefully.

"Allow me to present my friends," she said slowly, as if remembering her manners. "Sheriff Kichline, Mrs. Joseph Fredericks and Mrs. Jacob Lewis."

A carriage passed at a brisk pace, its wind causing their skirts to sway in its wake.

He bowed to the ladies. "I am pleased to make your acquaintance."

"Sheriff, is it?" Mrs. Lewis asked. "Yes, madam. I twice had the pleasure of serving Northampton County as sheriff."

"Is yours a German accent?" Blonde Mrs. Fredericks giggled into her gloved hand. "Of course, you would be friends with our dear little Mrs. Hough." She patted "dear little Mrs. Hough's" shoulder. "I just love how your people speak as if they are always clearing their throats."

He glanced at Greta, who'd blushed scarlet and turned away, feeling a sudden need to defend her. He resisted, however, since his presence clearly disconcerted her.

"You are easily amused then," he told Mrs. Fredericks. Judging by her unchanging expression, he doubted she realized he'd insulted her.

"What brings you to our city?" Mrs. Lewis stressed "our" as if she were a Spanish Inquisitor.

"I'm serving as a delegate to the Provincial Convention."

Her expression reflected such a sudden drop in temperature he half expected to see icicles form along her jawline. "I hardly think it appropriate for a *German* to presume to make demands upon a British King. After all, we are his loyal subjects, are we not ladies? *We* know *our* place."

"Oh, yes, of course," Mrs. Frederick said as Greta nodded slowly, looking down at her feet.

"Very well, then." Peter tipped his hat and bowed his head. "I wish you a good evening, madams."

He wasn't surprised when they didn't answer him as etiquette dictated, and he turned on his heel to continue walking to the river. His stomach felt as if he'd just eaten a bushel of Alpheus Shotwell's notoriously over-ripe tomatoes from the Famer's Market.

"We missed you after the session today." Samuel Miles addressed him as they relaxed in the comfortable parlor sipping port. The fire warmed their faces while a stiff wind banged the windows.

"I needed to be alone a bit."

Miles reached for his pipe and filled the bowl. "Those meetings become as dull as pond water the longer they last. And yet they are so necessary."

He felt distracted, in the room but not of it.

"My friend, you seem out of sorts tonight." Miles leaned back in his chair.

He decided not to say anything about his unpleasant encounter with Greta, but Peter knew his associate would understand the other incident. "At the London Coffee House near the river, I saw slave traders preparing for an auction tomorrow—men opening the mouths of men, women, and children, inspecting them as if they were animals and not human beings." His eyes narrowed as his voice deepened with revulsion. "One young boy was made to walk and bend in certain ways as a buyer pinched his bony limbs. He and all the others were dressed in little more than filthy rags, shivering in the cold." His teeth clenched.

Miles grimaced, then voiced his own convictions. "Here we are fighting for our freedom from a tyrant while under our very noses, His Majesty's government flaunts this deplorable trade. This is a new land, one I believe God set apart to perpetuate liberty to all captives, including these pitiable slaves, yet the Crown has soiled our noble colonies with an ancient, stinking institution."

Peter had never seen his friend so upset.

"No wonder you've been out of sorts this evening," Miles continued. "Any decent man would be."

Sparks from a kindling log snapped in the grate.

Peter spoke up. "I hope the Continental Congress takes our resolution seriously to prohibit the future importation of slaves to Pennsylvania. Perhaps other colonies will make similar motions."

"One can only hope—hope and pray."

After a long moment, Peter looked in his friend's eyes. "Yes, and maybe there is something else we can do."

His brisk strides and rigid posture reflected his determination as he walked down Market Street toward the Coffee House. The auction was already in progress. His breakfast, what little he'd managed to eat, sat like a Philadelphia cobblestone in his stomach as he stood among the buyers. A portly fellow with hair the color of faded straw paraded three men, a woman, and a little girl, who were chained together, across a wooden platform anchored by large barrels on either end. Potential customers lit fat cigars and eyed the chattel while Peter swallowed an impulse to make a whip of cords and drive them out of the City of Brotherly Love.

"I'll take the woman," a man called out.

Peter saw her clutch the child to her legs, chains banging against her body, eyes pleading, desperate. He could barely stand to watch the scene playing out.

"Will you take the girl too?" the auctioneer asked. "She's a strong little thing."

"I'm not paying full price for it." The scrappy-looking farmer pointed at the child, whose nose ran unaddressed. "You ought to throw her in for nothing."

"You must be jesting my good man. She's worth more than the mother—you'll get more years out of her."

Peter steadied himself, resisting yet another urge, this time to take his walking stick and thrash the auctioneer.

"I'll pay one-fourth, and that's my final offer."

"I can get more for her if I sell her alone." The auctioneer's tricorn slipped to a cockeyed position, and he adjusted the hat.

The woman gripped her child like a lioness, at once fierce and vulnerable before a powerful hunter.

"Do I have another offer on this fine young girl?" When none came, he scowled at the buyer. "Very well. I hope you realize what a bargain you're getting, sir."

Two burly assistants unbound and delivered the mother and child to their new owner while currency changed hands. Peter's blood pressure rose like the wind as an unshaven man pushed the boy Peter had seen the night before onto the platform.

"Now, here's a fine specimen! About six years old, in good health and strong, despite being thin. He'll work hard for years and years. Who'll open the bidding at fifty pounds?"

Peter's right hand shot into the brisk morning air.

The auctioneer pointed in his direction. "I have fifty pounds. Who'll give me fifty-five?"

A man near the platform raised his hand. The boy stood trembling in his pathetic torn pants and shirt, head bowed.

"I have fifty-five, fifty-five—who'll bid fifty-eight?"

Peter thrust his hand upward.

"I have fifty-eight. Who'll give me sixty?"

The other man beat Peter to the punch.

"I have sixty. Who'll give me sixty-two?"

"Sixty-five!" Peter called.

"This fine man knows a bargain! I have sixty-five. Will someone give me sixty-eight?"

"Sixty-eight!"

"Seventy-five!" Peter jumped over several numbers and landed at this one, hoping to discourage his competitor. Muttering broke out through the crowd.

"Seventy-five! Will anyone give me seventy-six for this fine lad?"

Peter glanced in the direction of the other hand, pleased when the space above the man's head remained clear.

"I have seventy-five going once, seventy-five going twice—sold, to the tall German for seventy-five pounds!"

Only then did the boy look up, his dark brown eyes finding Peter's.

"You had quite a time in Philadelphia." Sitting in her Bedminster parlor with her husband and her sons, Peter's mother leaned over and placed her hand on his shoulder. "I am proud of you." She smiled, still very much in possession of her original teeth, though they were slightly stained and crowded.

Charles grinned. "I thought you were looking forward to taking life easier."

Peter felt the years roll away; they were boy-cubs wrestling each other back in Germany while their mother clucked at them to get out from under her feet and go play outside. "Yes, well, you know what our good mother always says."

"To whom much is given is much required." Her eyes twinkled.

He bowed in her direction. "You trained me well, Mother."

"What do you think your wife will say when you come through the door with two slaves?" their stepfather asked.

163

"If you will excuse me, Father Koppelger, I have every intention of treating them as indentured servants. I'll train them at the mills and help them make their own way in the world when they're ready."

Peter had discovered while making the transaction the boy had lost his mother in the middle passage and his father had been sold at a prior auction. The young man he'd also purchased was in his twenties and had looked after the boy in their absence, and Peter didn't want them to bear any more separations.

Koppelger pursed his lips, nodding. "A fine gesture, son."

"Slavery is something we must do away with if we are to be truly free, and your good mother shares my sentiments."

The grandfather clock marked time in the background, and Peter breathed deeply of his parents' home fragrances—cinnamon, cloves, and ginger mingling with the scent of burning pine logs.

Andrew changed the subject. "What do you think, brother, will the King accept our resolutions?"

"I'm afraid such a gesture is highly unlikely."

"Well, I'm ready to fight him and his red-coated minions." The fire's glow reflected in Andrew's eyes.

"Maybe peace can still come," Charles said hopefully.

Peter smiled at his siblings. Charles might not breathe fire like Andrew, or be in the forefront of nearly every aspect of civic life like him, but he could always be counted upon to get involved when needed. And he would be needed, Peter knew. They all would.

CHAPTER SEVENTEEN

Erin and Melissa were discussing recent events over a pot of Earl Grey and a plate of chocolate dipped biscotti. Her friend's dishwasher hummed in the background.

"I think you should do it," Melissa said.

Erin looked into the amber-colored mug, feeling a little too bashful for eye contact. "I guess I wasn't thinking anything like this would happen so soon after …"

"I understand." Melissa sipped her tea. "Did I ever tell you I was engaged before Tim and I met?"

Now Erin looked up, into her pal's blue eyes. "No, you didn't."

She nodded. "We met while I was a junior at Gettysburg College. He wasn't right for me, but being young and not thinking clearly, I was drawn to him anyway. I hadn't dated anyone seriously before, and I think the idea of someone being crazy about me was just so …" She seemed to be looking for the right word. "… enticing."

Erin felt highly curious, wanting to ask a dozen questions but figuring Melissa needed to roll out her own story.

"Well, we got engaged, and somehow right after I said 'yes," alarm bells went off in my head. I suddenly realized I couldn't spend the rest of my life with someone who loved the Clash, not when I was into Whitney Houston."

Erin laughed. "That would've been a union of opposites!"

"That's for sure. Well, I ended up breaking the engagement, and although I was relieved, I also just wanted to crawl into a shell for a while and not go out with anybody else. I didn't really trust my instincts after that. The thing is, I happened to meet Tim just a month later, and I kept backing away from him at first. Starting a new relationship just seemed too soon, but fortunately, Tim wouldn't give up on me. I wasn't so sure about God's timing, but some of my friends encouraged me to trust him even if I didn't understand." She smiled and lifted her hands, palms up. "Here we are twenty-two years later."

Erin considered the implications for herself. "So, you think this could be God's way of, well, helping me get to know someone?" She couldn't bring herself to say "get serious," let alone "get serious with Paul." Just getting past a first date seemed a big enough wall to scale.

Melissa covered her friend's hand and squeezed. "From my perspective of knowing you as I do, go ahead. Go out with Paul. He seems like a good guy." Her eyes twinkled. "He's also really handsome." Erin blushed and laughed. "See what his character is like—if there might be a hint of a future with him, but don't necessarily dwell on the long-term." She made a "tsk" sound and shook her head. "I hope I'm making sense. It's not like you're going to marry the guy, but we need to admit the possibility is there. If I didn't think he was someone you should invest time in, I would tell you."

She couldn't believe her friend had used the "m" word, which seemed to hang between them. "What about Ethan? What if he hates the idea?"

"There's only one way to know, and that's to ask him. He's a big boy, and if he gives the stamp of approval to your seeing Paul, how about if you guys come here for dinner on your first date? I'd be happy to host, and maybe being in a familiar environment would make being with him easier for you."

Erin's eyes filled as she reached over and hugged her best friend.

"I think you should ask him," Pat Miles said, as if she'd just hung up from talking to Melissa. "I'm confident Ethan will tell you exactly what he thinks." She dipped her chin and grinned, the look of an insider.

"No doubt about that," her husband added, fiddling with tangled fishing lures.

"But you're alright with my seeing someone?" Erin's mind was a Fort Knox of doubts.

Her mother-in-law smiled. "Yes, dear, I'm alright with your seeing someone, as long as he treats you and Ethan well."

Al nodded in agreement as he looked up from his tackle box. "That goes for me too. If he's not a good person, I'll pull out my shotgun and drive him right off the porch."

"You don't have a porch," Erin said, a smile traveling up the sides of her mouth.

"But I do have a shotgun."

They broke into hearty laughter.

Ethan stroked his dog's back as his mom told him about Paul Bassett's asking her on a date. The sun was finally beginning to set behind the row of elms in their back yard as they sat on the sunroom floor feeling the last of its warmth.

"I like Paul and would enjoy going out with him, but if getting to know him feels wrong to you, I won't do it." Erin trembled as she spoke, tracing a finger along the swirling pattern of the Oriental rug.

Ethan pressed his lips together. "I like him, too, Mom. He seems nice.

I think it's cool he has our dog's last name."

"I know! What's with that?" She patted Toby's head, growing more subdued. "I didn't think I'd want to go out with anyone, at least not for a long time." She wasn't sure how many of her feelings she should be disclosing to a nine-year-old and decided less was probably more.

"Don't worry, Dad told me to expect this."

Erin felt as if her son had spilled a big container of Italian water ice on her bare legs. "Dad told you to expect this?" She was a Mynah bird.

"Yep. He said some day you'd date someone, and he was okay with that, and I should be too, and I should help you."

"He did?"

"Uh-huh. He said he wanted you to get married again someday and be happy, like you were with him."

There was no holding back tears, no matter how hard she tried.

"He did tell me, though, to make sure the guy was good to you, and to me, or else …"

"Or else what?" Her sense of humor began staging a comeback.

"I should go over to Grandpa's, get his shotgun, and drive him off the porch."

"We don't have a porch," she said, arching her eyebrows.

Ethan smirked. "No, but Grandpa has a shotgun."

The ringing phone jangled her awake at 5:14 a.m., interrupting a deep sleep. At first, Erin thought she was dreaming the incessant noise, then she started climbing to consciousness and groped for the phone on the night table. "Hello," she said, her voice froggy.

"Is this Erin Miles?"

"Yes. Who is this?" Her abruptness sounded rude in her ears.

"I'm a nurse from St. Luke's Warren Hospital."

She sat straight up, instantly awake, the cobwebs vacuumed from the corners of her mind. "What's happened?"

"We have your father, Tony Pelleriti, here in the emergency room. I'm afraid he's had a heart attack."

"Is he, is he …"

"We've got him stabilized and he's quite alert, but we're going to be running some tests. There's a possibility he may need a catheterization."

"So, he's going to make it?"

"We're very optimistic. Fortunately, he called your brother as soon as he started having chest pains, and your brother called the paramedics."

"Is my brother there?"

"He is. Would you like to speak with him?

"Yes, please." She let out a loud sigh.

"Hi, Erin. How are you?"

"I should be asking you, Allen."

"Well, I'm okay, and I think Dad will be too. They're doing some tests, and they'll know more about the extent of the heart attack and what happens next once they get the results."

"The nurse, or whoever I just talked to, said something about a catheterization."

"Yeah, the heart specialist mentioned the possibility and said Dad might even need a bypass. Everything depends on what they find through the tests."

"So, he's in pretty serious condition?"

"I'd say so, but he's stable. He was awake when I got here, and he even cracked a joke about not liking 'horsepitals.'"

She smiled. "That's Dad alright. Listen, let me get a shower and wake up Ethan, then I'll be there as soon as I can." She hesitated. "Do you think I should bring Ethan?"

"Um, maybe not. We'll probably be here a while. He could stay with

Tanya, though—she has off today, or maybe Mom. Then again, you never know about Mom where Dad is concerned."

She knew. "I'll call my in-laws. They're always happy to help."

"They seemed really nice when I was at, well, the funeral, and your graduation party." He paused. "Okay, don't hurry too much. Don't get into an accident or anything."

"I won't. I'll be there as soon as I can."

Erin sat with her father as he snoozed and thought about opening what would surely be an overflowing email inbox. Since early Wednesday morning's phone call, she hadn't had the time, energy, or focus to do anything except be at the hospital while her dad underwent a triple bypass. She'd barely managed to drive back and forth so she could be with Ethan as well. With Tony out of immediate danger and on his way to what the doctors said should be a full recovery, she felt ready to face the world again. Gone had been thoughts about what things to do with Ethan on summer vacation, her moribund job search or going out on a date with Paul Bassett. She'd toyed with the idea of calling him and telling him about her dad, but she hadn't had the stamina.

She'd also been thinking about how much her father meant to her and how happy she was to be fully immersed in his life at this stage of her own. She looked over at him, noting the way the hospital gown hung loosely around his shoulders but thankful for his returning color. He looked so peaceful, and she was grateful to God he hadn't died. She wanted him to stay around long enough to get to know him as an adult, to be close to him the way she'd been before the divorce.

She considered going to the cafeteria since the bowl of corn flakes and Tabasco sauce she'd begun the day with had faded quickly, but she decided instead to check her correspondence before trekking to the dining area. When Erin opened her email, she wasn't surprised to discover fifty-seven messages, excluding a plethora of ads in her junk mail folder. What did draw her attention was a message from Herman Weinreich at Lafayette:

> *Hello Erin!*
>
> *I hope you're doing well. I really enjoyed seeing you a few weeks ago. There's something I'd like to discuss with you. Give me a call at your earliest convenience.*
>
> *Herman.*

She noticed a phone number after his name, then looked at the date— July 14—last Thursday. She decided to take a walk and call him from the visitors' lounge if no one was around, curious to find out what was on her former professor's mind. When she found the room empty except for a television tuned to a close-captioned rerun of *The Brady Bunch*, she tapped in the number on her cellphone. Standing at the window, she fixed her eyes on the encircling mountains holding Phillipsburg in their steady embrace. He answered on the third ring.

"Herman Weinreich here."

"Hello, uh, Herman, this is Erin Miles. I just got your email."

"Erin! How good to hear from you! How are you?"

"Doing well, thanks. I apologize for not calling sooner. My dad's been in the hospital, and I'm just catching up with my email."

"Is he alright?" Concerned filled his voice.

"He had a heart attack, then a triple bypass, so he's been through a lot, but he's recovering beautifully."

"Thank goodness! You've been through so much lately. And how's that son of yours?"

"Ethan's doing well."

"Good. Are you in Easton?"

"Close by. I'm across the river at St. Luke's Warren. Lately, I've been up here more than I've been in Lansdale." She surprised herself by not referring to Lansdale as "home."

He paused. "I wanted to speak with you because I'm wondering if you've found a teaching position yet."

She was glad he couldn't see her cringe. "I'm afraid the nearest I've come is a community college in Alpena, Michigan. Let's not even talk about the school in Siloam Springs, Arkansas."

Weinreich laughed. "Somehow, I can't picture Erin Miles in Alpena, Michigan, or Siloam Springs, Arkansas, although they may be nice enough."

"I agree on both counts." Her smile helped release some muscle tension.

"Listen, I have an opening in my department for a one-year position while my tenured guy goes on sabbatical, and I wonder if you might be interested."

Her emotions shifted from tired and worried to a thrill of joy racing up her spine. "Really?"

"You'd be teaching two courses of Early American, 1600-1840, in the fall along with a senior seminar in Early American and one on Creating a Nation, basically covering the Federalist Period. Then in the spring, you'd have the second part of the intro courses, plus upper-level classes on Reconstruction through 1900. You'd basically be needed on campus three days a week, and you could organize your office hours around those times."

"How wonderful! I'm definitely interested." Although there wasn't anything professional about her enthusiasm, this was Herman Weinreich she was talking to.

"I'm afraid the pay isn't great, and the position is just for a year."

When he mentioned the salary, Erin noted the numbers were nearly twice what she'd been making at Hatfield College as an adjunct.

"I should let you know, however, there are some things stirring in the department that could potentially turn this into a long-term proposition.

I don't know how you feel about something so tentative, or about the commute—the first classes meet at 8:20."

She went through a series of mental gymnastics. She wouldn't be able to see Ethan off to school and make her first class on time, but surely, she could work something out—maybe with one of the neighbors who didn't have an outside job. She could always rely on her in-laws, but three days a week was a lot to ask for, especially since they were active in the community and their church. A nanny perhaps? She'd have to mull that over.

"I don't see a problem with the salary," she finally said, "and about the position being temporary, well, I haven't really been able to think too far into the future since my husband died. You might say I'm just taking life a step at a time." In contrast to her now-calm and measured response, Erin's mind was busily throwing possibilities at her.

"I completely understand. You know, Erin, maybe being back home at Lafayette would be good for you now." He paused. "If it helps any, I can also throw in benefits for the year."

"Definitely!" Medical insurance had been one of her major concerns about not finding another teaching job.

"So, would you like to come in and discuss the particulars while you're up here?"

"I would. I'll stet be staying up here tonight."

"Can you meet for breakfast tomorrow morning?"

"I was planning to go to church at ten, but I could see you around eight or right after church."

"Let's do eight. In the meantime, think the offer over."

When she hung up, Erin took a deep breath. She wouldn't need to look for a job outside of Philadelphia or the Lehigh Valley, a possibility she hadn't really allowed herself to consider, not when she was getting to know her family and her hometown with a fresh set of eyes.

CHAPTER EIGHTEEN

Frau Hamster shooed the boy into the dining room where Peter and Catherine sat awaiting breakfast, Baby Elizabeth swaddled nearby in the cradle that had rocked all the other Kichlines. Joe minced toward the table bearing *The Pennsylvania Gazette* and paused at Peter's side.

"Geben Sie Herr Kichline die zeitung," she told Joe, who looked up at her, his hands trembling. "News-paper," she said, uttering one of the few English words she'd bothered to learn. Her gnarled finger pointed first to the paper, then at Peter, then she gave the boy a slight shove in former sheriff's direction.

He smiled at Joe, who stood before him still holding the paper, looking startled. Joe had filled out over the past four months and was far less jumpy than at the beginning when the sound of a dog barking or a knock at the front door had sent him diving under the nearest piece of furniture.

Frau Hamster huffed, and her hands flew to her narrow hips. *"Nun, gehen Sie dann! Sind Sie bescheuert?"*

Peter stifled an urge to scold the woman for asking if Joe were stupid, as well as a laugh. Notwithstanding the ornery housekeeper's assertiveness with the boy, Peter also had witnessed moments of tenderness between them, like the time he found the feisty *hausfrau* handing Joe a large molasses cookie while patting his curly head. She'd also been diligent to fatten the child and teach him simple chores, such as fetching water and kindling. Early on Peter and Catherine had decided to let William stay in the house with Joe on the third floor until they adjusted to their new environment. When that time came, William would move to the sawmill house and learn the trade from Peter Horeback, as well as help out with the new church. The latter was progressing slowly because the hard winter's heavy snows and frigid temperatures had delayed construction.

"*Ja, I werde do it.*" Joe thrust the paper into Peter's waiting hand.

"Frau Hamster, this boy is coming along splendidly, but we must to do something about his speech patterns," Peter said. "His use of German and English is not only confusing, but also a source of mirth."

Catherine spoke up. "Now that Joe is more established, perhaps I should take over the job of teaching him English."

"I greatly approve and the sooner the better." Peter smiled as he unfolded the paper.

Frau Hamster began serving hot rolls and sausage, but urgent headlines about battles at Lexington and Concord threatened to commandeer his appetite. A few weeks earlier, hundreds of British troops had marched against colonists in a surprise attempt to seize ammunition. They'd been pushed back by militiamen whose alarm had been sounded by a Boston silversmith and member of the Sons of Liberty. Within a short time, some fifteen thousand patriots from throughout New England had surrounded Boston.

Catherine looked at him, seeming to read his mind. "Bad news?"

He nodded. "Blood has been spilled. Shots have been fired."

She looked at her husband, her eyes appearing steady and clear. "Is this the beginning, then, of war?"

He had learned not to mince words with his clever wife, which would be to insult her strong intelligence. She didn't need to be coddled and certainly not condescended to. He shot as straight with her as he did with the other members of the Committee of Safety.

"I believe you may be correct, my dear."

Her face blanched, as if she'd suddenly found herself standing at the edge of an embankment. "Is there no turning back?"

Frau Hamster paused with the sausages to his left, looking intently at Peter.

"I believe events may have gone too far for us to turn back." No one said anything else until Peter lifted his voice to give thanks for the food, then they ate in silence for a few minutes. He looked around the table and realized his older daughter was missing. "Where is Susannah this morning?"

Catherine finished cutting a piece of sausage as she answered. "She's gone to the grist mill."

He frowned, feeling irritated in general. "Why would she be at the grist mill, and so early?"

His wife's mouth turned up at the corners. "She said she had an errand to run."

This made no sense. "Come now, my good wife, what kind of errand would Susannah have to run at the grist mill?"

"She heard Andrew tell Jacob that Mr. Konk was going to be coming today for a rather large order, and Susannah didn't want to miss seeing him."

"Whatever for?" This was unwelcome information. "What business could she possibly have with Wilhelm Konk?"

"My dear husband, her business isn't with Mr. Konk, but with Hans."

He found himself snorting. "She's a child."

"Perhaps you still see her that way, but she is fifteen after all."

He pictured the scene at the Konk farm several months earlier when he'd spied Susannah and Hans talking earnestly, their faces aglow. He'd had the unwelcome thought that her forming an attachment at her age, let alone with a Moravian, wasn't the best idea or the right timing. Peter put his napkin on the table and rose, his hunger having abandoned him. "If you'll excuse me. I don't wish to be late for the meeting."

For a disconcerting moment, he couldn't remember if he were in Easton at the courthouse, or in Philadelphia at Carpenters' Hall. The buildings bore such a striking resemblance to each other, and the names and faces around the table, including Lewis Gordon, Jacob Arndt, and John Oakley, were virtually the same. The voices spilling through the open windows were, however, decidedly more *Deutsch*, plus he had just left his good wife and the comforts of his own home, not that of Samuel Miles. Robert Traill sat poised over his ledger taking notes as Gordon read an impassioned letter from the Committee of Correspondence for the City and Liberties of Philadelphia bearing an April 18 date. As he neared the end of the communication, Gordon uttered the words of Virginia's Patrick Henry spoken several weeks earlier and which had spread like a flame throughout the colonies:

"It is vain, sir, to extenuate the matter. Gentleman may cry 'Peace, Peace,' but there is no peace. The war is actually begun! The next gale that sweeps from the north will bring to our ears the clash of resounding arms! Our brethren are already in the field! Why stand we here idle?"

When Gordon finished, he set the document aside and let a few moments pass before saying, "With utmost urgency, I believe Pennsylvania's Committees must begin to provide for our defense in light of the recent fighting and deaths of our noble brothers in Massachusetts."

Peter nodded his head, along with his fellow committeemen.

"Long has Boston and the surrounding countryside borne the brunt of British cruelty, and the time for them to stand alone against the might of the King has come to an end. We must all stand together," Gordon said.

The laughter of children filtered in from the street, a poignant, though chilling, reminder of all that was at stake as the colonies positioned themselves to oppose in open warfare the world's most powerful military. For a moment, Peter thought it truly was madness to do such a thing, but then he corrected himself. *How can we be wrong to defend ourselves against a Tyrant, to protect our liberties and ensure a better future for those children outside—for all our children?*

"I completely agree," Oakley said. "Soon the British will be coming after us right here in Easton. Mark my words!" He tapped his right forefinger on the table three times, hard, with each word.

Arndt pressed his lips together and pounded the table with his fist. "This kind of action cannot go unanswered by the rest of the colonies. We need to show the King we are determined to oppose such indignities."

Peter took his time before he spoke. "I would like to make a motion to have each of Northampton County's townships form themselves into companies, choose proper officers, and provide adequate arms."

"I second the motion," Arndt said. "How much do we consider adequate?"

The men looked to Peter, who'd seen action during the French and Indian War and who knew a good deal about firearms from his days as Sheriff. "Well, let me see." He made a few calculations on a piece of paper, figuring how many men they needed and what each should have at his disposal. He concluded, "I believe each man should possess one good firelock, one pound of powder, four pounds of lead, a sufficient quantity of flint, and a cartridge box."

"I think that's reasonable," Oakley said.

"Please make a note of those amounts, Mr. Traill," Gordon said. "I also believe we should call to order a general meeting of the whole county committee on, say, Monday the twenty-second at 10 o'clock to make a report to us regarding their execution of these resolves. Do you believe that amount of time gives adequate time to prepare, Mr. Kichline?"

"Yes, I believe two weeks should suffice."

"Well, then, Mr. Traill, would you write letters to the several committeemen of the respective townships giving them notice of these resolves and recommending to them the same mode of proceeding accordingly?"

"Yes, Mr. Gordon, I will do so right away."

"I would like you to answer the letter from Philadelphia informing that committee of our actions first."

"I will send the same by Mr. Towers tomorrow."

"Mr. Kichline, will you do us the honor of becoming Captain of the Easton Company and bringing together such men as can serve this township to the best of their abilities and loyalties?"

He didn't have to think twice.

Not a man was absent on the twenty-second when the full Committee met at the courthouse. Ziba Wiggins wore not only his best waistcoat but his sternest demeanor as he attempted to seat the men according to their townships while keeping bystanders outside and away from the open doors. Since there were so many windows, however, he failed at preventing the curious from crowding beneath them.

Seeing his sweat-streaked red face, Peter clapped his old friend on the back. "You've done a fine job, Mr. Wiggins. Don't fret over the window situation. We'll manage nicely."

"I'll make sure all the gentlemen have water at the tables."

"Take your time, my friend. We'll be here a while."

A stray rooster flapped its wings haplessly at the front door, squawking and cackling as if someone had stepped on it, which is probably exactly what had happened.

"Who let that rooster in here?" Wiggins cried out, moving quickly toward the door. He shooed the frantic creature with his arms as the committeemen who'd witnessed the scene had a good chuckle.

"Comic relief," Robert Traill told John Oakley.

"Indeed. We'll need more of that before this sober day has ended."

Peter took note of his friend's shirt which had wilted in the heat, perspiration clinging to the man's eyebrows and around his mouth. Lewis Gordon was speaking himself into a puddle.

"Because this Committee maintains the British Ministry are fully determined and bent upon the total extinction and utter destruction of American liberty, we resolve to avert as much as possible being reduced to so abject a degree of slavery. Therefore, we have unanimously resolved that this Committee will abide by and carry into execution all such measures as the Continental Congress shall in their wisdom from time to time adopt for the preservation of American liberty."

Including war.

"That the association for our mutual preservation and security now forming in this county be earnestly recommended to all the freemen therein, and that they provide themselves immediately with all necessary arms and ammunition, and that they muster as often as possible to make themselves expert in the military art."

Peter had already begun doing so with his men. They knew how to handle a weapon, but they needed more military discipline and order. He swiped at a gnat and when the tiny insect persisted, he gently clapped it between his hands.

Gordon continued reading the resolutions. "No powder may be expended except upon urgent occasions, and all storekeepers are forbidden to sell or dispose of any arms or ammunition without the consent or approbation of one or more of this Committee."

There's going to be trouble with some of the Moravians. They aren't going to help the cause, but they're insisting upon keeping their arms.

"Whereas some who, though willing and desirous to learn the manual exercises are yet unprovided with arms, we therefore resolve that the standing committee shall apply to the Justice Grand Jury and Board of Commissioners to supply such deficiencies. Furthermore, these resolves shall be published in the English and German newspapers."

Gordon paused to take a long swig of water, carefully dabbed at his upper lip and continued. "There remains one further question—whether such townships or any part of them who shall refuse to agree to the general association of this county shall not be considered as enemies to this county and all dealings and commerce whatsoever shall be forborne with them, unless they do agree to act in concert with this county in general by the twentieth day of June next." He took a deep breath. "All in favor please signify by saying 'aye.'"

A concert of "ayes" reverberated through the crammed courthouse.

"All opposed will signify by saying 'nay.'"

The only sound came from outside where, although all conversation had ceased, the cacophony of local beasts and birds continued unabated.

"The motion has been approved unanimously." Gordon moved some documents around, apparently looking for something. "Our last order of business today is to review the returns of our various captains from their townships to see how many subscribers we have to the general association of militiamen."

After all twenty-six townships had reported, Robert Traill did some quick addition, then announced his results. Northampton County had produced just over two thousand, five hundred men to drill in the art of war. Eighty-seven hailed from Easton, the largest contingent of one hundred forty-two came from Lower Saucon, and the smallest, at twenty-five, was from Penn.

Peter wished they had a pastor in the room. A meeting such as this required some sort of prayer or benediction. They were going to need the Almighty's strength, favor, and wisdom if they were ever going to pull this off.

The meeting dispersed slowly, the men taking their time greeting one another and hearing stories from the townships. "Most of the people are standing with us, but we're not getting support from the Moravians," said one. Another nodded. "What if they don't comply?" Peter was concerned about this issue too—an image of his friend, Wilhelm Konk, filling his mind. For the first time in their lengthy relationship, he wasn't happy thinking about this good man. What trying times these were! He gazed at the faces of the men standing around, and although he considered most of them upstanding and capable, a few left him with lingering doubts about their fitness to train farmers to engage in war, or confront those who would refuse to support independence.

By the time he left the courthouse, he was spent, thirsty, and hungry. The crowds had mostly dispersed, but there stood Catherine. When their eyes met, he saw in her face the reflection of his own steadfastness.

CHAPTER NINETEEN

Her laundry stretched as far as the Great Wall of China and as high as the Pyramid at Giza. Maybe Mount Everest. How long had she been neglecting the wrinkled, soiled, stinking pile? A week? Two weeks? The last several days blurred in her memory, a succession of drives up the Northeast Extension across 78 or 22, however the mood struck. Then there'd been dealing with a succession of physicians and their assistants, wading through maddening telephone prompts, and trying to persuade her recalcitrant father to go to rehab to recover—that he wasn't ready to return home. Sadly, there wasn't anyone to take care of him, and he refused to go to Allen's or her house. Nevertheless, he wouldn't be able to clean or cook or do his laundry or his shopping for a few weeks. She sighed as she surveyed her stack of dirty clothes, sheets, and towels. Tony didn't seem to understand his being home with only visiting nurses a few days a week wouldn't get his basic needs met. Those duties would end up falling to Erin and her brother, even as they chauffeured their mother around. He had remained adamant, however, and home he went.

She began sorting whites, darks, and towels into heaps on the family room floor, wondering how many times Ethan had gone swimming anyway. She hadn't even realized he had four swim trunks, let alone nine beach towels. As she separated the laundry, Erin reviewed all her own missed appointments over the past several days, including their two dental check-ups, a trip to see the Phillies—she'd ended up giving her tickets to Melissa and Tim—a neighborhood block party, a bridal shower for a young friend at church, and haircuts for Ethan and her. Her son had begun looking something like Sonny Bono in the mid-1960s. Then, there was Paul. She made up her mind to call him as soon as she got the first load in the washing machine. Melissa had repeated her offer to have them over for dinner, which Erin liked because her friends could begin forming an opinion of Paul and honestly share their thoughts with her afterward. In addition, Paul could see her on her own turf, not that Easton wasn't her turf, but Lansdale was where she'd made her adult life. She wondered if she could make the time for something fun, however. Didn't someone somewhere need her? *This is ridiculous. I need to take care of myself too.*

Ten minutes and a strong cup of coffee later, she found and called Paul's number, feeling her temples tingle as she waited for him to answer.

"Hello, this is Paul."

When she heard his mellow voice, she melted. He not only looked like B.J. Hunnicutt, he sounded like him too. "Hi, Paul, this is Erin. Erin Miles." She gripped the phone tighter, feeling quite stupid. Did he know other Erins? Should she have just said "Erin" and not given her last name? She wasn't sure.

"Well, hello Erin Miles! How are you?"

"I'm pretty good—now—and you?"

"Never better." He paused. "You said 'now.' Were you ... ill?"

The perfect opening.

"I wasn't, but my father had a heart attack shortly after Heritage Day, and I've been running back and forth ever since. I'm just now tackling a proverbial Machu Picchu of laundry." She hoped telling him would ease any doubts he might be harboring.

"I'm sorry to hear about your father. How's he doing?"

"He's mostly alright now. He had a triple bypass and did well, but unfortunately, he insisted on going home instead of rehab to recover."

"And that's meant more work for you."

He got this.

"I'm happy to help both my parents, but being there for them has been challenging." She hoped she wasn't whining.

"You have a brother, right?"

"Yes, and we've been sharing the load.

There was a relaxed silence.

"I'll bet you're exhausted."

"Just about."

"How's Ethan doing?"

"You know kids—resilient. Clueless." She swallowed a complaint about her nine-year-old's failure to appreciate the demands being made on her as he asserted his own.

"He's a good kid."

She sat in her favorite sunroom recliner, and Toby settled his bulk on top of her feet. "Yes, he is. I, uh, I'm sorry I haven't called."

"How could you? You haven't had a moment to yourself, although I must admit you did have me worried there for a while."

She wished he could see her sheepish look. "I, uh, would like to see you."

"You would?" He sounded like an excited sixteen-year-old.

"My friend Melissa and her husband would like us to come to dinner at their house this Saturday night if that works for you. Would, uh, would that be okay?"

"I'd love to. They live in Lansdale, right?"

"Yes, not far from me." She was already figuring out what she'd wear, maybe the new sundress she'd bought at the start of summer and hadn't had a chance to put on yet.

"I'll be there with bells on," he said, reminding her of some of Jim's cornier expressions. "Well, maybe not bells, but I'll definitely be there."

Halfway through her battle of the bulging laundry, after running to the grocery store and taking Ethan to his friend Jake's house to swim, her cellphone buzzed. She was going to let the call go to voicemail while she finished putting away three bags of frozen veggies and two half gallons of ice cream, but then she saw the ID: "Hatfield College." She wondered what that could be about. She hadn't had any contact with the school since she'd left a year ago.

"Hello, this is Erin."

"Erin, Barry Sanders at Hatfield. How are you?"

"Well, hello, Barry. I'm doing quite well, and you?" She closed the freezer door after tossing a package of yellow corn into the bottom compartment.

"Never better. I heard you recently earned your doctorate. Congratulations!"

"Thank you." She leaned against the cool granite of the kitchen island.

"I know you worked really hard to get the degree."

He wanted something. He was probably going to ask her to come back and teach English Comp, but oh, she was going to feel good letting him know about Lafayette's offer. She wasn't bitter, not anymore, but the sting of Hatfield's earlier rejection hadn't entirely gone away.

"Yes, I worked hard, but the effort was worth the price," she said in her most civil tone.

"Listen, I have some news." He cleared his throat. Erin thought he sounded uncomfortable. "You know the guy we hired last year to teach history?"

She knew. "Yes."

"Well, I'm sorry to say he didn't work out for us."

She was a scent hound, ready to go after the fox. Dare she? Why not? "What happened?" she asked.

The dean didn't seem put off by her directness. "I suppose this was a classic case of a bad fit. We thought he'd bring needed diversity to Hatfield, you know, coming from the Deep South, having his doctorate in pre-Columbian American History, but when he got here, he never hit his stride, and his wife was homesick."

Erin sensed there was more, but she chose not to press for details, waiting instead for him to continue.

"We let him go at the end of the spring semester, which puts us in a bit of a pickle."

I'll say.

"Rather than begin a new search, we've decided to extend the job to you since you were our next choice after him last year, and now you have your doctorate. This would be tenure-track. You'd be teaching American history, but some other courses as well such as European and maybe Latin American in a pinch."

Erin was speechless. The direction of her life had started to become clearer after Lafayette's position opened, but now, she could no longer see where she was going.

"Who was the old-time baseball player who said something like, 'It's déjà vu all over again?'"

"Hmm, let me see—I think he said some other pretty funny stuff." Melissa squeezed fresh lemon into her iced tea. "You know my dad really likes baseball, and he watches games constantly all summer long, which drives my mother nuts."

Erin recognized the "I'm-about-to-go-off-on-a-tangent" look on her friend's face. The thing to do was just wait for the moment to pass, then pull back the leash, like she did whenever Toby wanted to chase a squirrel on their walks.

"He subscribes to all the games on cable, and they have a split screen TV, along with two sets, and my mother can't figure out how he keeps track of all the different things going on. Even with all the games he watches at one time, baseball still puts me right to sleep." She reached for an Oreo. "Sorry I don't have anything homemade."

"Don't be sorry! I came over here on the spur of the moment. Do you have any hummus though?"

"Um, yes, but no pita chips."

"I don't want chips. I want to dip my Oreos in hummus."

"O-kay." Melissa rose from her kitchen chair and went to the refrigerator. "What were you going to tell me about déjà vu? You know, I get that feeling sometimes, like when I was at Whole Foods the other day deciding whether to get Braeburn or Fuji apples ..."

"I was just thinking about the old baseball player who said, 'It's déjà vu all over again.' Anyway, I brought him up because something happened an hour ago, and I just have to talk to you. I even stopped doing my laundry, and you know how much I have. Thanks for dropping what you were doing."

"I never mind getting out of dusting. Ugh!" Melissa put the container of red pepper hummus on the table and cracked open the lid.

"Remember last year when I sat here telling you I wasn't get the teaching job at Hatfield?"

"I still have trouble believing they did that to you." She reached into a drawer, pulled out a spreading knife and stabbed the hummus. "I'm so happy you have the job at Lafayette. Just think—your alma mater—and

Easton!"

Melissa's cat wandered into the room and started slinking around Erin's ankles, so Erin closed her eyes and counted slowly to ten. Slinking cats made her skeevy, but she would never tell Melissa, who adored the calico. That was one secret she kept from her bestie.

"Lo and behold, Barry Sanders—Dean Barry Sanders—called me an hour ago and told me the professor they hired last year didn't work out—'he wasn't a good fit'—and he offered me the job." Erin watched Melissa's eyes expand exponentially.

"You're kidding!"

Was her mood excitement? Indignation? Erin couldn't tell. "Believe me, I couldn't make something like this up."

"Holy cow." She shook her head back and forth so many times Erin began to look for coins to start popping out of her ears. "What are you going to do?"

"I have no idea, Melissa. I pretty much had everything worked out about going to Lafayette. I admit I've still been working through what to do about Ethan's getting off to school and back home without me three days a week, and taking care of my parents after school at least once or twice a week, but those have seemed manageable." She felt as if she'd just run a half-marathon.

Melissa let out a low whistle. "You sure are dealing with a lot."

"Yes, I am."

"Other things aside, how would you feel about teaching at Hatfield after what happened last year?"

Erin had wondered the same thing. "I must admit, there were some hard feelings initially, especially after Jim had just passed away, but I've forgiven the school for what happened. Everyone makes mistakes, and they were big enough to admit them and ask me for another chance." She was managing to convince herself of these things.

"Sometimes when I have a big decision to make, I make a list of pro's and con's. Do you think a list would help?"

"Maybe writing down my thoughts would help me organize them better."

"When do you have to let everyone know?"

"I need a couple of days to sort everything out."

"I'll be praying for God to make your way very clear."

"Thanks. I'm doing the same. Sometimes I wish he'd send signs—you know, clear signs like, and she lowered her voice, 'This is the way, go in it.'" She slid a cookie through the hummus and took a bite.

"I think he does, Erin. Maybe not a sign like on a street corner or highway, but if you're listening closely, he'll find a way to let you know what to do."

"Some people say we can't really know God's will for things like this, but if we follow what we know is right, we'll end up doing what we should."

"Yeah, I've heard that too, but you know, that sounds really sterile to me and cold." Melissa frowned. "I mean, if he cares about the fall of a tiny sparrow and knows how many hairs we have on our heads, why wouldn't he be involved even more in the details of our lives?"

"I sure think so."

"Then go with that. Erin, I believe he'll let you know what to do."

Her spirit started feeling lighter. Suddenly, she remembered something else. "Oh, Paul says he'd love to come for dinner this Saturday."

"Wonderful! I've been thinking about what to serve and …"

Erin stuck an index finger into the air and yelled, "Yogi Berra!"

Melissa grimaced. "What?"

"Yogi Berra! He's the baseball player who said, 'It's déjà vu all over again.'"

On one side of the list she wrote "Pros" and underneath, "Hatfield."

There followed several entries—I know the school. Nearby. Permanent position. Pick up where I left off. Stay put. Security. No changes regarding Ethan's schedule, or at least manageable ones. Stability. In the "Cons" column Erin listed—I'm their second choice. Harder to get to Easton and my parents. Not as good a school as Lafayette. Smaller department, so I'd be teaching more classes outside my area of expertise. For Lafayette's "Pros" she wrote, Alma mater. Easton. Love the school. Great school. Wonderful opportunity to teach American history exclusively. Near parents and family. Would get benefits, like at Hatfield, and the pay is comparable, if not better overall. Cons: I'd have a harder time organizing my home life— Ethan's school schedule and after-school activities. The nearly hour-long commute. Only for one year—both pro and con. Still, there's a possibility of the job becoming permanent.

What would she do if the position did become permanent? Would she continue commuting? One of her professors had made a similar trek from Doylestown throughout her tenure at Lafayette, but did she have children? Erin wasn't sure. She asked herself if she'd want to move to Easton. She was firmly ensconced in Lansdale, but would she want to continue living there now that she was closer to her family, as well as her family history? Emotionally, she was leaning toward Lafayette, but she didn't know how to clear the hurdles. A mental picture of Paul Bassett materialized in her mind's eye, and although she didn't want to base her or Ethan's lives on what might happen with the endearing man, Erin liked the thought of Paul being out there. Certainly, he was no reason to base a major decision around. She flipped her pen onto the desk. In a way, she wished Barry Sanders had never called. Life would be so much easier.

As she stared in the direction of her bookshelves, Erin spied a small clay plate Ethan had made in Sunday School when he was six and had given to her on her birthday. The object bore a butterfly motif, along with a saying she'd seen so often she didn't even notice the words anymore. But now she did, and she felt chills.

"Trust in the Lord with all your heart, and do not lean on your own understanding. In all your ways acknowledge him, and he will make your paths straight."

CHAPTER TWENTY

He dozed in his favorite chair, but in his dreams, he was anything but relaxed as he mustered his "Associators," the nearly ninety men who made up his Easton Company.

"*Gegenwartige Arme!*"

Citizen soldiers in tattered shirts and breeches, preparing to face down the King's most disciplined, decorated, and decked out Redcoats lined up before him. His men's early lives, and generations before theirs, had been played out under tyrants who treated them like pawns on royal chessboards with little hope of ever bettering themselves or their posterity. They objected to the British Crown's imposition of burdensome taxes and chafed at being told they couldn't settle further than the Appalachians. To them, America stood for the freedom to pursue one's God-given talents and purpose, and by golly, they weren't going to yield to yet another despot.

"*Gegenwartige Arme durch Zahlen! Eins!*"

Peter called out orders in German since few of the farmers could speak English. In his dream, he moved up and down the ranks as he'd done earlier that day, teaching them how to stand properly, how to position their rifles and to load and reload quickly—skills he'd learned during the French and Indian War. At this point, they were looking like they'd just come out of the Bachmann after downing one too many pints, stumbling over one another and holding their weapons all cockeyed.

The men were laughing now, acknowledging not only their lack of military prowess but their clumsiness with the English language. One farmer, his chin jutting forward, stated loudly, *"Wir können nicht Englisch sprechen, aber wir können Englisch schießen!"* Peter clapped him on the shoulder and smiled as the other men in the Easton Company laughed at the joke—"We can't speak English, but we can shoot English!"

"Father. Father!"

He gazed through the crusty blur of sleep-laden eyes, his tongue feeling like he'd swallowed dust. "What is it, Jacob?"

"Father, Mr. Gress is here. There's a meeting of the elders at his house with the new minister. They're expecting you."

"Oh!" He sat up with a start, hoping Christian Gress wasn't able to see his rumpled condition, noticing Joe stirring in the chair next to his. "Thank you, son. Would you please tell him I'll be there in fifteen minutes?"

"Certainly, Father."

Peter moved his head to the left, then to the right and rolled his shoulders, hearing them click and crunch. When he heard the sound of the front door closing, he rose and stretched, smiling down at the small boy who couldn't seem to do enough for him. Joe jumped up and cocked his head, as if looking for instructions, but Peter put a hand on his shoulder. "I am fine," he said. He'd planned to take only a brief nap after the muster and before the elders' gathering, wondering why Catherine hadn't woken him. Spying a mug of once-hot apple cider on a side table, he sipped the lukewarm liquid and puckered his lips. How long had he been asleep? A glance at the mantel clock caused him to gasp. "Three hours!" He saw Catherine limping down the hall toward him.

"Well, hello. Do you feel rested?"

"I'm more vexed than rested. I'm late for a meeting." His glance bored into her brown eyes. "Why did you let me sleep so long?"

Joe looked at him, then Catherine. "Go to the kitchen, Joe." She motioned for him to leave, and he scooted. "Peter Kichline, I can't be expected to keep up with your impossible schedule." Her arms crossed over her chest. "How you can keep up with yourself is beyond me. If you're not meeting with the elders over calling a pastor or building the church, you're at Committee of Safety meetings, in effect running not only this village but the entire county."

She was on a roll, and he stood like a man and took her tirade.

"If you're not with the Committee, you're in Philadelphia, and if you're not there, you're running the mills or mustering your troops." She pointed a finger at him. "You are wearing yourself thin. You might be strong and vigorous and wanting to do what needs to be done, but darling, you can't do everything."

The effect of her words was like being slapped sharply. He opened his mouth, but nothing came out, so instead he placed his hands on her slender shoulders and looked in her eyes, which were mirroring concern and love. "I'll do something about my schedule, but first I must get to that meeting. They're counting on me."

"Yes, and I'm counting on you to let something go. Soon."

He kissed her cheek and went to the hall for his coat.

The Reverend Martin Rodenheimer housed a thundering voice in a slight body. He was about five feet three with a slim face and thinning blonde hair. *Earnest* was Peter's first impression of the young man from Philadelphia whom he guessed to be in his mid-twenties.

Elias Shook spoke first. "When did your people come to America?"

Christian Gress's wife interrupted. "Is there anything else I can get you, gentlemen?"

"No, thank you, my dear." Gress smiled as she retreated to the back of their house.

The pastor sipped his cup of tea, closed his eyes momentarily, then placed the beverage on a nearby table where it remained for the rest of the meeting. Apparently, Frau Gress hadn't mastered a formula for Liberty Tea—the rest of the elders' cups also remained suspiciously full.

"My father is from Switzerland, but he met my mother in Holland after moving there. Both of them came to know Reverend Michael Schlatter there as well."

"Is your father also a pastor?" Shook asked.

Peter already knew but let Rodenheimer tell his own story. "He is a rather earnest churchman, an elder in Philadelphia, sir, but not a pastor. He and my mother arrived in Philadelphia with my oldest brother in 1752, and I was born there the following year."

"Where did you study for the ministry?" asked Michael Butz.

"The College of New Jersey, sir."

"Are you then a Presbyterian?"

"While I am familiar with the tenets of that faith, Mr. Butz, I am of the German Reformed persuasion."

A look of relief passed across the elders' faces, and Peter smiled. He detected a slight lisp in the young man's speech, but Rodenheimer bore no traces of self-consciousness about the flaw. He could imagine him thundering from their new pulpit once the church was completed.

"Have you served any other churches?" Peter asked.

"I have preached many times in New Jersey and Pennsylvania, good sir, but this will be my first church, should you decide to extend the call to me."

"You know this is a union church," Jacob Pfeiffer said, good Lutheran that he was.

"I am comfortable with such an arrangement. I think brothers in the faith need to dwell in unity. I myself am at home wherever true believers are."

Pfeiffer leaned forward. "Can you preach in German? You have to preach in German."

"Yes, sir. I have mostly preached in German."

Peter leaned forward to take a cookie from a tray Mrs. Gress had left for the elders, his hunger from drilling catching up with him. Propriety and not knowing what he'd wash the treat down with kept him from devouring the entire batch.

The questioning continued—did he have a wife? No. The prospect of one? No. Could he preach in the school house until the church was completed? Yes, of course. Would he help further the building along? There was the rub.

"We seem to have come to a standstill," Christian Gress said. "Many of us are preparing for the possibility of war and are otherwise occupied."

"As is understandable," Rodenheimer said. "I would do all I could to complete the building. I am not averse to wielding a hammer myself."

The pastor didn't flinch when sniggers broke out.

"I may not look like much, but our Creator has given me strength few people see at first glance." His placid expression told Peter the minister hadn't taken offense. "I helped my father build our home in Philadelphia."

With his customary bluntness, Michael Butz brought up another matter. "My good man, where do you stand in the current climate—with the colonists or with the Crown?"

Rodenheimer didn't hesitate. "I am with the colonists, sir, and unafraid to speak my mind."

Peter knew they had found their man.

They were finishing supper when Andrew came to his father, who'd been planning on reading a book in the parlor, something he hadn't had the chance to do for many weeks. "May I have a word, sir?"

"Yes, of course. You look like something's on your mind."

Andrew looked out of the corner of his eyes at his sister. "Could we speak alone, I mean just the men?" He smiled. "And Joe."

Peter led the way to the front room where he sat with two of his sons and Joe while the rest of the household cleaned up. "What's on your mind, son?"

"Jacob and I were talking recently about how we haven't seen Mr. Konk in over three months. Actually, he failed to pick up his last order."

He let this information sink in.

"We're wondering if this might have something to do with the counties being under Committees of Safety and raising up Associators."

Peter pinched his lips together. "That could very well be. I know this has caused distress for the Moravian community." He paused. "I wonder why you didn't tell me sooner."

"We tried, Father," Jacob said, "but we seldom see you anymore."

He nodded. "I appreciate your telling me now."

"Should we do anything?" Andrew asked. "Mr. Konk's orders are large as you know and are missed. We're doing well, but we'd rather not lose his business or his friendship."

Peter looked toward the dining room where Susannah was helping clear the table. "I'll pay him a visit the first chance I get."

He hadn't wanted Susannah to go with him, but in her girlish enthusiasm, she was up and dressed and in her riding gear before he could say otherwise. He knew he could've forbidden her, but he decided not to. Maybe she could soften the situation, at least he hoped so. He knew as well as anyone this might not go well.

At the end of their journey to Hanover Township, they found Konk and his three sons in the fields under a semi-cloudy late spring sky. Wilhelm looked up from his work to see them, paused momentarily, then returned to his plow. Hans made eye contact with Susannah, glanced at his father and looked back down.

Peter had expected as much. He pulled the reins on his horse and sidled near the men. He noticed Susannah gaze at Hans, her face drawn. "Good day, Herr Konk."

The farmer grunted.

"My family and I have missed you and wondered how you might be getting along. Is everyone well?"

"You can see we are." Konk stopped what he was doing and strode directly up to Peter and Susannah. "You should know we've taken our business to Bethlehem."

The words hit Peter like bullets, which he deflected in his spirit. "I see. Might this have something to do with our present troubles?"

"You would be right about that, Herr Kichline. Your Committee has no right to dictate how my family lives." The red in his cheeks spread all the way to his ears. "We are still under the King of England's authority, and I will not bow to the wishes of those who would usurp his power. We Moravians have good lives here, and we are a peaceful people. You know the command—'Let every soul be subject unto the higher powers.'" He stopped momentarily then spoke the next few words slowly, deliberately, "'For there is no power but of God.' He leaned closer, his eyes as frozen as icicles. "'The powers that be are ordained of God.'"

A rebuke rose in his throat, but he swallowed the words, sensing they would fall on deaf ears. Oh, but he hated to see this friendship end.

"And now if you would, please, this is still my land, and you are no longer welcome here."

He heard Susannah gasp and turned to see tears streaking down her cheeks. He fought a desire to dismount his horse and pummel his old friend for making her cry. He could take the snub well enough, but he didn't feel half so generous when considering what this meant to Susannah.

He tipped his hat and pulled the reins of his horse, but not before seeing Hans gazing furtively at Susannah. "Let's go, my dear. We're clearly not wanted here anymore."

CHAPTER TWENTY-ONE

Erin had turned out Ethan's light, kissed his forehead and patted Toby as the dog snuggled next to her son. Moonlight sieved through the blinds, which Ethan insisted stay open.

"Mom?"

"Yes, honey?" She paused at the foot of the twin bed noticing Ethan's feet were inches from the bottom. Soon boy and dog would outgrow the arrangement, and she wondered what size bed to buy next time around. Jim would have known. He had always seemed to know just what to do. What would he have to say about Lafayette and Hatfield? In reality, she thought she knew. He'd review her pros and cons list with her, then conclude, "Follow your heart." The thing was, Erin didn't know exactly where her heart was.

"You used to work, didn't you?"

"Yes, Ethan, I taught at Hatfield College, remember?"

"Sort of. You didn't teach last year, though."

"You're right. I was finishing my doctorate."

"And now you're a doctor, right?"

"Right."

"Are you going to teach again, Mom?"

"Yes."

"Where?"

She sat on the end of the bed, feeling Ethan's feet underneath. "I'm not sure, hon. I actually have two offers I'm considering."

"Really?" Through the shadows, she saw him sit up, and his feet slipped away from her. "Where?"

"Hatfield has asked me to come back and teach full time, but Lafayette just offered me a one-year position, which could turn into something permanent." Erin felt weird discussing her situation with a nine-year-old.

"You went to Lafayette."

"Uh-huh."

"It's cool they want you to come back."

"Yes, I think so, too."

"So, if you went to Hatfield, we'd stay here and everything would be the same."

"Something like that." She stroked Toby's back.

"If you went to Lafayette, would we have to move?"

"Not exactly."

"Why not?"

Was she hearing disappointment in his voice? "I would just be teaching three days a week, so I could commute. I would have to get someone, though, to get you on and off the bus."

"I'm no baby! I can get on the bus myself." His indignation sparked like lightning.

First, she smiled to herself imagining Ethan getting organized enough in the morning to make the bus on time. Then she shuddered, picturing him wandering through the neighborhood after school unsupervised. No way. No how.

"What about Grammy Audrey and Grandpa? We'd be closer to them if we lived in Easton, and you know how they need us now."

Wow! Erin had just assumed her son would hate the idea of moving. "Yes, we would be closer, and they do need us more." She paused. "Are you saying you'd like to live in Easton?"

"Sure. There's always such cool stuff to do there."

"I like Easton too."

"And you grew up there, so, why don't we?"

Children could be so straightforward. They never really understood how complicated life was.

"Wouldn't you miss this house? And your school and friends, especially Jake?"

"Well, yeah, but Easton isn't far from here, and he could come and visit me, right?"

"Yes, of course."

"Well, I'm all for living in Easton." He burrowed back down to a reclining position as if the matter were settled. "I think you should teach at Lafayette."

On the way to her bedroom, Erin wondered whether this was a case of foolishness being bound up in the heart of a child, or out of the mouths of babes oft times come gems.

This was going to be one of those nights. Restless. Unable to find the right position. Dozing off only to be moving at turnpike speed inside dreams as confusing as her present state of mind. She was at a doctor's appointment with her dad, but the waiting room was more like a combination Jiffy Lube and deli. They'd taken a number and were waiting for a woman in blue scrubs to call them so her dad could get some sort of oil change, whether to his body or his car Erin didn't know.

"So, you'd be moving back home, then?" her dad asked. "It's about time. You know what Yogi Berra said—'There's no place like home.'"

"That wasn't Yogi Berra, Dad. Judy Garland said that in *The Wizard of Oz*."

Audrey made a sudden appearance, her hair green and her shoes—some sort of Reeboks with holes in the toes. "Yes, but someone else said 'You can't go home again.'"

"Yogi Berra said that, too," Tony said.

"You never knew anything." Her mother scowled at her ex-husband. "Pontius Pilate said it."

Erin interjected herself into the conversation. "You're both wrong. Thomas Wolfe wrote a book called *You Can't Go Home Again* in 1940."

Blank stares. Then Audrey said, "Well, he didn't go to college, you know."

"And neither did you," came Tony's response.

"At least she did."

"I know. I got the bills."

"Like fun you did! She put herself through school."

Erin woke up, her hair damp against her forehead, her breath short. Maybe she didn't want to go home at all. Maybe, she thought, she should just stay in Lansdale, at a safe distance.

Ethan was still sleeping, and she didn't bother to wake him. She needed time to think, to process the dreams and the questions, to ponder whether to put her hair up or keep it down for her "date" with Paul. She turned on her phone and checked the weather forecast—ninety degrees by noon with a high of ninety-five by six and eighty-five percent humidity. Erin moved closer to the sunroom windows feeling the heat against them even at seven-thirty, noting how brown the grass had become. She didn't know how to use the sprinklers Jim had bought before he died and felt guilty for letting the grass he'd so carefully tended get so shriveled. Toby waddled up to her and leaned against her right leg. "Well, Toby, I hope Melissa and Tim don't want to eat outside. I'm already melting, and I won't make a very good impression if I'm sweating tonight." Her reflection in the window reminded her to use extra smoothing products in her hair.

She opened the door for him to go out and went back into the kitchen to turn on the coffeemaker. While Toby did his business, including barking at the neighbors' two dogs, she pulled last night's leftover barbecue from the refrigerator along with a container of peach yogurt. Then she grabbed a box of Froot Loops from the pantry and began mixing the items together in a cereal bowl. When Erin called Toby back inside, she filled his dish with dog food, sat at the table and opened her tablet to check emails. There was one from Sydney Stordahl, with whom she'd shared news of her job possibilities. She was eager to get her DAR friend's take on the decision.

Hey Erin, I missed seeing you at the summer social the other day, and I hope your father is out of the woods and on the way to full recovery. I thought the turn-out was pretty good considering how hot it was. I'm actually considering cracking an egg on the hood of my Jeep this morning to see what happens! I got to thinking about your job offers—congrats on them, by the by. How great to have two possibilities at a time when one teaching position is as hard to come by as reruns of The Governor and JJ. *Do you remember that show? Nah, you're probably waaaay too young. Anyway, those jobs seem like a win-win situation to me, although I'm selfish enough to want you to stay and be groomed for leadership in the Valley Forge Chapter. Nonetheless, I started thinking about something after you left. You've been given an amazing gift—knowing your ancestors up close and personal. Not many people are as near to their foremothers and fathers geographically as you are. I can't imagine what it would be like to grow up in the same place mine lived!*

Anyway, are you familiar with a translation of the Bible called the Pilgrim Bible? It was first printed in 1948 and originally intended for young people or those who were young in their faith. My parents gave me a copy when I was confirmed in yikes, 1969! The Bible is KJV with many helpful footnotes. Needless to say, since it is KJV, I rarely looked at it as a teenager! The other night, I was reading something from Isaiah in preparation for a talk I'll be giving at a DAR chapter, and I came across the following—"build the old waste places, raise up the foundations of many generations and be called the repairer of the breach, the restorer of paths to dwell in." The footnote struck a beautiful chord and made me think: Paths that lead home. WOW! What wonderful imagery for you based on what you've shared with me about your parents' needs, etc. Who knows? Maybe you're being raised up to spread awareness of your ancestors in the Lehigh Valley while healing some of the stuff your present family has had to deal with, like death and divorce and just plain old junk. Paths that lead home!

She dropped her spoon, which clanked against the table.

The doorbell rang, and Erin exchanged glances with Melissa. Should she wait for her friend to answer or go herself?

"There's your date!" Tim said, looking up from a platter he was filling with ribeye steaks. "Would you like to let him in?"

"Sure."

Melissa winked at her. "Go ahead, Erin."

She walked through the entry way with little bubbles knocking around in her stomach, and when she opened the front door, they expanded to the size of a hot-air balloon. Her mouth fell open, and she was sure she was wide-eyed. Why was Paul wearing Jim's shirt? This didn't make any sense, none at all. In a state of momentary confusion, she half-wondered how Paul had entered Jim's closet and taken that Madras shirt. Funny, they were the same size.

Paul was grinning, but not like a Cheshire Cat. As if to cover sudden nervousness, he said, "Yes, I sometimes have that effect on women."

She tried to free herself from the initial shock, but she couldn't seem to move. *Pull yourself together!* "Sorry about that," was the best she could manage. "Come in." She prayed she wouldn't call him "Jim." What were the chances of Paul having the same shirt as her dead husband and choosing to wear it today?

"May I say you look lovely?"

"Yes, you may. Thanks." Her legs felt as wobbly as they usually did after a glass of wine. Should she shake his hand, maybe let him kiss her cheek? *At least close your mouth!*

"I have a little something for you."

He was holding a bag, possibly from the State Store, as well as a cluster of vibrant wildflowers in shades of yellow, magenta, purple, and orange. Paul handed the bouquet to her.

"How lovely!" Though obviously handpicked, he'd nicely arranged them.

"I found these earlier today near the site of Colonel Kichline's sawmill where they were growing along the bank. I've been researching a book about the early mills in the area, so I was over there." His blue eyes gleamed, looking pleased with himself.

"How thoughtful of you! Thank you." She was recovering her equilibrium, trying not to stare at that shirt.

"I'm sorry for the packaging. Hopefully Melissa has a vase you can put them in until you get home." He'd wrapped the flowers in a wet paper towel tucked inside aluminum foil.

"I'm sure she does."

She led him into the kitchen. "Paul, I think you'll remember Melissa, and this is Tim."

"I certainly do." He reached across the island and shook first Tim's, then Melissa's hands.

"We're glad you could come," Melissa said.

"Thanks for inviting me."

"We promise we won't make you sit outside today. What a scorcher!" Tim commented.

"For that, I'm truly grateful." Paul handed the package to Melissa, and she slid a bottle of red wine from the paper bag.

"Why, thank you, Paul. I'll open this to breathe. It'll go great with the steak we're having." She looked at the flowers Erin held. "Those are so pretty!"

"Aren't they? Paul found them near the place my Grandfather Peter had his sawmill."

"Well, that was sweet! I'll get a vase."

While Melissa busied herself with the wine and flowers, Erin took what she hoped weren't obvious deep breaths, attempting to calm herself.

"Where's Ethan tonight?" Paul asked.

"Melissa and Tim's son took him and his best friend to the trampoline park."

"That sounds like fun." He looked at Erin and smiled, so completely at ease she began to settle down.

"So, Paul, how long did it take you to get here?" Tim asked.

"Not long at all. I just came down the Northeast Extension to Lansdale—about fifty minutes."

"That's still a long commute," Erin muttered.

"Excuse me?"

Realizing she'd spoken her thoughts, she blushed. "Oh, just thinking out loud."

"Erin's been trying to figure out which job to take," Tim said, apparently unaware Paul knew nothing about what was going on.

He tilted his head to the right. "You have a few job offers then?"

Tim had thrown Erin in the deep end. "Yes, yes, I do." She pushed herself to the surface, trying not to sputter. She'd been hoping for more of a gradual introduction to this conversation. "I used to teach at Hatfield College, and last year I applied for a full-time history position, but I didn't have my doctorate yet. The guy they hired hasn't worked out, and they asked me to take the job."

"How wonderful for you!" Paul's grin couldn't have been more genuine.

"That's not all, though," Tim said, covering the meat with a sheet of foil. "She also got an offer from Lafayette."

She wished Tim would let her tell her own story, but not wanting to appear rude, she played along.

"Lafayette!" Paul's eyes warmed to a soft glow.

"It's just for a year, but there's a possibility the job could become permanent."

He pressed his lips together then said, "You have quite a choice to make there."

"Can I get you something to drink, Paul?" Melissa interrupted the conversation. Erin could've hugged her, wanting more time to acclimate to Paul's presence before going any deeper about her future.

Paul leaned back in the dining room chair and sighed. "I don't mind saying that's the best meal I've had in a long time." He pointed to his empty plate. "What an amazing cake! I just love anything chocolate, and this was moist and dense and ..." Another sigh.

"I'm so glad you enjoyed dessert," Melissa said. "That's a favorite at our church potlucks. In fact, I think every woman there has made this at one time or another."

"I think I'd like to come to one of those potlucks." Paul smiled in Erin's direction, but his mouth fell slightly open when she picked up a leftover celery stick and ran it through her slice of cake.

"You'll have to excuse her," Melissa said. "She does strange things with food."

Tim piped up. "One time, I saw her make a kind of patty out of crab dip and a Klondike Bar."

"I think her food tastes are charming," Paul said.

Neither he nor Erin noticed the look that passed between Melissa and her husband.

In his forthright way, Tim asked, "Do you go to church, Paul?"

Erin wanted to slap her friend on the arm. Although she wanted to know since her faith was important to her, she wanted to find out more casually than this direct question.

Paul sipped his coffee and looked across the table to his host. "I do, as a matter of fact."

"Let me guess," Melissa said, "you go to the church Erin's ancestors helped build."

"Not exactly, although I've attended some services there and like the place very much. I actually go to First Presbyterian Church, Bethlehem."

"How did you end up there?" Tim asked.

"When I first moved to Easton, I hadn't been going to church at all. My parents weren't very religious. When I came to the Lehigh Valley looking to put down roots, when I began researching the lives of the founders—like your family, Erin—I was touched to learn how much their faith motivated and encouraged them. I mentioned this to a friend one night over dinner, and he invited me to go to church with him in Bethlehem, so I did. The place felt like home to me from the start, and I've been going ever since." He smiled in Erin's direction.

She couldn't have hoped for a better answer to Tim's question. The outlines of Paul's life were falling in pleasant places.

As she'd greeted Paul at the door when the evening was young, now she walked him outside into the deepening night shadows and the sticky embrace of the day's lingering humidity. He'd said his goodbyes to the Greys, and even Tim took his wife's subtle hint about hanging back while Erin saw their guest to the door.

"I'm really glad you invited me tonight," Paul said, leaning against his car. "I like Tim and Melissa."

"They're good friends and good people. I'm pleased you came, and you like them."

"So, you live close by?"

"Less than a mile."

Crickets chirped. Someone opened and closed a car door several houses away.

"You have some big decisions to make."

"Yes, I sure do."

"I'll say a prayer for you."

She smiled. "Thanks. I appreciate knowing you will. I want to make the right choice."

"Understandably." Paul reached out and put his hand on her right shoulder, and she shivered in spite of the temperature. "I just want you to know, Erin, whatever you decide, I'll be here for you and Ethan. It doesn't matter if you're in Easton or Lansdale."

"Thank you," she whispered, feeling her throat catch.

He leaned across the short distance between them and kissed her cheek.

CHAPTER TWENTY-TWO

"What can I get for you, Sheriff Kichline?" The woman everyone still referred to as Frau Eckert still called him by his previous title. He'd stopped trying to correct her.

"I'll have ale."

"And for you, Mr. Traill?"

"The same."

She had plenty of help, but she always saw to his needs personally, and since they were both safely remarried, he felt more relaxed about her ministrations.

"Thanks for meeting me on such short notice, Peter. There's something I want to discuss with you apart from the other Committee members, at least initially." He worked his big hands, folding and unfolding them on the table.

"What's on your mind?" Peter leaned forward, studying his friend's expression for a clue.

Traill moved in his direction and lowered his voice. "I'm concerned about how many townships aren't providing their fair share of arms, ammunition, and men. When their committeemen report to me, I find out about the shortages."

Peter closed his eyes for a moment. "I've been getting snatches of information myself, but nothing conclusive until just now."

Other customers chattered in the background, the twin smells of tobacco smoke and autumn leaves intermingling. Frau Eckert returned to the table with a tray bearing their drinks and placed them before the men.

Traill thanked her and when she departed, he asked Peter, "What do you think should be done?"

"Perhaps the townships are not just being negligent but have legitimate reasons why they're falling behind."

"I didn't consider that possibility. I suppose I've been too busy feeling upset about their lack of compliance."

"There may be a little of both issues coming into play here."

"We need someone to investigate."

The words hovered between them. To Peter, they sounded oh, so familiar.

"How many townships are we talking about here?" Lewis Gordon asked at the next meeting.

"Six as far as I can tell," Traill said, then proceeded to recite the names on his list.

Gordon tapped his fingers on the table. "Do we have any idea why they're falling behind?"

"If I may address the issue," Peter said. "Those particular townships have dwellings scattered far and wide, so organizing their men into companies as well as collecting township payments for arms and ammunition is no simple task."

"I begin to understand the issue," said Jacob Arndt.

Henry Kooken nodded. "What should we do about this?"

"We can certainly address the issue when all the township committeemen gather with us again," Lewis said.

"But when will that be?" Kooken asked, spreading his hands. "We don't have a date yet."

Arndt leaned back in his chair, placing his hands behind his head. "I say the sooner, the better."

Gordon spoke, "I have an idea. Mr. Kichline, would you visit the committeemen in advance of the next meeting, say around the first of October? Find out what is going on and come up with solutions to their problems. You're especially good with this sort of thing, and you know this county like few other men, given your many years as Sheriff. Doing so would give us about three weeks to assess the situation."

Peter could see himself on horseback, riding from township to township, interviewing six committeemen in addition to drilling his own company, overseeing the church building project, not to mention both his mills, in the space of three weeks. He was also still functioning as a Justice of the Court of Common Pleas and Quarter Sessions. How could one man possibly fulfill all those responsibilities? He could just hear his good wife giving him another earful about being over-committed, which helped him reach a conclusion.

"I will be happy to meet with township committeemen, Mr. Gordon. However, the task would be carried out more efficiently if two or even three of us take it on, especially since we only have three weeks."

Gordon pursed his lips; the other men nodded their agreement with Peter. "Yes, yes, this is a large undertaking, let alone for one man. What say Mr. Arndt, you take two townships, and Mr. Traill, you take two?"

Peter smiled to himself. He hadn't thought Gordon would call upon Robert Traill, who wasn't exactly the most fit man among them.

"I'll be glad to help," Traill said.

217

Jacob Arndt agreed. "As will I."

"Then let's go through the list and assign the townships to each of you. If you incur expenses, the Committee will cover them. And let's set our next meeting for October second. Is everyone in agreement? All in favor, say 'Aye.'"

"Ayes" echoed through the room.

He stopped by the church before going home for the midday meal, pleased to see the outside looking mostly finished except for stairs and walkways. The Georgian style of the building lent a gentle elegance to the landscape, and Peter imagined generations of Eastonians worshiping in this place down through the ages, including his descendants. He stepped around a pile of lumber and took a broad step inside, hearing sawing and the pounding of nails. The smell of freshly cut wood caused his nostrils to twitch.

"Mister Kichline!"

He turned to see the Reverend Rodenheimer. "Pastor." He shook hands with the young man.

"I'm happy to see you."

"Likewise." Peter looked around and seeing William, gave him a wave. The man smiled and returned the gesture.

Rodenheimer followed Peter's glance. "William does absolute wonders as a carpenter. I believe God has gifted his hands, as well as his spirit."

Peter noted the pastor's now-familiar lisp. "I get the same impression."

"He showed me designs for the altar, pulpit, and pews which are simple, but refined. He is also a natural leader, and the men are quite willing to follow his advice."

"I look forward to the day when he'll be able to set off on his own."

Rodenheimer looked at him carefully. "I agree with you, sir. We need to give the Negroes a chance at freedom and independence, just as we're seeking for ourselves." He moved his arm in a graceful arc. "As you can see, we aren't far from finishing the church."

"Do you have any idea when we might be able to worship?"

"My goal is Christmas. I've spoken to Mr. Tannenberg, who is scheduled to be here in a few days to begin work on the organ."

"Will he have enough time to be ready for Christmas? An organ seems to be a complicated proposition."

"Perhaps, but even if he is not, we can still hold services if everything else is in place. Would you like to see what the men are doing?"

"I would indeed." Peter felt his shoulders relax as he meandered through sawdust and tools, greeting the workers. Most of them were townsmen volunteering their time, among them his brother-in-law, Frederick Gwinner. He already felt at home here.

Peter leaned down and kissed his wife's cheek. He'd planned to be out the door by seven. How the hands on the mantel clock had progressed to seven-fifteen so quickly he'd never know.

"You must eat something before you go." Catherine inclined her head toward the table's generous contents, her straight, rigid posture communicating more than her words.

"My dear, I need to be in Mount Bethel by nine with another pressing interview afterward." He started backing away, his consideration of the miles he had to cover and the conversations he'd be having with township committeemen running through his mind. When he bumped into something, he looked down to find Frau Hamster standing in his path like a stone wall.

Catherine's voice was firm. "You can spare ten minutes for breakfast."

"Honestly, Father, we hardly see you anymore," Susannah said.

No doubt about it, the females were ganging up on him. Andrew and Jacob looked down at their plates while Joe glanced up in Peter's direction.

"I am sorry for that, *Liebling*, but there is urgent duty to perform."

Catherine rose, walked over to him as the housekeeper backed away and guided her husband back to his seat at the head of the table. "Frau Hamster will make sure you're on your way in ten minutes."

"*Ja! Ja!*" the woman said, nodding repeatedly.

Peter felt cornered, almost surly, until he saw concern reflected in his family members' faces. They were right. A man did have to eat.

He stood in the hallway, scowling. He'd totally forgotten what he was going to do.

"Peter, are you alright? You seem confused." Catherine held a sleeping Baby Elizabeth in her arms.

He heard her saying something and decided he'd better start listening. As he focused on her face, he saw unfamiliar lines underneath her eyes. For some reason, he suddenly felt every one of his nearly fifty-three years. "I'm fine." He sprinkled his words with a measure of sternness.

She tilted her head to the right. "Are you coming or going?"

He wasn't entirely sure. Was he presiding over the Quarter Sessions today or going to the Committee of Observation meeting? He looked up at the ceiling beams. No, maybe the church elders were gathering to discuss the building. Or was that meeting tomorrow? He kicked at the baseboard.

"Peter?" Her eyes now were enlarged, as if she'd just seen an intruder.

He cast a shamefaced look in her direction and quickly called upon his reserves of dignity and firmness to disguise his confusion and shame.

Was he feeling like the time he'd lost his mother in the marketplace as a small boy or more like his feeble old grandfather who'd spent his last months sitting by the fire drooling? His wife stared at him with a look that would've roused his company of soldiers to attention.

For a moment, he felt as if he were back in the early days of Easton, breaking bread in the home of a dear and faithful friend, but the times had changed, and all of them had as well. His oldest son sat at the head of the table where his father-in-law had once presided—Peter Jr. sitting opposite his wife, Sarah, who was in her mother's former place. Caspar Doll was at the side now with his wife, who'd come into town with him and opposite the Dolls were Peter, Catherine, Andrew, Jacob, and Susannah. Frau Hamster had remained at home to feed herself, William, and Joe, and to look after the baby.

"What a fine meal, Sarah! You do your mother and me proud," Caspar Doll said.

The young woman blushed "Thank you, Papa, but Mama and Catherine deserve much of the credit."

Margaretha Doll made a tsking sound. "I didn't get here soon enough to do more than deliver a crumb cake."

"And I only contributed rolls, and Frau Hamster gave me a hand with those," Catherine said. She was smiling at her daughter-in-law who was roughly the same age as herself.

Susannah's youthful enthusiasm bubbled over. "Sarah's always been a wonderful cook. I used to bake with her and my Mother Anna when I was a little girl. Do you remember, Sarah?"

Peter surely did. Being at this table, enjoying good food and pleasant company soothed his spirit after the rigors of this day. He was also glad to see the recent unpleasantness with the Konks hadn't dimmed Susannah's spirit after her initial sulk.

Jacob leaned into his father's space, looking as if he were plenty tired of small talk. "I'm eager to know what happened today, sir."

Peter nodded, then said, "The Committee chose well-qualified people to serve as a Standing and Corresponding Committee to supplement our own work. The captains and other officers of the townships divided the county into districts …"

"… and formed the Associated Companies into battalions." Caspar Doll completed his sentence.

"What a lot of work," Andrew said, forking a piece of ham from the platter. When the meat fell apart, he used a serving spoon to gather all the pieces and transfer them to his plate.

"We also chose field officers," Doll said.

"So, Father, how are you going to support the cause?" Sarah asked, filling his outstretched plate with a generous mound of buttered egg noodles.

Doll sat up taller. "I will be captain of the Plainfield Company."

"I always said Papa knew how to command the troops," Margaretha commented, her eyes full of amusement.

"He had to be with all us daughters," Sarah said. "We needed bossing."

"Oh, I believe your mother was good enough at that," Doll joked, which produced a flashing of his wife's eyes and the uplift of her chin. Everyone laughed.

"What about you, Papa?" Susannah asked. Peter turned to Catherine, who appeared to be holding her breath. Before he could speak, Doll interrupted.

"I'll tell you what your good father will be doing."

Peter was happy to let his friend do the telling. Besides, he had his eye on the beets and noodles.

"We ended up dividing Northampton County into four districts, or battalions, made up of seven townships, and your good father was named Colonel of the First Battalion." He leaned back, his chest expansive.

Peter avoided his wife's eyes.

Doll continued. "The First Battalion will be made up of Easton, Williamstown, Lower Saucon, Forks, Bethlehem, Plainfield, and Mount Bethel."

Jacob let out a low whistle. "Wow, Father! That's terrific! I want to join."

"Me, too," Andrew said.

Although their patriotic zeal pleased him, Peter sensed this wasn't the best time to discuss how and when they might get involved.

His daughter-in-law put down her fork. "But Father Kichline, how will you manage? You're already so busy."

I won't have to manage everything." He wiped his mouth with the napkin and put the cloth back on his lap. "I've been stretched too thin as it is, and the other members of the Committee agreed to relieve me of my political duties—they'll appoint a few new members instead." He glanced at Catherine, who seemed to be breathing again.

She extinguished the candle on her nightstand. "I'm relieved you won't be carrying all those responsibilities, Peter."

He pulled the covers up to his chin and rolled over to face her, enjoying the nip of autumn filling their bedchamber. "I am too. I much prefer being out in the field with the men to sitting in meetings." He yawned. "And now that Pastor Rodenheimer has things under control at the church, I won't be needed for as many meetings there either."

She ran her hand along his strong forearm and nuzzled closer. "There's only so much of you to go around you know."

He smiled in the darkness. "I promise there will always be enough for you."

CHAPTER TWENTY-THREE

Erin crossed her right leg over her left trying to find a comfortable spot on the waiting room chair. How she yearned for a bottle of disinfectant to ward off the sinus drainage, red noses, and hacking coughs of patients with their shredded tissues and mysteriously damp sleeves. She checked her watch—ten forty-five. They'd been sitting there nearly an hour in conditions the Geneva Convention would surely consideration inhumane.

Her father seemed to read her thoughts. "He's usually late."

She nodded her head, attempting to stuff her outrage over the wait without so much as an apology from the placid-looking receptionist with a nose ring. The place smelled of menthol cough drops and cigarette smoke clinging to someone's shirt and hair. A young man sitting across the room sneezed loud enough to wake a sleeping teenager, and Erin flinched when she saw him wipe a greenish-yellow discharge from his nose. At that moment, the door to the inner sanctum opened, and a nurse in bulging tights consulted her clipboard. "Tony Pelleriti." She looked into the teaming room with its tired, huddled masses.

Erin grabbed her bag and leaped up.

"Huh?"

"They just called you, Dad. Do you want me to come back with you?" Erin bent down and raised her voice so he could hear her better. This was the first time she'd ever been to a doctor's appointment with him, marking yet another step toward relational intimacy with the man she'd been estranged from for several years of her youth.

"Of course."

The woman greeted him as they approached her. "Hello, Tony. How are you?"

"I'm fine now, but I may end up with pneumonia after sitting out there for an hour."

She gave a laugh. "There does seem to be a lot going around."

Erin decided if she did move to Easton, she most certainly was not going to use her father's primary care physician. Erin followed her dad and the nurse down a narrow hallway to a chair where he sat for his blood pressure and temperature readings. Then the nurse had him stand back up to be weighed.

"Everything's normal," she said, as if she'd contributed.

Erin was just glad the woman wasn't taking her blood pressure.

The nurse took them to a small examining room where Erin stood in a corner while her dad answered some questions, and the woman typed his answers on a laptop. Then she closed the lid. "Doctor will be with you shortly. You take care now, Tony."

"Shortly" turned out to be another twenty minutes. Erin tried to keep her dad's spirits up by discussing baseball standings and the coming season's prospects for the Eagles. She had thought several times about telling him she had a big career choice to make, one with considerable ramifications for her personal and family life, but each time, something held her back. When she initiated conversations with her dad, he tended not to hear her, going onto another subject altogether. She would need his full attention if she were to feel comfortable enough to tell him what was going on in her life. This wasn't the right time anyway, not when his mind was understandably on his health.

The doctor finally showed up, a lean man somewhere around Erin's age who looked the exact opposite of his waiting room—crisp, neat, and dressed according to the latest issue of *GQ*. "Good morning, Tony, and how are you today?" He reached out and shook the old man's hand.

"I'm good, but you really need to do something about the wait. We've been here all morning."

"I know, and I do apologize." He turned to Erin. "Is this your daughter?"

"Yes, this is Erin Miles."

"Nice to meet you, Erin."

"I'm glad to meet you too," she said, shaking his cold hand.

"She's a doctor too, you know."

The man gave a slight bow of his head. "Is that right?"

"Yes, but I'm a PhD."

"Do you teach?"

"Uh, yes. History."

"Where?"

Without thinking she said, "I have some offers I'm considering."

Tony appeared not to have heard, gazing instead at the physician, ready to be examined.

"Well, good luck then."

"Thank you."

"Now then, Tony, how have you been since being discharged from the hospital?"

"Just fine, doc. Feeling good as new."

"I understand you chose not to go to rehab."

"I didn't need to." Tony's jaw tightened.

The doctor looked at Erin as if for validation, and she shrugged.

"Are you having any pain?"

"Not really. Well, maybe a twinge here and there, just a little soreness."

"Likely from the surgery." He typed on his own laptop. "Are you sleeping well?"

"Pretty much. I sleep in my chair because I'm more comfortable sitting up."

"You don't live alone, do you?"

"Of course, I do." Tony gave a huff. "Why wouldn't I?"

The doctor didn't answer. "Are you able to keep up with your cooking and cleaning?"

"I'm managing."

Another look passed between Erin and the general practitioner. In her mind's eye, she envisioned the state of her dad's apartment—dirty dishes spilling from the sink onto the counter, floors thick with grime, furry windowsills, and a bathroom like a construction site Porta Potty. Had her father been able to do laundry? She wasn't sure, but his wrinkled shirt offered a clue. The physician typed something.

"I'm going to order you in-home occupational therapy for a few weeks, as well as some house help, until you get back on your feet completely."

Erin sighed quietly, vastly relieved. If Mohammed wouldn't go to the mountain, the mountain would come to Mohammed.

"How about if I buy you some lunch at the diner?" Tony looked eager to stay in his daughter's company.

"Thanks, Dad, but I can't today." She was already a half an hour late getting to her mom's to deliver the stamps, cash, and bananas Audrey had told her she needed.

"Why not? Do you have somewhere else you have to go?"

"Actually, I do. I have some errands I need to run for Mom."

"How is she?"

"Except for her vision, she's doing well." Erin started the car, willing the air-conditioning to kick in quickly, feeling uncomfortable discussing her mom with her dad.

"That's good. Tell her I was asking about her."

"Uh, okay." Why had she said that, for Pete's sake? Mentioning Tony to Audrey would be like pouring gas on a fire pit—kaboom! A sense of duty prompted her to ask, "Do you need anything at the store?"

"Hmm, I could use some milk and bread, and maybe some salad fixings, and ..."

An hour later, she showed up at Audrey's apartment wishing she could peel her clammy clothes from her body the way she would take the rind off an orange.

"I've been waiting for you, so worried something happened. Where have you been?"

"Believe me, you don't want to know."

Before going home to Lansdale, she felt a strong need to reclaim the charm of Easton and her connection to Colonel Kichline and all the other ancestors who'd walked those streets through the centuries. She hadn't told Audrey about the jobs at Lafayette or Hatfield either. Only Pat and Al knew. "We'll support you and Ethan either way," her mother-in-law had told her two days ago, which was good. Erin, however, had been hoping for more direct advice, a billboard maybe, the digital kind flashing from the sides of the Pennsylvania Turnpike.

Going over the toll bridge, she turned right at the second exit and pointed Mr. Scott in the direction of College Hill and Lafayette. She would drive around the storied streets and see whether she could picture herself being there for the next year, perhaps longer. She smiled as she drove past Gates Hall where she'd lived her senior year, remembering the two janitors who woke the floor each morning when the female would call out the male worker's name in a high-pitched voice—"Rus-sell!" Then she turned onto High Street and drove past the Williams Center for the Arts, the old field house and Markle Hall where she'd had her admissions interview. She recalled how thrilled she'd been at the idea of being a Lafayette student and easily pictured her acceptance letter with its distinguished seal bearing the likeness of the Marquis— *"Congratulations. You've been accepted as a student into the class of 1993 at Lafayette College."*

She would've parked in the lot behind Markle and walked around campus, but she was content to drive, seeing the familiar paths she'd once trodden as a happy 'Pard. In place of the earlier smells, frustrations, and worries of the day were peace and a sense of belonging to the hilltop school where her adult life had begun. There she'd started building her own foundation on more solid rock, leaving behind the sinking sand of her parents' failed marriage and the unstable years following. She belonged here in a way she never could at Hatfield College, as much as she'd enjoyed teaching there. Who knew? Maybe one of her ancestors had helped start Lafayette back in the 1820s, and her roots went even deeper than the years she'd spent there. With her current track record, she wouldn't be a bit surprised. Her thoughts turned into prayer. *Is this where I should be, Lord?*

Reluctant to leave the serenity of College Hill, Erin drove toward her Aunt Jane's where many early, happy memories gathered in her memory. When she reached the house and parked in front, she did a double-take—a dark-haired woman in a suit was standing at the edge of the lawn next to a "For Sale" sign. Now the lady was looking at her and mouthing words. Erin slid down her window. "Excuse me?"

"Yes, hello! I was wondering if I could be of some help."

"This house is for sale?"

"Yes, it just went on the market today. Are you interested?"

"My aunt used to live here. I sort of grew up in this house, I mean I spent a lot of time here when I was a kid."

"Would you like to see the inside?"

"Really?"

"Sure. Just park in the driveway, and I'll show you around."

Erin felt as if she'd entered a broad daylight, much happier version of the old *Twilight Zone*. She used to watch the black and white reruns with her cousins, then have nightmares afterwards.

When she got out of the car, the woman extended her hand. "I'm Deana Kloetzli."

"Erin Miles."

"Nice to meet you."

Deana led Erin past the lawn that could pass for a fairway at Green Pond Country Club, including flower beds where weeds apparently were off-limits. "The place looks wonderful. I always loved this house."

"Are you from Easton?"

"I grew up across the river, but I was in Easton a lot. Are you?"

"Wilson Borough." Deana reached the expansive front porch where a colorful wreath of wildflowers graced the door. As she started opening the lock box, she asked "Who was your aunt?"

"Her name was Jane Anderson."

"Jane Anderson." Deana paused, looking up. "Did she show dogs or something?"

"Yes. She had some champions when I was growing up, but after she and my uncle divorced, she remarried and moved to Massachusetts."

"I'm guessing the present owners must've bought the house from your aunt because they've lived here a good many years."

She wished her aunt and uncle had stayed together, that this place could've remained part of her life. A year after they had divorced, Erin's parents split up, and the following years of her youth lacked the joy of the previous times.

When they entered the foyer, she took a sharp breath as she beheld a brighter, even better version of the home she'd once known. The owners had an affinity for white furniture and soft paint accented by pops of subtle color on the window treatments, sofas, and seat cushions. The floor plan was more open than Erin remembered with the kitchen flowing seamlessly into the family room where a once-red-brick fireplace now featured river rocks. She smiled as her mind replayed a scene from years ago when her cousin Emma and her boyfriend, a Lafayette student, had painted everyone's faces with glow-in-the-dark liquid, doused the lights, and scooted around the hardwood floors singing Indian songs and chants he'd learned as a summer camp counselor. She wondered what had happened to him after he graduated and no longer dated Emma.

"Is the house the way you remember it, Erin?"

She brought herself back to the present. "Yes, and no. This looks like some sort of magazine spread! Everything is so perfect. I especially love all the Colonial Williamsburg touches. My aunt would've liked them, too."

Deana smiled. "Funny you should mention that. The owner is a designer and used to live in Williamsburg before coming to Easton. So, let me show you the kitchen, baths, and bedrooms. There are all new stainless-steel appliances, granite counter tops, tile in the bathrooms, and the views of Easton, Phillipsburg, and the rivers are to die for."

She sighed. "Yes, I remember those views." In her life, no other scenes had ever matched them.

Fifteen minutes later, Erin stood looking out of a window in the master bedroom taking in the "killer" scene when she suddenly remembered a dream she'd had the year before. In the vision of that night, she'd been at her Grammy Ott's old neighborhood among run-down houses, feeling the emotional weight of their decay. Suddenly new buildings rose among them with pristine views of the Delaware and Lehigh Rivers and Easton itself gleaming in the dazzling light of transformation. As she had awakened, a verse had echoed in her spirit, "I will restore the years that the locusts have eaten."

Now, pursing her lips, she wondered whether this renovated house might be part of her own renewal.

"Where's Ethan?"

"Al took him to Merrymead for ice cream." Erin's mother-in-law pointed to a glass pitcher. "I just made some iced tea. Would you like a glass?"

"Yes, thanks!" She made herself at home, taking a seat at the table while Pat gathered tumblers and filled them with ice. She was glad they were alone.

"How was your father's appointment?"

"He's doing much better, and the doctor is going to get some house help for him." She laughed. "Believe me, he needs help. My dad's idea of cleaning up is moving a basket of laundry from his bed to the floor."

"Heaven knows you and your brother can't be cleaning and doing laundry on top of taking him and your mom to appointments and running errands for them."

"True." She jumped to the chase. "There's something else I'm dying to tell you, Mom."

Bringing the tea to the table, Pat placed the drinks before Erin and herself and sat down. "You look ready to burst."

Her story spilled out as her mother-in-law listened quietly, occasionally sipping her tea and nodding at just the right places. As Erin finished, her lips were trembling. "There's just one problem. I feel peaceful about the prospect of teaching at Lafayette, and I'm thrilled I might be able to buy my aunt's old house, but …" She reached for a tissue from the counter. "Thinking of leaving you and Melissa and my neighbors and my church really hurts." She swallowed down a sob. "Jim and I built our house from the ground up, and we brought Ethan home from the hospital to it. I …" She couldn't continue. Pat handed her the box of tissues and pulled out one for herself.

A few minutes later, Pat spoke. "I'm wondering … Erin, would you be able to buy your aunt's house and keep it for visits to Easton, like a retreat or vacation house? I know how much you love your home town and how you'd like to be there for so many reasons."

"Yes, that's an option, but when I think about commuting to teach at Lafayette, I don't really know how to work out my schedule with Ethan's."

"You know Al and I will help however we can."

"Thank you so much. You've always been there for us. I …"

Pat's smile reassured Erin. "And always will be."

She felt like Noah's dove, searching for a place to land, unable to find one just yet.

She was running late Sunday morning and unable to assemble more than a glass of grapefruit juice and a leftover bean burrito for breakfast before getting Ethan to Sunday School. He'd refused her offer of the same with a turned-up nose. "No thanks, Mom. Our teacher always brings donut holes." She took herself to the adult education class in the parlor and went straight to the coffee cart while the leader asked everyone to find a seat. After pouring a cup, she sat next to Melissa and Tim, then she spotted Al and Pat in the row in front of her. They turned around and whispered, "Good morning, Erin." Melissa shot Erin a knowing smile—they'd talked for an hour on the phone last night.

"How are you this morning?" Melissa whispered.

"Doing well. Still deciding where to live, but happy I've chosen Lafayette."

Doug Griffith, a church elder whose appearance accurately matched his office, stood at the lectern. "This morning, we're continuing our summer series in which we're hearing from many of the missionaries our church supports. I love how we get to put names to actual faces and hear their stories, don't you?" The nodding of many heads commenced. "Today we have Dwight and Marlene Alexander from Shalom Ministries in the Poconos. Before I introduce them, let's open with prayer."

Erin prepared herself for a lengthy appeal because Doug was known for mentioning every possible need he could think of, from a neighbor's lost cat to the pastor's cousin's daughter's upcoming hernia surgery, as well as petitions for a dozen world leaders, each by name. She was pleasantly surprised when he limited himself to prayers for the President and one of the deacons, who was going in for hip surgery in two days.

Then the missionary couple came up front, the woman standing to the side while her husband addressed the class first. "Thank you very much for inviting us. We love this church and always enjoy worshiping with you. As Mr. Griffith said, I'm Dwight, and this is my wife, Marlene, and we're with Shalom Ministries." He clicked on a PowerPoint slide show featuring their organization's logo, a juxtaposition of Hebrew and English letters against the backdrop of a wooded mountain lake and a log cabin. "Does anyone know what the word 'shalom' means?"

Erin waited a beat and when no one said anything, spoke up. "Shalom means 'peace.'"

Dwight pointed in her direction. "You're right. Our ministry seeks to be a place of peace for missionaries who've come home on furlough—men, women, and children who are often burned out from giving completely to others in their fields of service, who need to find rest for their souls but who often don't have the financial resources for a peaceful retreat or vacation. We give them the ability to come away by themselves and rest before heading off to raise their support again, which is itself quite stressful, and then to return to their mission fields. Some don't even have a home to go to when they come back to the States, and most of their worldly goods are in storage.

"Just this week a couple contacted us. They're from Lansdale and due to return from Guatemala for a year at the end of August with their three young children. The problem they have is there's no place to stay. Their parents have downsized and don't have room for them long-term. I assured them God would somehow answer their need."

Prickles spread along Erin's shoulder blades, then down her back. Pat Miles turned her head to the left and glanced at her. Melissa leaned closer. "Did you hear that?"

Yes, Erin had heard. Sunlight splashed through the windows, enveloping her in its warm embrace as she had sudden clarity. She would rent her Lansdale home to the missionary family and live with Ethan in her aunt's house—Erin's house. She had found her own peace, her own shalom. Peace like a river.

CHAPTER TWENTY-FOUR

The autumn woods fringing the parade ground combusted in a blaze of crimson, gold, and red, the sun's rays setting them afire. Peter inhaled the smoky coolness of the air and the glorious sight in one big gulp as he surveyed his men, who were not so bountifully arrayed, who'd come from farms and fields to train in the art of war. Their dedication moved him. He knew the sacrifices they and their families were making to engage in mustering exercises. The recent image of a little girl toddling around a chicken coop feeding the flock while her older brothers and sisters tended the larger animals and assisted their mother to bring in the harvest had become a symbol to him of their patriotism. He looked down the second row and saw their husband and father standing straight, shoulders back. Then Peter noticed a little man slipping into the ranks with mincing steps, as if trying to evade detection. How many times was this now? He leaned over to question his subordinate.

"Captain Horn, who is that diminutive fellow over there?" He used his head like a pointer, indicating where to find the young man. Horses neighed in the near distance, a crow cawed overhead.

The captain's eyes shifted to the very spot, and he nodded. "Ah, yes, Colonel Kichline, that would be Andrew Drunkenmiller." His expression tightened. "He is always late, always dragging his feet. Falls asleep half the time."

"Do you know anything about him?"

"No, sir, I do not, but I intend to."

Peter sensed his subordinate would like nothing more than to teach the young man a lesson about tardiness, but something inside made Peter shy away from such discipline. "After we drill, I'll have a word with him myself."

Horn looked in Peter's eyes and although he said, "Of course, sir," the downward turn of his lips communicated his disappointment.

"Would you begin the drill, Captain?"

"Yes, sir." He nodded toward the drummer to get the man's attention and when the blustery rhythm ended moments later, called out, "Come to order men!"

Peter began walking up and down the rows, touching a man's shoulders to stand straighter, adjusting cartridge boxes and patting protruding stomachs. He even took several deep breaths and sucked in his own belly to demonstrate proper military bearing. Then he came to the fellow who was the object of his curiosity—barely a man at that, completely smooth-faced except for a smattering of blemishes, so slender he would have made an excellent scarecrow.

"Young man, I'd like a word after the drilling."

His face blanched; he looked down at his boots. "Y-yes, s-sir."

The rest of the men were drinking water from their canteens and conversing in groups before leaving for home and hearth. He found the boy on the edge of the crowd, looking in Peter's direction, shivering, although the temperature was in the low sixties.

"Come with me." He motioned toward a copse of vermillion trees, and the lad dutifully followed. Seeing a large rock, Peter nodded toward it for the boy to sit, then Peter did as well. "You are Andrew Drunkenmiller, are you not?"

"I am sir."

"Which township are you from?"

"L-lower S-saucon, sir."

"How did you get here today?"

"I walked."

Peter took in the dusty boots, loose at the seams. "That's quite a distance."

"*Ja.*" He seemed to will himself to look up and spoke in broken English. "I am very sorry to be so often late."

"Are you late because you have far to come?"

Andrew hesitated a moment. "Partly, sir. You see, I can't come until my work is done and until … my father won't miss me."

Peter moved his head slightly to the right. "Your father doesn't know you're mustering?"

"*Nein*, sir."

"And why would that be?" He anticipated the answer.

"We are Moravians, sir. He doesn't believe in what we do."

"I see." Peter remained silent a moment. "And you do?"

"Yes, sir, with all *mein* heart."

Peter clapped him on the shoulder. "What would happen if he knew?"

"I do not exactly know, sir, but I want freedom from the British more." Although the voice warbled, Andrew's conviction was steady. For a long moment, Peter couldn't find his own voice.

"Father, I want to join you too."

Jacob had come into the parlor to speak with his father after a late November dinner. Peter had been anticipating this conversation for several weeks and watched as Catherine rose discreetly from her chair and left the room. Peter set aside his copy of Marcus Aurelius' *Meditations.*

The young man perching on the very edge of the chair appeared ready to spring up like a mountain lion. Jacob began breathlessly, "The church is nearly finished, Father, and building in Easton is slowing down because, as you know, this is our slow season, so there's nothing claiming my attention except being in the militia, which is on everyone's minds, and every man who can should be joining." He slowed down for a second. "Peter and Andrew have joined, and Uncle Frederick is drilling. I want to be a soldier, to do my part." He sat taller as if to add to his stature, as well as his argument.

Peter tented his fingers. "If I were you, I would think the same way."

Relief splashed over Jacob's face. His shoulders relaxed. "Then you understand."

"I was young once myself." He smiled. "Having strong convictions is good when the cause is right."

"This one is."

He nodded in agreement. "You may have your chance, Jacob, and I wouldn't deny you, but let's use our heads as well as our passions."

The young man frowned, his mood changing. "I'm not sure what you mean."

"I don't know what's ahead for us. If we must fight—and I think relations with Britain indicate we're coming to that—we need to have a plan for our family."

"What kind of plan?" Jacob sat on his hands.

"Peter Jr. and Uncle Frederick are the heads of their own families and must make their own decisions. Andrew is twenty-three, also old enough to make his own way, and although he remains under this roof, he's becoming increasingly independent, especially at the mill." He noticed Jacob's mouth open and anticipated what he was about to say. "Your help has made his success possible. You're excellent at milling yourself." He sat still for a moment, hearing the baby cry on the second floor and Catherine's footsteps on the stairs. "Jacob, I need you here, to begin taking a bigger role in the mill, and should Andrew and I be called away, I'm going to need you to be the man of this house, someone I can rely upon." He reached over and grasped his son's burly arm. "None of us knows what is going to happen, but I do know difficulties lay ahead. Can I count on you to help our family through them?"

Jacob met his gaze. "Yes, Father, you can."

"Thank you."

After a moment, "Father, may I please drill with the men, if doing so doesn't interfere with my mill work?"

Peter pressed his lips together, considering what seemed a reasonable request. "I see value in that. And who knows—you may yet have a turn at soldiering by the time these troubles are over." In his heart, he earnestly hoped not.

Peter gazed into the parlor from the bottom of the stairs, hearing the laughter of several church women as they spun and talked. Catherine, Susannah, and Elizabeth Traill had been talking about creating a Daughters of Liberty group in Easton, and the discussion had turned into action. Their commitment to freedom ran as deeply as his own.

He entered the room with a bow. "Good day, ladies."

Spinning wheels filled the parlor. Frau Hamster and Joe fluttered about, refilling goblets and replenishing plates of cakes and cookies.

"Good day, Herr Kichline."

"Good day, Papa!"

"Good day, husband."

"I want to thank you ladies for your hard work. I appreciate your dedication very much, and so do the men." He paused. "So, what are you spinning today?"

"Wool, Papa. We're going to make cloth for uniforms."

"You are doing a fine thing here." He started to say something about how they were giving as much as the men, but his mouth remained at half-staff when he saw Catherine's reaction to Joe's placement of a seed cake on her plate. His good wife looked at the delectable treat, her face turning as white as the cap she wore, and she covered her mouth and bolted from her seat, almost knocking over her spinning wheel in her haste. The eyes of every female in the room, young, old, and in between, followed her retreating figure. She caught Peter's gaze for a split second as she ran past him, Frau Hamster on her heels. When he swallowed, his saliva felt as hard as one of Meyer Hart's horehound drops. He'd seen that look before.

"Peter, darling, I assure you. I am well enough to walk to church."

He wasn't convinced. "That you may be, but I would feel much better using the carriage. The streets are slippery after yesterday's snowfall."

She smiled and shook her head. "You worry too much about me."

"I admire your strength, but please indulge your husband and let me take you and Baby Elizabeth to church in the carriage."

She sighed and smiled at the same time. "If you insist."

"I do."

Susannah giggled as she entered the hallway, tying the ribbons of her bonnet. "Is there room for me as well?"

"There is always room for you, daughter. Frau Hamster should ride with us as well."

She grinned upon learning she wouldn't have to trudge through the cold after all.

"I'd rather walk, Father," Jacob said, looking toward his older brother.

"And I'll go with him." Andrew looked around. "We can go with Joe and William."

Peter appraised the domestic scene, his smile rising from a deep inner well of contentment, and he felt a need to say something on this auspicious occasion. "What a fine family I have! I want to thank you for all the things each of you did to help bring about this new church building. Even more than the courthouse, a church is a crowning jewel in any village, and this one will shine especially brightly. I'm happy the first service is on Christmas Eve." He was used to giving speeches and having people listen, but he also liked to think he knew when to stop.

Transformed. Peter had seen the building hundreds of times, inside, outside, from every unromantic aspect of its finances and building materials, right down to the hardware supplied by his brother-in-law, Frederick Gwinner, and by Meyer Hart. Nevertheless, Peter was seeing this church for the very first time.

Catherine squeezed his arm as he led the family through the doors. "This place is beautiful." Her voice was a kind of hush.

"Oh, Papa!" Susannah exclaimed under her breath. "Is this for real?"

He nodded. "Yes, dear one. At long last, Easton has a church."

"Welcome, Kichlines!" Elder Gress greeted them as they stepped further inside. "A happy Christmas to you." Joy so illuminated his weathered face the wrinkles had all but fled.

"And to you as well, Herr Gress." Peter pumped his hand as his lungs filled with the scents of burning beeswax candles and newly cut evergreen boughs.

"Magnificent, isn't it?" Gress's eyes misted as he looked in the direction of the sanctuary, which was filling rapidly.

Out of the blue, Peter recalled the cathedrals of his native Germany, the splendor of vaulted ceilings and spires so high they appeared to pierce the very heavens, as well as the ornate woodwork and statuary of the Roman Catholic churches. This simple house of worship was every bit as earnest, if not opulent, which was exactly what he preferred.

"Yes, this is a truly magnificent church. You've done a splendid job."

Gress's cheeks flushed. "I? Oh, but I was just a small part of this project. You …"

Peter cut him off. "To God be the glory."

Gress shook his hand again, then Peter led his family down the aisle, past a man who appeared to be Anthony Esser, but then again when had Peter ever seen the man smile? Lewis Gordon waved from two pews away, and Peter nodded in his direction. There were Ziba Wiggins and Frau Eckert, the innkeeper John Rinker, Daniel Labar, the shoemaker, and blacksmith Christopher Bittenbender, along with dozens more people whose lives and business he was as familiar with as their own family members. As a two-term sheriff, he knew enough about the people of Easton—enough about human nature—to have turned him into a veritable cynic if he'd been so inclined. He knew who imbibed to excess, which shopkeeper used dishonest scales, who was cruel to his animals and stingy with his wife and children. He also was deeply aware of his own shortcomings, his quick temper and impatience, the fear he battled when a family member was ill. He studied the way candlelight gentled everyone's countenances until they appeared quite transformed, a version of their very best selves. Was he being allowed a tiny glimpse of Heaven?

His long legs carried him to the third pew from the front on the right, just behind Robert and Elizabeth Traill. Peter stood to the side to allow his offspring and servants to enter first, followed by Catherine, with him anchoring the end. His entourage spilled into half of the pew behind them as well, and when Peter Jr. and Sarah came, followed by Frederick and his family, they rounded out the space, exchanging greetings with the rest of the Kichline clan.

"The church looks wonderful, Father," Peter Jr. said leaning forward, clapping his father's right shoulder.

"I'm well pleased. And how are you and Sarah tonight?" he asked in a low voice.

"Very well, thank you. I see the organ isn't ready just yet."

"No, we'll be singing acapella for a little while."

Peter shook hands with Robert Traill and nodded toward Elizabeth, then he sat in silence, contemplating the crowded pews and the serenity of this mystical evening of snow and pure light. He felt as if he'd just enjoyed the best meal and conversation a man could have in this world.

A hum like bees filled the sanctuary, the congregants apparently too excited to remain completely silent as they usually were when gathering for worship. Ten minutes later, Pastor Rodenheimer took his place in a chair carved by William's gifted hands. Though physically the chair might have dwarfed the minister, his spirit made up for what was lacking in his stature. Peter caught his glance, nodded, smiled. Out of the corner of his eyes, he noticed Meyer Hart sitting by himself on the other side. He would make it a point to see the man afterward.

He felt as swamped by well-wishers as the pastor himself when the poignant service ended an hour and a half later, exuberance flowing in and through the building like the swelling of the Delaware and Lehigh Rivers in early spring. Joy filled his spirit until he thought his grin might wrap clear around to the back of his head, then start all over again. He didn't wish to be abrupt with anyone, but while he spoke to each person who desired a word, he kept an eye on Meyer Hart, who was himself surrounded by well-wishers.

"What a night and what a service!" Frederick Gwinner actually hugged Peter, which startled him as much as if his brother-in-law had started undressing in public. Then Frederick embraced his sister.

"Yes, brother, what a beautiful service!" Catherine hung on to her hat.

"And where is our good Frau Hamster?"

"If you will excuse me, there's someone I must see." Peter left them and threaded his way through the teeming main aisle, able to see Hart from the vantage point of his height, nodding and smiling politely as he went. Finally, he reached the shopkeeper and waited until Frau Eckert and Ziba Wiggins finished talking with him.

"Herr Kichline! How good to see you!" Wiggins said. "We shall long remember this splendid service."

"Indeed we shall, Mr. Wiggins." He nodded. "Frau Eckert."

She touched her right hand to her heart. "We've never known anything quite like this." Her breath caused him to step back.

"Well, my dear, let's be going," Wiggins said. "Good evening, Sher, uh, Mister Kichline."

Peter turned to Meyer Hart and grasped his hand. "How very nice to see you tonight."

Hart's face appeared to have absorbed the candlelight. "Ah, my friend. The pleasure is indeed mine."

"I admit while your presence delights me, I'm also surprised."

"I feel welcome here, as if your fellowship is wide enough to take in an old Hebrew like myself."

"Indeed, you are welcome here. We do, after all, worship the same God."

Hart nodded. "That we do."

Pastor Rodenheimer joined them. "This building is here in no small measure due to your generosity, Mr. Hart."

The old storekeeper shook his hoary head and waved his right hand. "I did very little."

"I must disagree," Peter said. "Your gift of nails meant a great deal."

Rodenheimer quoted from the book of Luke. "'For mine eyes have seen Thy salvation, which Thou hast prepared before the face of all people, a light to lighten the Gentiles and the glory of Thy people Israel.'"

Peter glanced at his old friend, whose faded eyes had begun to water.

"I can't help but wonder," Hart said, "what this village will be going through in the next year given the present troubles with England. I think we are fortunate to have this house of prayer and worship for such a time as this."

He noticed the minister staring toward the front of the church, and while he followed the gaze, Peter wasn't seeing what the man of God was seeing. Finally, Rodenheimer added a benediction to their conversation.

"This will be a house of prayer for all the nations, and before the passing of many days, people of many nations will indeed gather here, and they will find rest for their souls and healing for their wounds ..."

A chill shot up Peter's left calf.

ABOUT THE AUTHOR

At fifteen, Rebecca Price Janney faced-off with the editor of her local newspaper. She wanted to write for the paper; he nearly laughed her out of the office. Then she displayed her ace—a portfolio of celebrity interviews she'd written for a bigger paper's teen supplement. By the next month she was covering the Philadelphia Phillies. During Rebecca's senior year in high school, *Seventeen* published her first magazine article and in conjunction with the Columbia Scholastic Press Association, named her a runner-up in their teen-of-the-year contest. She's now the author of nineteen published books including two mystery series, as well as hundreds of magazine and newspaper articles.

Her other books include: *Great Women in American History*, *Great Stories in American History*, *Great Events in American History*, and *Great Letters in American History*, along with *Harriet Tubman*, *Then Comes Marriage?* and *Who Goes There?* A popular speaker, Rebecca also appears on radio and TV shows. She's a graduate of Lafayette College and Princeton Theological Seminary, and she received her doctorate from Biblical Seminary where she focused on the role of women in American history. She lives with her husband and son in suburban Philadelphia.

For more information visit www.rebeccapricejanney.com

Dr. Rebecca Price Janney

Author of 20 Published Books/Historian/Speaker

www.rebeccapricejanney.com

Twitter: @rebeccajanney

Easton in the Valley and Easton at the Forks

The Easton Series

(Elk Lake Publishing)

Other Books by Rebecca Price Janney:

Great Events in American History (AMG)

Great Women in American History (Moody)

Great Stories in American History (Horizon)

Great Letters in American History (Heart of Dakota)

Harriet Tubman (Bethany House)

Who Goes There? (Moody)

Then Comes Marriage? (Moody)

The Heather Reed Mystery Series (Word)

The Impossible Dreamers Series (Multnomah)

Look for the final book in the

Easton Series

Coming in the summer of 2018!

The valley of decision is a challenging place to be—join Peter Kichline and Erin Miles as they make life-changing choices

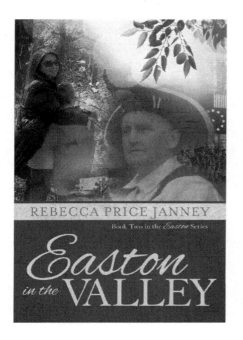

David E. Fessenden, Author of The Exploding Speakeasy

In book one of the *Easton Series*, get to know two people, two hundred years apart joined by life experiences, family ties, and a winsome place that beckons "Come home."

Available in bookstores and from online retailers.

Elk Lake
PUBLISHING™